CADIA STANDS

More tales of the Astra Militarum from Black Library

GLORY IMPERIALIS
An omnibus edition of the novels *Imperial Glory* by Richard Williams,
Commissar by Andy Hoare and *Iron Guard* by Mark Clapham

SHADOWSWORD
A novel by Guy Haley

BANEBLADE
A novel by Guy Haley

ASTRA MILITARUM
An anthology by various authors

YARRICK: THE PYRES OF ARMAGEDDON
A Commissar Yarrick novel by David Annandale

YARRICK: IMPERIAL CREED
A Commissar Yarrick novel by David Annandale

YARRICK: CHAINS OF GOLGOTHA
A Commissar Yarrick novella by David Annandale

HONOUR IMPERIALIS
An omnibus edition of the novels *Cadian Blood* by
Aaron Dembski-Bowden, *Redemption Corps* by Rob Sanders and
Dead Men Walking by Steve Lyons

STRAKEN
An 'Iron Hand' Straken novel by Toby Frost

THE MACHARIAN CRUSADE
An omnibus edition of the novels *Angels of Fire*, *Fist of Demetrius* and
Fall of Macharius by William King

• GAUNT'S GHOSTS •
By Dan Abnett

THE FOUNDING
An omnibus edition containing books 1–3:
First and Only, *Ghostmaker* and *Necropolis*

THE SAINT
An omnibus edition containing books 4–7:
Honour Guard, *The Guns of Tanith*, *Straight Silver* and *Sabbat Martyr*

THE LOST
An omnibus edition containing books 8–11:
Traitor General, *His Last Command*, *The Armour of Contempt* and *Only in Death*

BOOK 12: BLOOD PACT
BOOK 13: SALVATION'S REACH
BOOK 14: THE WARMASTER

CADIA STANDS

JUSTIN D HILL

BLACK LIBRARY

A BLACK LIBRARY PUBLICATION

First published in 2017.
This edition published in Great Britain in 2019 by
Black Library,
Games Workshop Ltd.,
Willow Road,
Nottingham, NG7 2WS, UK.

10 9 8 7 6 5 4 3

Produced by Games Workshop in Nottingham.
Cover illustration by Mikhail Savier.

See Black Library on the internet at

blacklibrary.com

Find out more about Games Workshop
and the world of Warhammer 40,000 at

games-workshop.com

Printed and bound by CPI Group (UK) Ltd, Croydon, CR0 4YY

*For Loremasters Issy and Teddy – who've always known their Blood Angels
from their Ultramarines, from their Sons of Horus.*

It is the 41st millennium. For more than a hundred centuries the Emperor has sat immobile on the Golden Throne of Earth. He is the Master of Mankind by the will of the gods, and master of a million worlds by the might of His inexhaustible armies. He is a rotting carcass writhing invisibly with power from the Dark Age of Technology. He is the Carrion Lord of the Imperium for whom a thousand souls are sacrificed every day, so that He may never truly die.

Yet even in His deathless state, the Emperor continues His eternal vigilance. Mighty battlefleets cross the daemon-infested miasma of the warp, the only route between distant stars, their way lit by the Astronomican, the psychic manifestation of the Emperor's will. Vast armies give battle in His name on uncounted worlds. Greatest amongst His soldiers are the Adeptus Astartes, the Space Marines, bioengineered super-warriors. Their comrades in arms are legion: the Astra Militarum and countless planetary defence forces, the ever-vigilant Inquisition and the tech-priests of the Adeptus Mechanicus to name only a few. But for all their multitudes, they are barely enough to hold off the ever-present threat from aliens, heretics, mutants – and worse.

To be a man in such times is to be one amongst untold billions. It is to live in the cruellest and most bloody regime imaginable. These are the tales of those times. Forget the power of technology and science, for so much has been forgotten, never to be re-learned. Forget the promise of progress and understanding, for in the grim dark future there is only war. There is no peace amongst the stars, only an eternity of carnage and slaughter, and the laughter of thirsting gods.

PROLOGUE

BORDERS OF
THE SEGMENTUM OBSCURUS

She is four. It is time to learn.

Her father lifts her into the night sky. On other planets, the vision above would be a velvet-black sky, the cold white light of ten thousand stars, or the strange beauty of a crescent moon. But she is Cadian, and the sky is not dark and star-studded; it glows with the swirling, lurid bruise of the Eye of Terror that stares back down like a cyclops' orb. The only twinkle comes not from stars, but from reflected sunlight catching the adamantium plates of low-orbit defence platforms.

She starts to tense. Sometimes the eye is purple, sometimes green, sometimes darker patches of unnamed colour. Her father's voice brings her back.

'That is the Eye of Terror. The prison of our enemy,' he hisses. 'We are the padlock that keeps them trapped. That is why they hate us.'

'All of us?' she asks.

'All,' he says.

There is a long pause as she stares upwards. 'Even Mother?'

'Yes,' he tells her, 'even Mother.'

There is a pause. She tastes blood in her throat. She wipes her nose and her finger comes away smeared with red. She cannot stop staring into the Eye even though she feels sick. She knows this is a test that she must pass, and she will not give up.

'Does he hate *me*?' she asks, sniffing the blood back.

'Yes. The Despoiler hates you.'

There is another pause. 'He wants to take our world from us?'

His voice is close to her ear. She can feel the breath of his words on her skin and in the tangled curls of her hair. He is passing on what he learned as a child. 'The Despoiler wants our world to *burn*.'

Vomit rises in her throat. She swallows the bile back, and stares deep into the darkest pits of the iris as if looking for a face there, a being to whom she can address her words. At first she sees nothing but then – there! – in the darkest patches of purple light, there is a plume of pale clouds.

'What do you see?' her father demands, but she cannot speak as she gasps for breath. His fingers are tight. 'Speak, child. Have faith! The Emperor protects!'

The breath comes with a sudden shock as blood begins to drip from her nostrils. 'A face!' she says, her voice beginning to break with fear. She squirms for a moment. She wants this to stop, but his hands are firm on her arms, and he holds her up for a little longer. 'That is the Despoiler!'

he tells her and lifts her higher into the air. 'What do you want to say to him, who hates us all and wants to burn our world?'

Blood begins to pour from her nostrils. She will not look away. She will not give up. 'Never,' she says.

'I cannot hear you.'

'Never!' she says, louder this time.

'Tell him!'

The child shouts up into the night sky. 'Never! *Never*!'

The father brings his daughter down and holds her tight against the chest sections of his flak armour. 'Well done, child,' he says and feels relief. It is not easy to expose a child to such things. He watches his daughter walk back to their hab.

He is a Cadian and a father. He has done his duty.

For her, the true test is yet to come.

PART ONE
THE SUMMONS

ONE

ORBIT OVER CADIA

Below them, the planet was poised half in light and half in darkness.

Major Isaia Bendikt could not tell if a new day was coming on, or if the night was falling. He stood with Warmaster Ryse and his posse of command staff on the viewing platforms of the *Fidelitas Vector* and remembered how he'd left Cadia over twenty years before.

In those twenty years, he'd had more than his fair share of benighted ice-worlds, void-moons and jungle worlds with blood-sucking nanobes that dropped onto you from the branches above.

He'd seen the worst of the galaxy and now, looking down upon Cadia, he remembered his last moments on his home world.

A young Whiteshield, without a kill to his name.

* * *

Bendikt's father had never got the chance to go off-planet. He was one of the one in ten Cadian Shock Troopers whose draft drew them as a territorial guard. It was his life to stay at home and stand ready to protect Cadia. But war had not come, and that uneventful career was a shame that had discoloured his life.

When the sixteen-year-old Isaia Bendikt drew an off-world draft he was both proud and envious of his son. It was a hard thing for a dour father to express, so he'd done what many fathers had before him – bought a bottle of Arcady Pride and got both himself and Bendikt drunk.

Bendikt remembered the night clearly. They had been sitting at the round camp table that stood in the middle of the small sub-hab central room of their home. His father had drawn up the camp chairs and slammed the bottle down between them, set two shot glasses on the table.

He had forced a smile as he unscrewed the top, crumpled it up in his hand and threw it back over his shoulder, where it had rattled in the corner of the room. His mother had left them a few plates of boiled grox-slab and cabbage on the table. Bendikt had tried to line his stomach as his father poured them a shot glass each.

'Here,' he'd said and held out the brimming glass.

They'd tapped the rims against each other and tipped the glasses high. Shot by shot they'd drunk and slowly knocked the bottle back. When the muster bell rang there was only a little amasec in the bottom of the bottle. 'To your first kill!' his father had slurred. His mother, a thin, worn, earnest-looking woman, had joined in with the last toast.

It was a short walk to the muster point, where other Whiteshields were being loaded onto rail trucks, their apprehensive faces staring out from under their Cadian-pattern helmets. All the tracks led straight to the landing fields outside Kasr Tyrok.

Bendikt and his parents pushed through the crowds to find his truck. Both his mother and his father had last words for him, though he was damned if he could remember them. He was only sixteen and so drunk he could barely stand. There were no tears. It was poor form to show sadness when a Cadian was sent to fight. It was part of the rhythm of life: birth, training, conscription, death. It was natural that a young Whiteshield would go and kill the enemies of the Imperium.

Bendikt had imagined himself many times taking the straight route south, and never seeing his home again. Before climbing aboard, he checked himself one more time to make sure that in his drunken state he had not forgotten anything.

He had boots, webbing, jacket, belt, combat knife, las-rifle, three battery packs, Imperial Primer in his left breast pocket, water canteen in his right. He pulled in a deep breath. He was ready, he told himself, to face anything the galaxy could throw at him.

'So,' Bendikt said. They said goodbye to one another, and his mother briefly embraced him and stuffed a packet of folded brown paper into his jacket pocket. 'Grox-jerky,' she whispered.

She was a tough woman, brought up on a planet where the only trade was war, and little given to expressions of emotion.

'I want to thank both of you for giving me life. I promise you I will be all that a Cadian should,' he said. It was a speech he had prepared, but being drunk he stumbled on his words and left much of it out.

Then he saluted and turned to climb aboard the truck. He looked out to wave goodbye to his parents, but darkness was falling and they had already turned for home. That was the last Bendikt had ever seen or heard of his family. For the next twenty years, other Guardsmen had been his brothers and sisters, and the Emperor his father.

Bendikt found it hard to remember his father's face but had never forgotten the hug his father had given him, and feeling his father's thick arms wrap around him, his broad, rough hands on his back. His mother's voice had never left him; he could recall her whispering 'grox-jerky' into his ear, and those words stayed with him, and somehow came to mean 'Look after yourself', and even 'You are well-loved, my son.'

As Cadia revolved beneath them Warmaster Ryse put both hands to the carefully tooled brass railings and leaned forward, his breath misting a little on the chill of the foot-thick glass.

He wanted to mark this moment with something momentous, yet poetic and memorable. Something that could go in his memoirs when, and if, retirement came. As if sensing its moment, the Warmaster's servitor-scribe, an emaciated body with augmetic stylus right arm and waist-mounted scroll, shuffled forward, knocking a few other sycophants out of the way.

The scribe had come with the title of Warmaster and Ryse seemed to rather like having his every word taken down for posterity. And now that there was no more Deucalion Crusade for Ryse to lead, it had occurred to many of them that perhaps Ryse might not be a Warmaster much longer.

Perhaps, many were thinking, Ryse's star was on the wane, and it was time for them to find one that was rising.

Ryse coughed to clear his throat, then his bass-baritone rang out, 'We have returned to our mother in her time of direst need.'

There was more, and Bendikt thought the Warmaster's speech could have been better, but the Warmaster finished with a flourish, like an Imperial preacher waxing lyrical. 'Men shall not say that we forgot our duty, nor that we forgot from whence we came.'

As he spoke, there was the scratch of stylus on vellum, leaving a trail of precise minuscule, in neatly justified blocks of text. Bendikt could not help reading over the scribe's shoulder while Ryse paused as if waiting for it to catch up, letting the words ring through his head.

Bendikt looked away. The Warmaster turned, and as if picking him out for not paying due attention, asked, 'What do you think, Major Bendikt?'

'She looks peaceful enough to me,' Bendikt stammered.

Ryse smiled indulgently. 'Yes. Cadia sent out the call and we have returned. Her need has not been forgotten.' The motors of the Warmaster's bionic arm whined gently as he patted Bendikt on the back. No doubt he had meant this to be a human gesture, but Bendikt did not find the crude press of metal fingers comforting.

'How long until we disembark?' Ryse asked a thin, pale officer with a shock of white hair.

The officer snapped his heels together. 'Governor Porelska has sent his personal barge to bring you down, Warmaster. *Sacramentum* is being loaded onto it as we speak. As soon as it is stowed down, I will let you know, sir. The freight captain did not think it would be more than a few hours.'

Sacramentum was Ryse's Leviathan. A brass-worked marvel of gunnery and armour and engineering that had spearheaded at least two assaults on the hive world of Owwen.

'Good,' Ryse said. 'Good.' He was one of those men who liked to fill silences with his own voice. At that moment one of the adjutants touched the Warmaster's sleeve. The commander of a battalion of Mordians had arrived on the viewing deck. They were standing by the lift in a formal and uninviting group, waiting for an introduction.

'Ah!' Ryse said as if a passing chat with the Mordians was all he wanted in the world, and nodded to them all. 'Excuse me, gentlemen.'

As Ryse's entourage fell away only one other man remained, staring down at Cadia.

Bendikt took him in through the corner of his eye. He was a first-degree general from his epaulette, but he wore combat drab, not dress uniform, and had both hands placed firmly on the brass railing, his fists clenching it so tightly that his knuckles had gone white.

His boots had not been polished since embarkation. There were mud splatters on the hem of his coat and dried mud stains on his knees as well. That was a detail worthy of note: generals didn't often kneel, never mind in mud.

Bendikt couldn't hold himself back. 'Excuse me, sir,' he ventured. 'Are you General Creed?'

The man turned to him. He was broad and bull-necked, with close-shaven hair. His eyes were hard and intense. Bendikt coloured. 'Sorry. I mean, are you *the* General Creed?'

'Well, there are four generals named Creed last I counted.' The other man's eyes had a mischievous twinkle.

'General Ursarkar Creed?'

'Yes. I am one of two whose name is Ursarkar Creed. The other, a fine old man of three hundred and twenty years, has retired to the training world of Katak. I spent six months with him there, working with Catachans. Good bunch. General Ursarkar Creed had a particularly good stock of amasec, though I didn't think much of his stubs. They were a little too refined for me. I like something with a little more punch.'

Creed's mouth almost smiled. 'As he came first, *he* has the honour of being plain General Ursarkar Creed. Because I am the second, I am known as Ursarkar *E.* Creed.' He put out a hand and Bendikt returned the hard grip.

'I am honoured to meet you,' Bendikt said.

Creed seemed amused by the word. 'Honoured?'

'Yes,' Bendikt said. 'We were in the same draft.'

'Were we now?'

'Yes. I always thought that my career had gone well until I heard you had made general. The first of our draft.'

To make general by the age of forty years, Terran standard, was a feat almost unheard of.

Once he'd got over his envy, he'd studied Creed and his tactics, and when they'd been in the same warzone, Bendikt had followed Creed's career through memos and regimental dispatches.

'How do you feel? I mean, you've been predicting this recall for nearly two years now,' Bendikt said.

Creed seemed impressed, but there was no joy for him in being right. 'I have. You're right. It would have been better if the recall had started two years earlier.'

'And you were demoted for your troubles.'

'Only pending investigation. Ryse – should I say, Warmaster Ryse – stuck by me.'

'Is that because you saved the day on Relion V?'

Creed laughed. His breath smelled faintly of amasec. Creed was also famous for his prodigious appetite for the bottle. 'That's probably half the reason. The other half is that Ryse is no fool.'

There was a moment's pause as Creed took in Bendikt's uniform and regimental badge. 'You must be Major Isaia Bendikt of the Cadian One Hundred and First. Twice awarded the Valorous Unit Citation. You have one of the most highly decorated tank regiments in the whole of Cadia. Between you, your crew has won six Steel Crosses, four Steel Aquila and the Order of the Eagle's Claw.'

Bendikt's cheeks coloured and he didn't know what to say. 'Well, yes, sir. My regiment prides itself on its service to the Golden Throne.'

The smell of amasec grew stronger as Creed leaned in and spoke to Bendikt in a low, confidential voice. 'Did you ever think you would make it back to Cadia alive?'

Bendikt knew the statistics as well as any other: half of all able-bodied Cadians left the planet to fight across the Imperium of Man but fewer than one in a thousand of those ever returned. He barely needed to think. 'Never. You?'

Creed pursed his lips as his knuckles whitened again. Night was falling on Cadia and the Eye of Terror was starting to glow. There was a long pause. Creed smiled. 'Oh, I've always known that I would come back.'

Bendikt did not know how to answer that. He looked down at their home world – grey and blue in the half-light of her sun.

'And you really think Cadia is in danger?'

'The utmost danger.' Creed's nostrils flared. 'The whole

sector has been under attack for years. Plague. Treachery. Heresy. We see all these proud defences, but Cadia is like a kasr whose walls have already been undermined.'

Bendikt was lost for words again. They both looked up to the viewing dome above their heads. In the darkness of space they could see the turret lights of orbital defences, floating gun-rigs and the bright engine flares of patrolling frigates and stub-nosed defence monitors.

'You really think so?'

'I know so.' Creed smiled humourlessly, and his eyes flickered briefly across the room to where a rather embarrassed-looking Ryse was trying to explain a joke to the Mordian commander. 'Our enemies have planned for this for a thousand years. Maybe more. And we have grown complacent. Look. Ryse is more interested in little pleasantries with those dreadful Mordians than planning for the war. Cadian High Command is full of men like him. They have no idea how present the threat is. Even the High Lords of Terra suspect little, I guess. The Cadian Gate is in utmost danger and it is up to us – honest men like you and me – to ensure that she does not fall. Cadia cannot fall. She *will* not fall.'

There was a long pause.

Bendikt felt flattered by the word 'us', but he was shaken by the ominous warnings. 'What can we do?'

'We shall fight like bastards,' Creed said. 'And we have to be more devious than our foes.'

Bendikt smiled. 'Is that possible?'

'Life in the Guard has taught me three things,' Creed said. 'Endurance, grit and the understanding that with faith and courage and good leadership, anything is possible.'

'I hope you're right.'

Creed gave him a long look and leaned in once more. 'When I was young my drill sergeant had a favourite saying.'

'What is that?'

'Hope,' Creed said, 'is the first step on the road to disappointment.'

TWO

FIDELITAS VECTOR
SATELLITE EMBARKATION HANGARS
TYROK FIELDS

No one could remember the last time this had happened.

All year, the huge, draughty, impersonal chambers of the processing satellites filled with tithes of Cadian Whiteshields who would be loaded onto the cavernous decks of troop transports and delivered straight into the hungry wars of the Imperium of Man.

On Cadia, the rhythm of birth, training, conscription, graduation, embarkation and departure was as deeply felt and adhered to as the movement of the seasons from summer to winter, the rising of the sun, the fall of night.

Now, that natural sequence of life had gone into reverse. Troop transports were arriving fully laden, not empty. Years of tithes were returning within months. Veteran troops numbering in their millions. It was overloading even the efficient Cadian administrators. Long queues of troop transports hung in patient orbit and even War-master Ryse's personal transport, the *Fidelitas Vector*, had to wait for five days before she got her berth.

'The loading officer sends his apologies,' Warmaster Ryse's adjutant stated as the Warmaster took in his brief breakfast of recaff, fried slab and a pair of freshly poached eggs. He picked up his silver knife and fork and began to eat. The brooding threat had made him hungry.

The Warmaster ate his way through the five-day delay. Bendikt accepted any invitations he was given to Ryse's banquets. He'd spent long enough eating ration-grade food and could not pass up the fine table that the War-master kept.

Bendikt hoped to run into Ursarkar E. Creed once more, but he did not appear, and each time Bendikt made his way back to the troop decks after dinner with an air of disappointment.

On the last night, Bendikt was sitting at a table making conversation with a pair of veteran warriors. The first, to his right, called Lynch, claimed to have led the campaign to wipe out the xenos race called brynarr. 'They were not fighters,' he said as the servitor refilled his glass with dark red wine. He took a sip and put the cut-crystal glass back down. 'They were rather sentimental towards their pupae. It made them particularly easy to trap and kill. The sur-vival instinct was not natural to them.'

Bendikt nodded politely, as his eyes scanned the room for Creed's distinctive shape.

'Your name is Bendikt?' the man to his left said, read-ing Bendikt's place setting. 'Are you one of the Kasr Tyrok Bendikts?'

It was a question aristocratic Cadians asked him. 'No,' Bendikt said. 'I was born in the sub-hab of Kasr Halig.'

'The sub-hab?' the man said in surprise.

'Yes.'

'And now you're a major?'

Bendikt did not think he needed to answer that question. His epaulettes spoke for themselves. The general, whose place setting said he was named Grüber, took a sip of wine. 'How old are you, major?'

'Forty. Terran standard,' Bendikt said.

'The same age as General Creed?'

'Which General Creed?'

Grüber gave a little snort of surprise as he cut the smoked fish in half. 'Ursarkar Creed.'

'I think there are two General Ursarkar Creeds.' Bendikt took a sip of wine.

Grüber could not tell if he was being mocked. 'Ursarkar E. Creed,' he said.

Bendikt took a sip of wine. 'Ah! Yes, of course.'

'What did you think?'

'Very impressed.'

'Really?' Grüber said, and took another sip of wine. 'I've always found him a little overrated.'

Creed did not show up that night or any other. Bendikt made his excuses to Generals Grüber and Lynch and left early.

He spent the last full day of waiting for disembarkation in Hab-Hangar 07-85, playing Black Five with a pair of captains from the Fighting Jackals, Cadian 883rd Rifles.

The Fighting Jackals had got fat and complacent with their last posting on a settled world named Andromeda.

Bendikt didn't like being away from the front line, on principle. Downtime made men soft, and he'd found from personal experience that it gave men something to hope for: a life that they would never achieve.

It was Bendikt's duty to relieve them of their coin. In order to distract them he kept prompting the men to talk of Andromeda, but the more money they lost the less glowing their stories were. 'Well,' one of them said as he watched Bendikt shuffling the cards. 'There'd been a regiment of Catachans there before us. They were still putting the place back together.'

After an hour they were looking unhappy. 'Another game?' he suggested.

They shook their heads. Bendikt tipped the coin onto the table and began to count it up. Not bad, he thought. This lot should keep him going for a few days in the bars of Kasr Tyrok. A spectacular night, if that was all he had.

Bendikt slid the coins into his pocket, rose quickly and put out his hand. 'Good luck.'

Next morning shrill alarms rang out, and one by one, down the long hangar, the three rows of strip lumes flickered to life.

'Moving out,' Sergeant Tyson said.

'About time,' Bendikt said as he pushed himself up from his bed. Before him stretched half a mile of figures rising from their bunks, packing the last of their belongings into their backpacks.

Tyson took in the empty bottle of Arcady Pride in the bin. 'Good night last night, sir?'

The memories of his celebration came back to him. Bendikt nodded. 'Not bad,' he said. He threw the sheets back and reached for his uniform. His flak armour on the bottom, Cadian drab jacket folded neatly on top. He was still a Cadian, even when drunk.

'So, apparently, our orders have changed.' Tyson offered the latest order sheet to him, but Bendikt wasn't interested.

'Does it say where we are going?'

Tyson shook his head.

Their orders had changed at least six times in the journey. They would be manning an orbital defence platform. They would be a mobile reserve. They would be the spear-tip of a massive armoured column and sent to the outer planet of Kasr Holn as a first line of defence. Bendikt sighed. Sounded like a typical military mess. 'See if you can find someone who knows.'

'Yes, sir,' Tyson said.

Bendikt was up and dressed when his Colour Sergeant, Daal, came forward smartly and saluted.

'Everything packed and ready?' Bendikt asked.

Daal grinned. 'In truth, sir, they've been ready since the recall.'

It was true. As soon as they'd heard that they were returning to Cadia the men of the 101st had gone over their uniforms and equipment, polishing, repairing, sewing, fixing, sharpening, cleaning every button, web-pouch, blade, seam and item that they owned. It was all he expected. They were a crack unit. Elite of the elite. They barely needed leading, at times. They were like a sharp knife. All they needed was pointing in the right direction, and a little bit of pressure. They did the rest themselves.

'Good,' Bendikt said.

Daal was so excited he couldn't hold himself back. A

few moments later, as they stood over the recaff pot, he said, 'Gave second platoon a bit of a dressing-down.'

Bendikt nodded but said nothing. His head was hurting less.

'They got a little fresh last night.'

'Me too,' Bendikt said, and took a sip of the lukewarm recaff. This long into a voyage and the recycled water started to taste of oil and sterilants, and even with recaff this strong, you couldn't mask the flavour. He put the cup down. He couldn't drink any more of the stuff. 'When's our slot?'

'Zero nine hundred hours, ship time,' Daal said.

'Is ship time synced?'

'No. We're six hours, fifty-three minutes ahead of planet time. Apologies from the captain. There was not time in the flight from the Mandeville Point... Haste and all that.'

Bendikt nodded and looked at the empty bottle in the bin. Next drink, he thought, would be in the fleshpots of Kasr Tyrok. He could not wait.

As debarkation alarms rang, the ballast deck lights of the *Fidelitas Vector* flickered on, illuminating thousands of tanks and support vehicles, parked and waiting. For the journey, their machine-spirits had been stilled, but as long files of marching Guardsmen moved slowly down towards the Troop Processor Alpha 4, the armour was loaded straight onto landers and ferried to the planet.

The *Fidelitas Vector* trembled as vast decks filled with noise and fumes; Leman Russ tanks reversed towards the lander ramps, followed by vast tracked ammo carriers that creaked under the weight of man-sized Baneblade shells, armour-penetrating rounds and the massive, squat, building-levelling rocket shells for the Banehammer siege cannon.

Ryse was the first to leave the ship, on board the governor's personal barge, with his staff and the *Sacramentum*.

'Like rats,' Tyson said as they watched the governor's barge diminishing towards the planet.

The honour of following the Warmaster went to the Cadian 774th, 'Titan Killers', with their complement of three ancient Shadowswords. Next were the Cadian 993rd/57th, the 'Bluecaps', a thousand and ten veteran warriors who had spent the last three years fighting greenskins at close quarters on the jungle worlds of Semyon Prime.

Bendikt's 101st were scheduled to load onto a drop-ship late that morning, but their appointed time came and went while they were still waiting on the *Fidelitas Vector*. They were standing on a vast descent ramp, tilting steadily downwards to the loading decks.

Bendikt kept checking his chronometer. He'd been in queues like this before, where the Administratum had cocked up titanically, and they'd spent days in the exit corridors, waiting for their slot to come through.

'Looking forward to Cadia?' Tyson asked.

'Well, I think I missed out on the bars of Kasr Tyrok. But home. To be honest, no, not really.'

His adjutant looked a little crestfallen.

Bendikt sighed. 'I'll feel better when I touch down, I'm sure.'

'Sure you will, sir.'

Bendikt nodded. 'Still the little worse for wear.'

'I'll get you another recaff, sir.'

'Yes. Please do. And make this one stronger.'

Bendikt was still waiting for his recaff when at last the queue ahead of them began to move, and the Guardsmen stood up and started walking. For two hours they filed down through long, wide access ramps, still fuzzy with promethium fumes, into the troop processing plant.

It took three hours for their lander, a three-tiered ferry, to fill with their complement of inducted Guardsmen, tanks, ordnance and equipment, and then, with a dull metallic clang, the void-chambers were sealed, air-supply pipes and magnetic clamps disengaged, and the fat, ungainly landing craft fell towards the planet.

The atmosphere inside the lander was cramped and close. There were no windows. Nothing but the hunched shapes of men and equipment, and an air of tense apprehension. For most of their lives, being in a lander meant a new warzone, and there was nothing within the crowded, stuffy interior to distract the mind. Most of his men sat in rows on the floor, their knees pulled up to their chins, heads bowed, helmets on, eyes shut.

Bendikt's stomach lurched as the lander dropped from the battleship towards Cadia, but then there was the sense of release and of falling. He felt he ought to see how his troops were doing, and pulled himself up with one hand on the metal wall.

He made his way along the lines of waiting troops, swapping brief words with his men. He picked out one young lad. 'What's your name?'

'Georg, sir.'

'How long since you left Cadia?'

'A year and a half, sir.'

'Bet you didn't think you'd be returning so soon.'

'No, sir.'

'Got a girl back home?'

Georg's cheeks turned crimson as he grinned. 'Well. Yes...' He almost forgot to add 'sir'. 'She drew the planetary defence force.'

Bendikt nodded. 'Good luck,' he said.

Bendikt was about to pass on when Georg fumbled inside his coat and pulled out a well-thumbed pict of a young girl in Cadian drab, her hair tied back from her face. Bendikt took it. It was what you did when a man showed you his sweetheart. 'She looks like a fighter.'

Georg grinned. 'She was, sir. Galina. Fought against the draft decision. Went right up to Cadian High Command...' The sentence trailed off, and Bendikt finished it for him.

'But there was nothing they could do.'

Georg nodded. 'Nothing.'

Bendikt returned the picture. 'I hope she's not forgotten you.' But then Creed's words came back to him.

Hope paved the road to disappointment.

Last time the Cadian 101st had fallen planetwards they'd been rocked by flakk fire from the opposing greenskins. It had been a terrifying descent. But this time there was no thunder of war, no evasive manoeuvres, no ping of shrapnel ringing on the outer hull.

They came in from the north, passing high over the ice-capped peaks of the Rezla Mountains and banking gently to the right. Slaved servo guns tracked the drop-ship as it burned off speed on a long descent over the northern polar regions, following the prescribed flight path that had been punched into the command consoles of its servitor docking crew.

The descent took the best part of two hours. It was a long, slow parabola, and by the time the landing gear was engaged and they felt the lander slow to a hover before finally touching down, the men's mood had turned almost jubilant. When the far doors opened, they started to laugh and joke and there was a great cheer when the vast landing ramps slammed down and the light and air of Cadia swept in.

Bendikt stood on the top of the landing craft ramp and breathed deeply. Before him was the vast military transit camp that was Tyrok Fields.

Cadian High Command had recalled all Cadian units. No one knew when this had ever happened before, and now, as he stood there and looked out across the miles and miles of Tyrok Fields, he was struck by the buzz of millions of Cadian Shock Troopers.

The enormity of it hit him, and he stood amazed, like a feral world savage seeing his first orbital craft. The vast flat plain had been turned into a city of tents, parked armour, piles of ordnance and rations, and supplementary supplies. Bendikt could not even begin to guess how many Guardsmen were camped here. They stretched away on all sides, as far as he could see. The hum of their activity was a constant roar. There had to be a million, at least. And on the far horizon, like a beast on the veldt, a Leviathan blared its horns in salute as a maniple of Warlord Titans strode southwards.

The Titans answered with a trumpet blast and rolled slowly towards him, like a gathering wave. Bendikt grinned.

He found himself hugging Tyson, slapping him on the back and laughing out loud.

They were home.

Looking back, Bendikt regretted how he spent his first day and a half back on Cadia.

He passed up the chance to visit Kasr Tyrok and went with Colour Sergeant Daal and his support staff to report in to the local Munitorum office to sort out their orders.

The Munitorum office was a low sandbagged shack in the corner of Camp 889. They took a ticket – D9973 – from a servitor-station and waited their turn. The wait was long, but this was Cadia, so it was orderly and disciplined – and the room was full of other Shock Troopers. They spent the time finding out if they'd ever been in the same warzone.

When their ticket was finally called, they were brought to a low camp desk, where a Munitorum clerk rested his hands on the table before him, on which there were ration packs, a sheaf of neat papers and a heavy metal aquila stamp.

'Cadian 101st,' he said by way of greeting.

Bendikt nodded and sat, resting his helmet on his lap.

The clerk checked his papers. 'Major Bendikt? Good. My great-uncle was in the 101st.'

'What was his name?'

'Oh, you wouldn't know him,' the clerk said. 'He was killed in his first engagement. Crashed Valkyrie.'

Bendikt had heard a hundred stories like that. He was tired and wanted nothing more than to be sitting in a bar, putting his money to good use. 'War's harsh,' he said.

The Munitorum clerk was an old man with wide-set

round eyes and a manner of cocking his head that reminded Bendikt of an eagle. But he was polite and efficient and supplied them with their ration books and chits for ammunition, winter boots, medical supplies and everything else that an army needed. 'Rations look thin,' Bendikt said as Daal looked at the daily food allowance.

The Munitorum official turned his head and stared down at him, before cocking it the other way. 'Siege footing,' he said.

'Already?' Daal said.

The clerk nodded.

Bendikt put his helmet back on. He thought he would check their orders. 'So we're supposed to be joining up with our tanks and the 74th Armoured Battalion of Northern Command.'

The official looked down at the scroll of servitor script that he was using. 'Hmm,' he said. 'Your orders seem to have changed.'

'Again?'

The man cocked his head again and looked at him. 'Yes. Your unit has been posted to Observation Post 9983.'

'Where's that?'

'I don't know.' The clerk's cheeks coloured. He clearly did not appreciate surprises like this. Not on his watch. 'Hmm,' he said, and frowned for a moment as he looked for the missing data. At last, he looked up with an expression of weary resignation. 'That is, I fear, classified.'

'So how do we get there?'

'I'm afraid I don't know.'

'And our armour and equipment?'

'I'm afraid–'

'You don't know.'

The man cocked his head to the side and nodded. 'Exactly.'

By the time Bendikt got back to their camp the transports had already set out to Kasr Tyrok.

'I could drive you,' Tyson offered.

'How long would it take?'

'Six hours.'

Bendikt seriously considered it for a moment, but it didn't make sense. If they left now they'd only have time to get there and then turn back round in time for embarkation. 'Kind of makes the whole idea pointless, don't you think?'

'I guess, sir.'

Bendikt cursed. The lights of the camp stretched out in all directions. He looked up at the lurid purple stain in the sky, and the Eye of Terror glaring down at him.

'I forgot how bright it is,' Bendikt said.

Tyson nodded. 'Frekking ugly, isn't it?'

'Yes,' Bendikt said. He'd missed Cadia, but he had not missed the night sky. The Eye of Terror was brighter than he remembered. Its green-and-purple light cast a shadow on the ground. It made him sick looking into it.

Never, he thought. An instinctive response.

Never.

A staff Centaur arrived at Bendikt's HQ tent an hour before dawn. 'Are you Major Bendikt?' a territorial officer asked as he made the sign of the aquila in a brisk, perfunctory way.

'Yes.'

'Your transport is waiting.'

'Good. To Observation Point 9983?'

'No. Air Base Alpha 443.'

'Tyson, have our orders been changed again?'

Tyson blushed. 'No.'

'Air Base Alpha is a transit hub.'

'Where are we going? To Observation Post 9983?'

The man checked his papers. There was a pause. 'I don't see where, I'm afraid.'

Bendikt's temper was starting to rise. 'We were told we are being sent to Observation Post 9983.'

The other officer's cheeks coloured. 'I don't know, but I have to make space. There's another lander coming in tomorrow during the parade.'

'What parade?'

'Volscani Cataphracts. There's an official welcome.'

Bendikt was pissed off. 'Never heard of them.'

THREE

OBSERVATION POST 9983

A Guardsman had few expectations, yet at the least he wanted to know where he was going to war. But no one had heard of Observation Post 9983 and the 101st had a deflated air about it as the men of the regiment gathered their kit and marched the distance to Air Base Alpha 443.

In the skies above Tyrok Fields fliers were swooping down, constantly emptying and refilling with regiments, as some made their way out to the kasr fortresses along ten-lane arterial highways, while vast planetary landers brought in fresh regiments.

'Any idea where this observation post is?' Colour Sergeant Daal asked as they saw the lines of Valkyries waiting.

'None,' Bendikt said. His temper was starting to fray. They hadn't come home to observe. They were the 101st, for Throne's sake. A figure ran out from the side door of one of the Valkyries. He had a data-slate in his hand and looked at it before saying, 'Major Bendikt?'

'Yes.'

'We're ready for you.'

'Know where we're going?'

The man pulled a face. 'Sorry.'

'What about our tanks?'

The man tilted his head. 'Sorry. Above my rank.'

Bendikt cursed under his breath. 'Daal. Get the men on board.'

They climbed up onto the aircraft, platoon by platoon.

'That's the lot,' Daal said as the last Guardsmen clambered aboard.

Bendikt looked about him one last time and nodded. 'Right. Let's find out where the hell we're heading.'

They left their Valkyrie's side doors open. Bendikt and Sergeant Daal stood staring out over Cadia.

It took six hours to cross the checkerboard of Tyrok Fields, and then they were over moors, with armoured regiments crossing the wilds like herds on the savannah. The wind was cold on their faces. It made their eyes water. They had to shout over the roar of the turbines. 'We're heading north-east,' Bendikt said. For what it mattered.

'So much for the drinking district of Kasr Tyrok,' Daal said.

Bendikt stood in the lee of the doorway and looked down. Homecoming was overrated, he thought. Whatever this observation post was, there had better be a damn good bar nearby.

A row of ten Leviathans was making its way across the plains below. Each one was a hundred yards tall, a hunched beetle of ceramite and gun barrels, trundling slowly along on massive tracks, with an honour guard of

Baneblade tanks looking diminutive next to them. They went in single file like a herd of giant grox.

Their Valkyrie tipped to the side as the men crowded in to see, squinting into the wind. The Valkyrie did a little salute and the signals officer of one of the Leviathans gave a short toot over the broadcasters to acknowledge them.

And then the Valkyries turned south towards the Central Massif, and the land beneath them was white with snow.

They landed at a bustling base high up in the moors of Cadia's Northern Massif. It was about as cold and bleak a place as you could imagine, but there was no time to get out. The Valkyries refuelled and then set off again, heading south.

They flew through the night and got what sleep they could.

Next morning the engines were wheezing in the thin atmosphere.

'Are we lost?' Daal asked.

Bendikt opened the doors a crack. They were halfway up a craggy black mountain with snow-capped peaks, heading towards a vast vertical cliff face under the summit. Clinging to the side of the cliff, two-thirds of the way up, was a tiny landing pad with a rockcrete parapet, a pair of slaved servo-bolters tracking their approach, and the tarpaulin cover of a Hydra platform, below which was a metal door.

There could not be a more bleak and deserted posting on Cadia, and it was there that they were heading.

'I do not believe this,' Bendikt said.

He glanced at the faces of his men. No one looked happy.

* * *

The landing pad was only big enough for one Valkyrie at a time. It was a dangerous approach, with mountain gusts buffeting them as they approached the cliff wall. Each Valkyrie hovered as the troops disembarked, and then the empty craft fell away as the next in the queue moved forward.

It seemed to take an age for Bendikt's craft to get its turn. As they waited, the co-pilot came back to brief them.

'We are low on fuel!' he shouted over the wind. 'Get your men off quick.'

Bendikt nodded. He was tense as they made their approach. The black cliff filled his vision as their Valkyrie moved in.

The co-pilot waved at them through the cockpit window.

'Ready!' Daal shouted, and stood at the doorway as they touched down. The men jumped out with all their kit, still perfectly presented, and ran over the ice-slick surface to the ramp that led down to the parapet.

Sergeant Dykene of Second Platoon was there, offering a steadying hand. 'Careful! Don't slip. It's three thousand yards until you hit the bottom.'

Bendikt didn't need a hand. He strode along the narrow parapet, and in through the metal blast doors into a vast reinforced chamber, where the air was warm and dry.

He strode forward. After the roar of wind and engines, the inner space seemed almost silent. He paused and listened. In the stillness, there was the distinctive low hum of maintenance engines.

He looked about. On the rockcrete wall, in chalk, were the crossed flag murals of all the regiments that had been quartered there. The names stretched away into the distant gloom. The last said Cadian 290th 'Steel Fists'.

'What the hell is this place?' Bendikt asked.

He turned and looked about at the cavernous chamber, and spotted a man in civilian uniform making his way straight towards him.

He had neatly combed grey hair, bushy black eyebrows and bright violet eyes.

'You are Major Bendikt?' the newcomer asked.

'Yes.'

The man's voice was light. 'My name is Rivald. I am the caretaker here. Welcome to Observation Post 9983.'

Observation Post 9983 was little more than an icicle-clad parapet and landing pad, clinging two-thirds of the way up a mile-high granite cliff face, under a looming over-hang of thick white ice. The parapet hugged the contours of the mountain, with loop-holes and firing ports staring out into two-thousand-yard drops, and an ancient Hydra plat-form, draped with tarpaulins, just visible under the snow.

It was a bleak, cold place, without road or access, apart from the landing pad, which was subject to treacherous updraughts and on which only the most skilled pilots would dare land. Why anyone would want to place a base here was something that troubled them all.

Bendikt summoned his vox operator, Mere.

'Made contact with Northern Command?'

'Yessir,' Mere said. 'There's an old vox relay system here. Beast of a thing.' He laughed. 'Could probably talk to the captain of the *Fidelitas Vector*.'

'Well, thank him for his hospitality,' Bendikt snapped. 'But first get someone in command. Find out what the hell we are doing here, and what the hell we are supposed to be observing.'

'Yessir.'

'Tyson. Has Armitage scouted out this place?'

'Yes.' Tyson sniffed. 'There's six floors that we know of. All going down into the mountain.'

'Six?' Bendikt said. 'That you know of?'

'Well, Armitage says there are doors on the third floor that he can't open.'

Bendikt cursed. 'Where's the caretaker... What's his name?'

'Rivald,' Tyson said. 'He appears to live in a series of officer habs, on the second floor.'

When Bendikt found him, Rivald was praying at a little shrine on the second floor. The doors of the shrine were open against the wall; from the flame of a stubby red candle, light flickered on the image of the Omnissiah, and fresh libations of oil dripped from the shallow sacrarium.

Rivald put up a hand to say that Bendikt should wait for a moment, and when he finished, he wiped the oil from his hands onto his apron. 'The machine-spirits here are very old,' he said as an apology. 'They need special care.'

Bendikt's temper had been rising with each moment he had to wait and Rivald seemed a safe person to vent it on.

'Listen,' Bendikt said. 'I don't give a frekk about the machines. My men had to cross the galaxy to get back to Cadia in her hour of need.' He felt like Warmaster Ryse, waxing lyrical, and his irritation grew. 'We're a tank regiment and we've been stuck halfway up a mountain in the middle of the Central Massif. Do you know what the hell this place is and why we're here?'

Rivald had a look in his eye that seemed to imply this

kind of conversation had happened before. He folded the metal doors back on the shrine and said, 'No.'

'Nothing?'

'I have guesses,' Rivald said. 'Come to my chamber.'

Rivald led him to a disused wing with brass fittings and polished nalwood doors. 'This was once the officers' lodgings,' he said. 'The main barracks are on the third floor. There's room for three thousand men here, at least. I've counted the beds. It keeps me busy between my duties.'

Rivald led him through a pair of double doors, marked with the sign of the aquila, and into a long corridor, lit by a single strip lume. The air had a musty, dry feel. The corridors were clean and neat, and in one of the rooms, a light was shining.

'This way, please,' Rivald said. 'This is my room.'

Bendikt followed him inside. It was a neat, plain cell. There was a camp bed, a three-drawered dresser, a poster of a red aquila and the bold text: The enemy is listening... Keep it to yourself!

The furniture was clearly much newer than the rockcrete fittings, which had an ancient, baroque feel to them.

Rivald motioned to him to sit down on a plain wooden chair.

Bendikt remained standing. 'What *is* this place?'

'Observation Post–'

Bendikt cut him off. 'Quit the grox-shit. Clearly not. Why do they need three thousand men here? What is there to watch? We're halfway up a mountain.'

'I can't tell you, I'm afraid. I came here twenty-five years ago.'

'And what do you do – exactly?'

'I keep the place running. I pray to the Golden Throne. I

keep the machine-spirits company. Sometimes units come. Like yours.'

'When?'

'A year ago. They were the Cadian 9034th Airborne. They were not happy to be here.'

'I can bet. How long did they stay?'

'Six months.'

Bendikt felt sick at the thought. 'Is there any way off this base?'

Rivald shook his head.

'There must be.'

'No.'

'Can we scale the mountain? Or go down? Are there ropes?'

'Others tried,' Rivald said, and frowned. 'I have seen it. There is nothing. Only the landing pad.'

'One landing pad. Three thousand men. There must be something here. My scouts said there are doors. On the third level…'

'Yes. They bear the name "Salvation 9983".'

'What does that mean?'

Rivald shook his head. 'I do not know.'

'Can you open them?'

'No.'

'Are you sure?'

The old man nodded.

'Well, frekk-all use they are then.'

There were footsteps in the corridor outside. Bendikt put his hand to his laspistol, but it was Tyson. He was breathless. He saluted as Bendikt slid the sidearm back into its holster. 'Sir! There's been an incident.' He took in a deep breath and the words spilled out all in one. 'The Governor of Cadia is dead.'

'Dead?'

Tyson nodded. 'There's been an occurrence at Tyrok Fields.'

'A battle?'

Tyson tried to explain. 'It was the Volscani, sir. They turned their guns on the governor. At the landing site.' He took a deep breath, and it all came out in a sentence. 'Some are saying, well, sir, it seems that the Volscani have turned *heretic*.'

FOUR

OBSERVATION POST 9983

Without facts all the Cadian 101st had was speculation, and that was not good. Without evidence, a Guardsman's mind turned to the worst possible eventualities as a child in the dark will imagine monsters.

Bendikt did not care where the enemy were. What they needed were facts. An enemy's location and strength. How best to kill them.

Bendikt ran through all the units he could think of and tried to get a link through to them, but the channels were overloaded with the bellowing of men in battle. The men and women of the Cadian 101st listened in stunned silence to the vox communications from the fields of Tyrok. Panicked shouts of surrounded units. Commanders desperately trying to locate their men. All the confusion and terror of war.

It sounded like hell.

Bendikt punched the wall in his fury. 'Powerless!' he

hissed, pacing up and down, trying to find an explanation for what was happening as the rumble of war shook Tyrok Fields. 'We're frekking powerless!'

Had some hothead gone rogue? A perceived insult, perhaps? The Eye of Terror drove men mad.

But as they listened, a thread of calm began to establish itself. It was one man's voice, cutting through the shouting and the screams. He gave commands. Calmed terrified men down. He started to bring the scattered survivors of Tyrok Fields together again into an army: fought chaos with order.

'That's Creed!' Bendikt said, and stood with one hand on the vox, as if standing next to the general. 'That's Ursarkar E. Creed!' he shouted. 'Get Creed on the vox. No, send him a message. Tell him Major Bendikt and the 101st are stranded at Observation Post 9983.'

Mere tried, but the vox channels were overloaded. After an hour of failing, he raised his hand. 'There's going to be an announcement, sir.'

The whole 101st gathered in a rough horseshoe about the vox.

'Men and women of Cadia.'

It was Creed. He was speaking intimately. It was as if he were in the room with them. They felt his closeness; it was part of his magic.

'We lost many today. Friends. Sons. Mothers. Daughters. Comrades. We withstood fire, bombardment, treachery and cowardice. And we did not flinch. We did not turn to ask if another would step up and take our place. We stood, we fought, and we strode forward into battle.'

There was the sound of distant cheers through the vox, and Bendikt's stomach ached. If only they could have been there, in the battle. He pictured the scene, the vast Tyrok Fields stretching away, fires burning, medicae units looking for the injured. Creed's bullish silhouette, with a greatcoat slung over his shoulders, cigar-stub in his hand.

'Today the High Command of Cadia have asked me to serve as Lord Castellan of Cadia.' There were more cheers. The atmosphere in the room was so quiet you could hear a man breathe.

Bendikt could imagine Creed's knuckles, white on the podium, waiting for the crowd to go silent. Creed's voice came again. 'I have accepted the honour.'

Bendikt and Daal exchanged looks.

There was a long pause, as the cheers of Tyrok Fields rang out.

Creed was waiting. Bendikt imagined him putting up his hands for silence. 'What happened today was no accident. It was no chance. This was orchestrated by a mind that has planned and plotted for thousands of years. The Despoiler.

'It is the hour that we have long foreseen. The chance to prove ourselves his match.'

More cheers.

'I offer you nothing but blood and battle. This is our part in a war that has lasted ten thousand years – and today, brothers, today we – you – have won a great victory that will be remembered for another ten thousand years, or as long as the Imperium of Mankind shall last!'

The sound of cheering was drowned out by a military band playing Flower of Cadia.

The broadcast was clearly over.

'Turn it off,' Bendikt told Mere.

There was stunned silence. Bendikt stood by the vox and looked into the faces of his soldiers. 'You heard what

Creed had to say and I know that you feel the same as me. We should be down there. Instead, we're here, in this Throne-forsaken observation platform. I'm going to do all I can to sort this mess out. You'll all have a chance to strike a blow against our foes. I promise you that.'

The next day dawn did not come.

The skies of Cadia turned black as the great fleets of Imperial Navy defence monitors and orbital defence platforms – the proud defences that he had seen, just days before, from the decks of the *Fidelitas Vector* – were swept aside by the vast fleet of the Black Legion. Massed cruisers, landers, crash-pods, the war-hosts of the Despoiler filled the skies.

Weeks turned to months, and the attitude changed from anger to despair; Creed's pronouncements over the vox became more impassioned. *'People of Cadia...'* each speech would begin.

'We have smashed an armoured column at Kasr Relon. The enemy has landed on Cadian soil in great force. We are the generation upon whose shoulders lies the heavy duty of sending them all to their deaths.'

Creed's deep voice remained a constant, even when he had bad news to share.

'People of Cadia. The walls of Kasr Batrok have been breached, but I am assured that the men there are fighting with grit and resolve, and it cannot be long before the enemy are trapped and isolated, and their forces entirely destroyed.'

'People of Cadia, hold strong! We are the barb that holds the foe. Reinforcements are on their way. The High Lords of Terra commend you for your sacrifices. Hold the line! Repel the enemy. Do not give ground.'

* * *

Each night, clots of black cruisers dropped flocks of landers that fell planetwards like flocks of carrion birds. They disgorged their full payloads, spewing out a disorganised sprawl of ritually scarred cultists, daemon engines and champions of the Dark Gods who killed their way to power.

Feral and hive worlds had been emptied of populations and loaded into vast hangars, and now they spilled out in maddened squads numbering thousands in each, charging in wild jubilation, screaming unholy names, losing themselves to prayer and abandon. They spewed out in such numbers that even the massed brigades and armoured columns of the Cadian Shock Troopers, the finest human warriors in the galaxy, were slowly driven back: trench by trench; redoubt by redoubt; and finally kasr by kasr.

Day after day, hour after hour, tons of ash coiled snake-like into the upper atmosphere, turning the planet dark.

Each day, Major Bendikt stood on the high parapet of Observation Post 9983 and watched in desperate impotence.

On the thirtieth day, he took out his scopes to watch the Black Fleet mass its power against his hometown of Kasr Halig. His tri-dome helmet cast a slanted shadow across his face as the broadside of lance batteries strobed the night of Cadia with long bars of incandescent white light. The lightning storm went on for hours, smothering the plain in dust and ash, and stitching an irregular pattern of mushroom clouds up into the high atmosphere. Kasr Halig was taking a fearful punishment.

Day by day its void shields flickered blue and then yellow. They were straining to the limits.

'Sir?'

Bendikt turned. Sergeant Tyson was making his way towards him, still pulling his thick, ice-world gloves on. Bendikt had been leaning far over the parapet and he pulled back as Tyson joined him.

'How do you think it's going down there?' Tyson asked.

The lance-lightning strobed their faces. 'They're taking a hell of a pounding.'

Tyson nodded.

'It won't be long,' Bendikt said.

Tyson's expression said it would not. He puffed out his cheeks. 'You should get some rest, sir,' he said.

Another furious broadside against the city rolled like thunder.

'I was born in that city,' Bendikt said. 'I know her switchback streets and armoured intersections like the butt of my lasrifle.'

They stood, lightning casting stark shadows across their faces as the orbital bombardment continued. The mountain beneath their feet trembled as a titanic explosion on the plains lit the clouds from within, like a distant, red nebula. There was a series of gathering blasts, each one big enough to show yellow through the gloom, and Bendikt felt his guts knot themselves together as the *boom!* rolled across the plain towards him.

The debris rose miles high: chunks of rockcrete, bastions, armouries and defenders, like dust, rising into the upper atmosphere.

Kasr Halig was no more.

The very fate of the Imperium of Man hung in the balance, and there was nothing he or his Cadian 101st could do. 'We can stay ready,' Tyson said by way of consolation. 'Stay fresh. We can keep ourselves sharp.'

Bendikt made no comment. He had no more words left. He was stuck on the mountain fastness, and Cadia was dying before his eyes.

On the one hundred and tenth day of the war, Bendikt was stripped to the waist doing press-ups when the vox-unit crackled. He fumbled for a moment, dusted his hands off. 'Tyson?'

The other man's voice was indistinct with the gale that was blowing outside.

'Say that again.' Bendikt had to raise his voice to be heard. 'Again,' he said. There was a long pause as his words echoed in the vast empty chamber. 'A Valkyrie? Are you sure?'

'*Yes,*' Tyson said. '*Coming in now.*'

Bendikt cursed as the link was dropped. He pulled his undershirt and flak-jacket on and started to hurry up through the empty hangars.

The vox link was re-established as he exited the stairwell. Tyson was calling his name. The urgency of his voice sent a chill of fear through Bendikt, the sound of his footsteps gathering speed until he was running.

'*Bendikt!*' Tyson said. '*You have to come. He's here!*' Tyson was practically shouting into the vox.

'Who?' Bendikt demanded.

Tyson could barely contain himself. '*It's frekking Creed! He's here.*'

PART TWO
THE WAR FOR CADIA

ONE

On the scuffed blackboard of the ruined schola the lesson for the day was still drawn in chalk. *Do not waste your tears; I was not born to watch the world grow dim...* For the students of Schola 5, Guild Quarter, Kasr Myrak, teaching had ended when the war for Cadia had begun, right there in mid-sentence, but Minka knew the end of the quote. Every Cadian knew it. She'd spent hours as a child reciting her Quotes Imperium. She paused.

Minka had been a student here just four years earlier. Her mind's eye looked back into her own past: the hall full of young cadets, girls with their hair cut military-short, boys leaning by the locker doors, the tall, bearded schola-major standing with one arm braced straight against the wall, talking armoured tactics with a slight, blonde cadet in ponytails.

Minka allowed herself a second's indulgence: she smelled the carbolic soap on her freshly pressed clothes, the metallic scent of gun lubricant on her hands, the thrill of an hour about to be spent in the Imperial chapel – but she could feel the impatience of her partner, Yegor – the last survivor of the 93rd Mordian Ironguard.

Medi-packs, guns, ammo, battery packs, food – there had to be something here of use.

Minka barely noticed the stink as she picked her way around the room, then into the officers' mess. Locker doors hung open, books and files and scraps of paper littered the floor. There was a bloodstain on the polished tiles, the puddle smeared where the body had been dragged away.

Three bodies lay half buried under the fallen roof-girders at the end of the corridor. They'd been there for weeks. The hollows of their eyes had filled with dust, as snow filled a winter footprint. She checked the pockets of the dead men and got half a lho-stick and a hand-worn aquila charm.

'Anything?' the Mordian asked.

'Just this.' She held out the aquila. She wasn't an idiot. She kept the lho-stick for herself.

Fighting broke out on Euphrates Street. There was a flash of a flare, the crump of a mortar, then the dull-rattle bursts of a distant autocannon. Neither paused. You only heard the shells that were meant for someone else.

Minka led them through a doorway into the enclosed square of the drill yard. The rockcrete slabs were marked with white lines. Someone had set up a water stand, but the metal drum was riddled with auto-rifle rounds, and the bottom was empty.

Minka pointed. 'Look!'

Yegor couldn't see anything.

'There,' she said, and took his arm. 'A gun barrel. Can you see it?'

Yegor squinted. 'Cover me,' he said.

Minka crouched in the corner of the yard, lascarbine to her shoulder, as Yegor carefully picked his hand- and footholds. He slipped back a little as he made his way to the broken window. The iron shutters hung by a single hinge. Yegor had to work his way round to the exposed side of the building. Minka caught his look and moved across the yard to cover him.

A pair of corpses hung from the cast-iron streetlights at the front of the school. The dead bodies revolved slowly on their axis. They had not been there yesterday. Minka slid her lascarbine forward. She gave a low warning whistle, and Yegor paused and pointed.

Heretic, his signal said. Minka nodded and put her carbine to her shoulder.

It was time to kill.

The captains of Battlefleet Cadia had kept their ships at the highest state of preparedness.

They had battered the Black Fleet on its approach to the planet, until the terrible understanding came to them that they had been trying to fend off only a single squadron of Abaddon's great armada.

When the full strength of the Despoiler had arrived at Cadia it had smashed its way through the veteran defences, orbital and fleet-based, and it had turned the skies of Cadia black, blotting out the sun and stars.

Landers, battleships, tankers and drop-ships had clustered over Cadia like flies on a corpse. Orbital bombardments had brought night as debris was thrown into the stratosphere, then the first landings brought millions of cultists onto the planet.

Where they came from or what these fanatics called themselves Minka didn't know or care. The cultists were undisciplined, untrained, unable to hold their own against the elite Cadian troops. All they had was madness and ferocity. It was like fighting rabid dogs.

In Kasr Myrak the loyalists had dubbed them 'the Unnamed'.

Minka let the Unnamed come forward. He was gaunt, hive-world pale, his hands shaking. There was blood about his mouth. It didn't look like his.

He had not seen her. Minka braced herself. The las-bolt hit him in the gut and he went down like a wounded spider, bent double, legs and arms scrabbling wildly in the air. The second shot hit him high in the chest. This time his body fell back against the rockcrete road slabs, and blood began to puddle about him.

Magister House lay in Unnamed territory, three blocks south, between Euphrates Street and Statue Square. Ratling sniper Belagg Grakk lay on the seventh floor and waited. He had been behind enemy lines for three days now. The fighting had swilled around and through the building, and passed on again, like a tornado, or a tidal wave. And now he was among them.

It was how he fought. A small, secret shadow waiting for his moment to strike. A mortar team here, an officer there, just enough to keep the enemy disoriented and wary. Eight floors up, with las-batteries for a hundred and fifty shots.

A hundred and fifty dead heretics.

Belagg crawled forward. An Unnamed war party was making their way along Chapel Street, hunched like they were running into a storm. Belagg picked out the leader. He wore a commissar's greatcoat and had a pair of heads hanging at his belt, a sword in his hand. The heads were fresh. One looked like demo-expert Drawling. The other like his bomb-maker, Eddard. Belagg didn't waste time checking. He flipped the safety off, sucked in a few long breaths, and aimed.

Nothing scared men more than a sniper shot, but the Unnamed didn't even pause. They didn't duck. Even the man he had shot. The las-bolt had hit him low in the back and his legs were gone. But he was pumped full of stimms and he moved like a two-legged lizard, arms dragging him along the street, a smear of blood on the rockcrete behind him.

Minka heard a shout. More Unnamed were coming. She hissed up at Yegor to be quick and he caught the end of the gun barrel and yanked. A stream of rockcrete dust slid down as he pulled himself higher. 'It's jammed,' he hissed back and lifted an iron girder to yank the ammo feed free. The square metal box set off an avalanche of rubble and dust. It hit the ground with a full thud of stubber rounds.

The Mordian put his shoulder under the girder. The shouts were coming closer. They must have seen the body.

'Come on!' Minka called and Yegor put a hand under the girder and gave it a shove. The fizz of a fuse gave her a bare moment's warning. She caught Yegor's eye. It was clear he understood.

The bomb went off.

* * *

Captain Rath Sturm had seen everything the galaxy could throw at him and had the scars, metal skull-plate and augmetic eye to prove it. He'd earned his veteran stripes on Armageddon. A man who'd fought greenskins was hard to scare.

He was the commander of the survivors within the city. He'd risen to that position, not by rank or promotion, but because he looked after each and every one of his fighters as if they were his own flesh and blood.

As the Unnamed hunted for survivors of the explosion, he came at a run, vaulting a sandbagged doorway, heavy inward-curved Brimlock kukri in one hand, bolt pistol in the other. The first three Unnamed spun backwards as the mass-reactive shells punched into them. The fourth was upon him before Rath could fire.

Rath ducked an axe and cut upwards, slashing the heretic's throat out with his heavy kukri, shouldered the corpse out of the way and drove forward.

He took position in a doorway. 'Find them!' Rath shouted to the men who followed in his wake. He did not look behind. He knew they would hear. He knew there were more Unnamed to kill. He shot them as they charged down the street.

Sergeant Taavi found Yegor first. He was still breathing, but not for long. He moved on. 'Here!' Guardsman Gunnel said.

There was a boot sticking out from the rubble. Taavi pulled at the blocks and threw them aside.

If one was Yegor the other had to be Minka. 'Is she dead?' Gunnel said.

'I don't know,' Taavi hissed as he pulled the blocks of rockcrete aside.

* * *

There was rockcrete in her mouth and nose. Minka kicked against the rubble as the hands reached down to free her. They dragged her up. She spat the grit from her mouth, stood unsteadily on her feet, carbine still in hand, and blinked her vision clear.

Someone was holding her face. It was Taavi – his wide blue eyes staring at her. His mouth was moving. The explosion was still ringing in her ears. She read his lips. 'Get back!' he was shouting, but she could not.

Taavi seemed to understand. He pointed. The blast had reshaped the rubble before her. It had reshaped Yegor too. His arm ended in a torn and ragged mess of cloth and flapping flesh. His legs were wrong; his body was folded in two.

'Get back!' Taavi shouted.

One of the heretics had an autogun with a round barrel. It flashed as it sprayed the wall above her head. Taavi shoved her but Minka would not leave.

'Yegor!' she shouted, but it was too late for debate.

She was thrown over a shoulder, her ribs bruising as whoever carried her jogged along, and found herself staring down at the ground, eight feet below her.

TWO

KASR MYRAK

When the war for Cadia had broken out, the defence of
Kasr Myrak lay in the hands of General Stahl, a typical
high-ranking Cadian veteran of a hundred and fifty years'
service. Drawn from the aristocracy, he was well liked and
effective, and put the defences into good order.

After the treachery at Tyrok Fields, Cadia was quickly
swamped by traitor forces and Kasr Myrak was surrounded
by a warband of perhaps ten million, who'd gathered like
insects on the plains.

They were a rabble. Their assaults had been haphazard
and largely ineffective against the superior Cadian training and discipline, and their manner of war disgusted the
defenders. It was heedless, disorganised, relied on bodies, not tactics, and at first the hopes of the Cadians had
been high.

Kasr Myrak's turn had come on the forty-second day of
the war for Cadia.

After the void shields of their larger neighbour, Kasr Halig, had been overloaded, the vast fortress had been torn apart by a series of explosions that went from magazine to magazine.

Finally, the atomic reactor went critical, and chunks of the city were thrown upwards by the force of the blast, leaving a crater half a mile deep. A huge part of the siege army had been destroyed in the explosions, but the elite forces – Iron Warriors and disciplined bands of traitor guard – had already started moving out.

It had taken three days for the siege armies of the heretics to surround Kasr Myrak. The Cadians had endured a relentless bombardment, partly from orbiting space ships, and partly from the vast armies on the plains. The Shock Troopers had retaliated with wall-mounted Basilisk batteries and vast tower-mounted defence lasers. They had pummelled the forces of the heretics with great blue-white bolts of energy that stabbed out into the gloom.

Each day the Unnamed attacked like rabid dogs: snarling and slathering, bounding on without fear or pain or order, deploying massed armoured and infantry assaults made up of untrained, inhuman scum.

On the fourth day of the assault, spotters reported the first sight of iron-clad Space Marines towering over the heretic hordes. Just the rumour of Iron Warriors had brought a solemn air to the mess halls and guard chambers within the outer bastion walls.

The Iron Warriors were here; every Guardsman knew that the fight for life had begun.

Overnight the heretic Space Marines raised great earthworks and began to push towards the outer walls, keeping up their momentum despite the approaching barrage.

Tech-priests detected the tremor of mole-mines excavating ponderously towards them, while a storm of lance strikes rained down on the void shields, making the air fizz with ozone.

For a week the fighting was ferocious and bloody. During the day flocks of arrow-shaped black bombers rained vast spiked frag charges and incendiary canisters down on the city streets. At night, the skies were barred with the beams of streaming search lights and the red tracer fire of Hydra defence platforms; each dawn brought the sight of the Iron Warriors' earthworks creeping gradually closer to the outer walls.

Demolition squads rushed out of armoured sally ports in up-armoured Chimeras, their multi-lasers spewing out searing bolts. The Cadians threw themselves at the Iron Warriors but had to fight their way through cultist slaves, who blunted their advance with melta bombs and demolition charges.

Few Cadians returned from these missions, but each attack slowed the relentless assault for precious hours. On the fifth day, troops on the West Gate felt the tremor of mole-mines approaching the walls and teams of Cadian civilians dug counter-mines. The Cadians sent in demolition squads of their own, then flooded the Iron Warriors' tunnels with toxic slime and radioactive coolants.

It was on the afternoon of the fifth day that the first Iron Warriors mole-mine exploded under the North-East Bastion. The blast was immense. A whole section of wall lifted into the air and then crashed down in ruins. With a howl, tens of thousands of cultists charged. The number and fury of their charge rocked the defenders back and brought them right up to the cliffs of rubble. A few cultists started to clamber up the sacred walls of the kasr before the blizzard of las and autocannon rounds cut them down in heaps.

On the sixth day, two more mole-mines exploded near the south gate, and there was ferocious fighting, this time hand to hand, as the heretics crested the rubble walls and had to be driven back with flamer and bayonet.

The battle went on into the night, with repeated assaults of daemon tanks, heretics and kill-teams of Black Legion Adeptus Astartes that swooped in, bolt pistols barking with each shot, chainswords spraying blood and gore across the walls.

On the seventh day, whole sections of the outer walls were reduced to ash and rockcrete rubble.

Rath's 94th kasrkin had held the line that night and the enemy's grand assault began after dawn – a frenzied, howling charge of mutants and heretics and those driven insane by the violence and the darkness.

Ten thousand Unnamed made the first charge. They died to a man, cut down by scathing salvos of disciplined lasrifle fire, withering support from heavy bolter and auto-cannon squads, and precise shots from the surviving gun turrets and bastions. The heretics lay in heaps ten-deep, when at last they fell back, mewling and howling curses at the defenders.

That evening a mole-mine penetrated the magazine, deep in the bowels of the rockcrete bastion. The armoured walls acted like a seal on the explosion, which vented out through the doors and loop-holes before it tore the ancient rockcrete fortress apart. The void shields flickered and fell. Under a barrage of orbital bombardments and massed assaults, the walls had been attacked at all points at once, hemmed in to the south banks of the Myrak River.

On the morning of the eighth day, the warband of the Black Legion champion Druxus Bale battered the defenders with close-range Vindicator shells. Once the Cadians had been driven back, Druxus' warbands charged across the open ground in Land Raiders that mounted the rubble cliffs, shrugging off a blizzard of las-fire.

Flamers gouted out under the smoke-filled sky. Assault ramps slammed down as bolters killed the last Guardsmen, then power armour-clad Black Legion warriors stormed out, the mass-reactive shells of their bolters hitting the defenders with unerring aim, punching through carapace and flak armour and exploding the Cadians from within.

The sudden, precise and overwhelming assault swept the defenders away from the Southern Gates and down into the city. The hand-to-hand fighting was fierce and brutal, as tens of thousands of heretics swarmed up behind them and drove the Cadians back.

General Stahl led the defence in person, a bodyguard of elite carapace-armoured kasrkin about him. For a moment they had thrown Druxus back, knocking Black Legion Terminators off the walls, but then the Chaos Warlord had shoved his way to the fore.

He was a giant warrior in baroque warplate, bald head covered with obscene tattoos. In the hands of the Chaos champion was a crackling sword of blue fire. He singled Stahl out.

'For Cadia!' the general shouted, and threw himself at the enemy. He had fenced with the finest in the Cadian Shock Troop, and with an heirloom power sword and faith in the Emperor, he felt sure of victory.

His first blow scored a deep groove in the Terminator's pauldron, the second drove through the layers of ablative armour – a fine blow that drove Druxus back for a moment.

But Druxus was ancient long before Stahl was born, and it took more than a power sword to lay him low. He caught the blade in his open hand and broke it in half with a crackle of energy.

Stahl refused to give way. He drew his hot-shot laspistol and stood his ground. 'In the name of the God Emperor of Mankind,' he shouted, as Druxus laughed.

'The False Emperor,' the Chaos champion snarled as he tossed away the shards of the power sword. He caught Stahl by the chest and threw him to the ground.

Stahl staggered back to his feet as his kasrkin ran to his side.

Druxus killed them all with a sweep of his axe that cut Stahl in half.

With the breach in the wall and the death of the commander, Kasr Myrak had, as far as the forces of the Black Legion were concerned, fallen. Iron Warriors, Black Legion and elite mortal units moved on to the next siege and left Kasr Myrak to be plundered by the maddened hordes of heretics and cultists.

Hopelessly outnumbered, the Cadians were driven back, block by block, exacting massive casualties on the enemy – but losses they could afford to take.

Rath was on the West Gate when that last assault began. His regiment, the 94th, 'Brothers of Death', massed heavy bolters that cleared broad kill zones about their bastion.

'Never!' he shouted shortly after the heretics' grand

assault began. Their manner of war disgusted Rath. It
relied on insane, bestial ferocity. It lacked training and
discipline. And worst of all, it was winning.

The next assault came minutes later, with the same
result. Rath cursed and shouted as the enemy fired wildly,
casually squandering supplies. The dead lay six-deep
before the eastern gate, where Rath stood with his men
when news broke that the southern walls had been
breached.

Cadia was not a planet; it was a fortress built on a planetary scale, its natural geography reshaped to allow defence
in depth. Its cities, known as kasr, were fortresses with
resident garrisons of hundreds of thousands designed,
not for the comfort of their inhabitants, but to be death
zones to invaders. Market places and street corners were
set with bunkers and redoubts and emplacements. They
were designed to be defended for months, or years, if
necessary. The long-dead architects of the Imperium had
made no concessions for comfort or fashion. Any attack
would be mired in tunnels, switchback roads, blockhouse
ground floors, overhanging buildings, with pill-boxes and
gun emplacements built into living rooms, public audi-
toriums and mess halls.

There were ammo dumps deep in the bunkers of baker-
ies and hab-blocks; hab-blocks with reinforced buttresses
and vision slits for windows; and there were bastions
with landing pads on their roofs, and roofs so thick with
reinforced rockcrete that they were practically invulner-
able to anything except the heaviest bombardment.

'Take to the city!' his commanding officer had shouted
to Rath. 'Make them pay for every inch! Understand?'

It was the last order Rath had been given by a superior officer. He was his own master now.

No one else knew how to drive him harder.

THREE

STATUE SQUARE

For the last six days, Rath's company had made their base along the south side of Statue Square. The monumental buildings there offered good cover from air attacks and they had a symbolic significance. The Cadians held on, despite all attacks.

The field hospital filled the narrow gap between the museum and the veterans' hall. Morag Geran had to turn sideways to enter the gap. He set Minka down with a gentleness that belied his size.

Before the war, all Minka had known about ogryns was that they were giant abhumans whose strength made up for a lack of intelligence. But Geran was anything but stupid. His wide mouth and blunt brown fangs did not work well on a human level. Speaking Gothic seemed like a great effort for him, as if he were trans-lating everything he said from grunts to words, but his mismatched eyes – one brown, one blue – spoke louder

JUSTIN D HILL

than his voice. He kept saying her name. 'Ninka. Ninka.'
His brows knotted, and he stared down at her, full of
compassion and worry.

'I'm fine.' Minka pushed herself up gingerly. Her body
hurt all over. Images came back to her: the explosion, the
darkness, Yegor crumpled in the dust.

'Frekk,' she said. 'There was a stubber.'

Geran looked almost bashful as he showed her the stubber with its ammo feed. 'I got it,' he said. He pulled the
bolt back. It pinged with a satisfying sound of a round
being loaded into the firing chamber. He grinned blunt
brown teeth. 'Works!' he said.

Minka forced a smile. It seemed a poor trade.

'I kill for Yegor,' Geran said.

'Good,' she said.

The six hundred men and women of Rath's company
were all that was left of the hundred and thirty thousand
defenders of Kasr Myrak who had started the siege a hundred and eight days earlier. Six hundred fighting men,
women and children – at the last count, which was two
days before. Two days of constant retreat, when they had
fallen back to the southern side of Statue Square.

They were Shock Troopers, mostly of the 94th, 45th,
772nd and Kasr Myrak's own 87th. But there were others
too, Whiteshields like Minka, civilians, and survivors of
other units who had come to fight on Cadia – regiments
whose roll calls had once numbered in the thousands,
but were now only a bare handful of names.

On that morning they held all the ruins between Statue
Square and the river, where the tightly packed habs and
warehouses and gantries lined the banks. They had about

74

a month left of fighting before they were all wiped out. Less, if the Unnamed kept up this rate of attack.

The Unnamed had been attacking solidly for fifteen days now, the waves of heretics rising and crashing and falling back, like the waves of the sea. The tide was rising as Medicae Rone cleared Minka and she dusted herself down and picked her way to the barricades on the south side of the blockaded street.

She looked out from the sandbagged doorway as the Unnamed came down the broad thoroughfare of Imperial Parade. Minka winced as she pulled her carbine to her shoulder, which hurt. Twenty, then fifty, and suddenly there were hundreds of them, a wall of bodies with axes and clubs and serrated knives. She aimed and fired and winced, and aimed again.

All around her Rath's company took up their positions. They lay behind loop-holes, knelt in sandbagged windows and doorways, perched in the ruins as the Unnamed charged into the open.

They howled as they charged, and were mown down by enfilading fire from heavy-weapons teams hidden in the flanking buildings on Gold Street and Museum Street. Minute after minute, hour after hour, they kept coming, until Minka's shoulder was agony and her trigger finger ached, and she willed – prayed – for this to be over.

'Hold fire,' Rath shouted suddenly. 'Hold your fire!'

Minka paused, and one by one the fighters about her lowered their rifles. But the Unnamed were still falling, and Minka suddenly saw what Rath had seen. Their enemies were falling to shots fired from behind.

'Think our relief has come?' Sergeant Taavi asked.

Rath gave him a withering look. There was no relief. 'The

forces of Chaos understand only force. What this means is that there's something bigger and tougher pushing the Unnamed forward. And we need to know who they are…'
He gave Taavi a meaningful look.

Five minutes later Sergeant Taavi was crouched in the sewer with five hand-picked men. He loosened his knife in its boot-sheath and nodded to the rest of his make-shift squad: Theo, Malfred, Ulant and Delunt.

'You should have kept your mouth shut,' Delunt said.

'Should have never joined the Guard.' Taavi laughed. He'd grown up in Kasr Myrak and if he was going to die it seemed fitting that he should be back here to do so.

He knew the sewers well. It had been part of his cadet training – to know the city above and below ground – and before the war, Taavi had known a pretty young cadet who lived in one of these blocks. They'd hung around in the sewers together until he was shipped off-world. Alyona was her name. Her smell came back to him, for a moment, despite the stink of smoke and ashes all about him. Taavi checked the grenade on his bandolier. He'd taken it from a fellow Cadian's corpse that morning, and he patted it for luck.

Rath's signal came – a simple *tap-tap, tap-tap-tap* of a finger on a vox-bead.

Taavi gave each of his squad a curt nod. His shotgun was loaded with all the shells he had left. He made a silent prayer to the Golden Throne and threw the wooden cover back.

Being small had never been a problem for Belagg Grakk. No taller than a human child, the ratling could clamber through holes that no man could ever get through. He pulled himself up, floor by floor, to a bedroom in what had been a well-appointed hab-block on the southern side of Statue Square. The broad pale wood floorboards were strewn with pages of books. There were clothes – grey with ash and dust – lying beside a split drawer. There was a hole in the wall where a missile had impacted, and a charred stink of explosives. He threw himself down on the floorboards by the window, crawled forward, breathing heavily, and pulled his long-las up beside him.

Below him, the streets as far as Euphrates Street were filled with columns of heretic fighters. He used his scope to find a target. An enemy tank commander, at the back of a column, standing in his turret, signalling to the driver behind him.

Belagg then pulled in three long, slow breaths to steady his aim. He lined up the man's head in the centre of the target. The distant torso bucked forward as the round hit him. The column slowed as the troops scanned for the sniper.

Belagg picked out a sergeant, marching alongside the tanks, gesticulating wildly to his men. He fired again, a head shot that dropped the heretic in an instant. The column had stopped now and he picked another. And fired.

Taavi was up and out in a moment, crouching in the entrance hall of a hab-block. There was a shape in the darkness where the doors used to be. He fired twice. Heard a low grunt of pain, pulled the grenade free. Kept moving.

Shots rang out in the street outside. A shadow leaped at him. He was on the fallen man in a second, smashing the butt of his gun into the heretic's face. Bones and teeth shattered under his blows.

Taavi ducked shots that hit the plaster above his head. Heretic voices were harsh and foreign. He threw himself against the hab wall and stole a glance through the empty window. Lasrifle shots sprayed the wall outside. Wooden splints flew up as the frames smouldered. Taavi felt the impacts through the wall at his back. He bit the pin and counted to five, tossing the grenade out into the street.

'Krak!' he shouted an instant before the explosive went off, filling the street with shrapnel.

Taavi leaped through the window and landed in the street. He fired one-handed, hitting a heretic full in the face. He ripped the autogun from the dying man's fingers.

Taavi was a Cadian. He'd learned to strip a gun before he was tall enough to reach a door handle. Children on Cadia did it blindfolded. He knew what it was from the weight and the balance.

Auto-rifle. Modified M40, Armageddon pattern. Round magazine. Thirty solid slugs. Heavy hitter.

Taavi's finger was already on the trigger as he swung round. He fired short bursts, knocking three heretics back against the far wall. A body shot took one out, a head shot slammed another sideways.

Taavi kept low, firing as bullets and las-bolts stitched the air about him.

A red-uniformed fighter appeared round the corner and ran at Taavi with an axe. Taavi let the auto-rifle buck in his hands as the solid slugs slammed into the heretic's chest. The heretic danced like a puppet on its strings. It was a glorious moment of excess.

The heretic fell dead a few feet away, black-spiked helmet ringing out against the rockcrete floor. Taavi crouched down and pulled the body over. The collar badge was stitched with two entwined letters, VC.

'Rath,' he hissed into the vox-bead. 'Contact. Guess who's in town?'

'The Sisters of Our Martyred Lady,' Rath said.

'You wish. Volscani Cataphracts.'

Rath laughed humourlessly. *'Great. Now get back here.'*

Taavi bundled his men to the sewer opening.

Theo was last back in. Taavi was about to follow when he felt vibrations through his boots. At the far end of Imperial Procession, the distinctive shape of a Leman Russ appeared from a side street, exhaust puffing black promethium fumes. It turned for a moment on its tracks and faced the street. Then another tank appeared, and another, their banners of human skin flapping wetly as they accelerated towards him.

'They've got tanks,' he voxed.

'How many?'

'Well, I saw six.'

Rath cursed. *'This will be fun.'*

At the south-eastern corner of Statue Square stood the ruins of a hab-block. The rest of the row was made up of monumental edifices: the vast hulk of the Veterans' Hall, and next to it the Museum of Resistance, with the inbuilt chapel to St Hallows. The buildings looked out onto the square, and up the triangular pediment of the museum the white marble figures of Cadian soldiers marched in step.

The vast buildings had given the Cadians a solid hundred and fifty yards of wall to defend, but it was different resisting tanks. The high ceilings and massive blocks would offer little defence against ordnance. One shot and

JUSTIN D HILL

the weight of the walls would crash down. That did not
hold them back; the defenders scrambled for position as
the Volscani armoured columns came on.

Minka ran up the broad steps of the Museum of Resistance. The inner hall of the museum was dark and empty
and scattered with paper, ration boxes and chips of stone.
From each of the three doorways, galleries opened up
ahead and to either side.

The exhibits of tanks and equipment and medals had
been locked away in the cellars or scavenged for the battle.
All that remained were the empty pedestals, the uniformed
mannequins – now bundled up against the wall – and the
battle-scarred banners of Kasr Myrak's home regiments.

She could hear the shouts from the rear of the museum,
where loop-holes and windows gave fine fields of fire
south, towards the Volscani attack. She took the Castellan
Hall, where two of Konn's squad were loading a missile
launcher. The rest had taken up position at the barricaded
windows – standing to fire, then ducking back again.

Geran was at the far end of the hall, hunched over the
heavy stubber, tongue between his teeth as he concen-
trated on loading a new ammo belt into it.

'Need help?' Minka shouted, but the ogryn growled as
he finally got the fiddly shells to load. He held the stubber
one-handed, hosed the street with rounds and grinned.
'You stand with me?'

Minka nodded. She took the opposite side of the window and risked a quick look. Volscani tanks were coming
down the road in single file. At the head was a Chimera,
its multi-laser turned forty-five degrees to the left. Shots
flared out in short bursts of red bolts. The tank commander was standing in the cupola. Minka fired three

times. Her aim was out. She cursed and fired once more, but her charge was running out.

Frekk, she cursed. But as she fumbled for a new battery pack a missile arced out from the museum windows and hit the Chimera on the nose.

There was a blast of white smoke, and then a pause before the turret of the Chimera was ripped off with a roar of yellow flame. Minka slammed a new las-battery into place as the burning Chimera was pushed aside, and the distinctive shape of a Demolisher-pattern Leman Russ filled the street.

The tank turned for a moment on its tracks, swivelling its fixed gun towards the back wall of the Museum of Resistance. Volscani squads started to charge. Geran unloaded his ripper gun in a furious fusillade of lead. There was a *ping!* as the magazine ran empty. Geran looked down confused and then there was a low roar as the Leman Russ fired. The shell hit the St Josmane wing. Through the open galleries, Minka saw the shoulders of the building seem to shrug for a moment before the whole facade collapsed into the street beside them.

The smoking Demolisher barrel swung towards where Minka stood as the Volscani started to scramble up into the museum. She had to grab Geran's arm with both hands. 'Come on!' she shouted. 'Quick!'

FOUR

THE MUSEUM OF RESISTANCE

Belagg knew he should be falling back, but the Volscani standard-bearer was oblivious, and the oblivious made the most satisfying targets. He aimed and fired, and paused to watch the round hit. The banner fell behind the ragged silhouette of the ruins.

There was a girder walk between this building and the next. He put one arm out to balance as he crossed the brief patch of open sky, then fell back behind cover into the next building. He carried on, dropping down two more floors into a ruin across the road from the Veterans' Hall.

He was walking quickly now, through a long hallway deep with papers as a forest in autumn is with leaves. Below him, he could hear the roar and shouts of battle. It didn't concern him. A sniper was separate from all that. He killed from a distance. He was barely seen, and then he was moving once more.

Belagg suddenly felt that he was being watched. He turned – nothing but the long empty hallway, open to the sky. There was a staircase that led down to street level, but the Volscani were making good progress, and he decided to take another high-beam walkway back into Hab Tyrok.

That feeling again.

He turned – quicker this time – nothing.

But Belagg had instincts, and now his heart was beating. He wiped the sweat from his palms, crouched down and looked all about him. He started forward and ran straight into a giant boot, in smooth blue-black plate. How anything this large and heavy had crept up on him, he could not guess, but he had seen enough of the Imperium of Man to know power armour when he saw it.

He had witnessed the Adeptus Astartes once before, fighting on a world named Hargal Prime, when he'd been lying in the upper branches of a coral tree as the sky filled with burning contrails. A drop pod had landed fifty feet to his right. It had smashed its way down through the stone branches of the forest and scored a long black line down the trunk of the coral tree. One door would not open, but the rest had slammed down and ten golden armoured Space Marines were out in a moment, splitting into two squads, and killing.

Belagg had watched in awe. The Adeptus Astartes had shrugged off the impacts from axe or crude ballistic weaponry. He had almost cried watching the beauty of their warfare. Then one of the warriors had turned towards him and pinpointed his position, bolter already raised to fire.

Belagg had gone stiff with terror, knowing that he would die. But the Space Marine had paused and nodded towards him as if to say, you and I are on the same side, little warrior.

That memory passed through Belagg as he looked up at the vast shape before him, from greave to knee plate, groin, piping, chest and head. Images were carved there that were hard to see, but he saw the pale wet skin, slapped over one pauldron, and knew from the holes therein that this *thing* had once been human. When his gaze reached the warrior's face Belagg immediately wished that he had not looked.

The Volscani Cataphracts swarmed through the holes in the museum wall, clearing each hall with flamers and grenades before storming on to the next. Minka was with Konn's squad and Geran as they retreated back through the galleries towards the entrance hall.

Geran used the stubber as a club, but he was bleeding from a dozen wounds as he brought up the rear. The last Minka saw of him he was standing in the ruin of a double doorway when suddenly the room was filled with long plumes of flaming promethium. The Volscani were only yards behind.

A shot grazed her shoulder armour. She threw herself through a doorway. The dark shape of a Volscani trooper was silhouetted by flames. Minka ducked and ran at him. Desperation drove her harder than she had ever thought she could fight. She rammed her bayonet into his chest. If he cried out she did not hear it.

A grenade skittered towards her. Konn was shouting at her.

She threw herself down on the ground as the explosion went off. The pain was sudden and hot and sharp. She put her hand up and saw her own blood.

A low whoosh and then a titanic explosion in the gallery

she had just been standing in. There were flames and dust. Minka had no idea which way was forward or back. A figure came through the smoke. It was Rath. He pulled her close and shouted into her ear. 'Get back across the square!'

Another shell impacted thirty yards to the right. She was down again, spitting dust from her mouth. Rath dragged her back up. She hung in her oversized uniform as Rath held her in one hand. He looked her in the eye to make sure that she understood. 'Get back! Go!' he shouted as another shell hit the museum walls.

The Space Marine stared down at Belagg. The giant wore a blunt blue helmet, with ornate brass fittings, wheezing pipes trailing off to either side and flickers of light playing over the dark blue armour. Its eyes were red, the red of coals in a darkened room – intense with the heat of hatred and cruelty. Belagg's hands began to shake. He dropped his long-las and desperately scrambled back.

He knew that he was trapped. He had a better chance of survival throwing himself off the building than staying here with this monster. Bestial, primary instinct told him that his impact would be a swifter and easier death.

The giant reached out towards him, but Belagg was small. He twisted and turned away and flung himself from the building.

He had a brief glimpse of Chapel Street rushing towards him. Parts of his life flashed through his mind as he fell. He regretted that he had not killed more heretics in his time. He regretted many things. But more than anything Belagg felt triumph that he had escaped death at the hands of this terrible monstrosity.

From eight storeys high, impact with the ground below should be brutal and instant. For a lowly member of the Astra Militarum, the prospect of a clean death was almost the best that a warrior could hope for.

That fact consoled Belagg in the seconds as he fell. He was oblivious to the physics of his situation. He did not care that the density of a planet's atmosphere determined how fast you fell. Speed was determined by the mass of an object and its resistance to air. Heavier objects fell faster than lighter ones.

All this was of passing interest to the ratling. In moments, he would be dead.

Speed was determined by the mass of an object and its resistance to air.

It was a lesson that the Night Lord, Asseb Krieg, had learned thousands of years in the past.

He was waiting for the ratling at the bottom of the building, as a child would wait to catch a toy that was dropped from a high window. He caught him in one hand and held him up, close to his face.

Inside the helmet, his Night Lord's lipless mouth smiled.

'No,' Asseb Krieg said as the ratling screamed. 'You're not dead.'

There was a long, delicious pause, as the Night Lord added, 'Yet.'

Taavi drew in a deep breath as the hab-block wall exploded outwards into the street. The Volscani armour was smashing its way towards them from three directions at once. Through the cloud of dust and debris came the blunt, scratched and heavily armoured front plates of a Leman

Russ Demolisher, the turret traversing towards the bunker. His squad didn't have anything that could hurt this beast.

Not unless…

'I've got it working,' Guardsman Rawlin hissed. He had a meltagun in his hand. It was one they'd found, but some heretic had done a frekk-job on it with a Ryza ammo charge that was never going to fit.

'You sure?'

Rawlin pulled a face. 'Sure,' he said.

'I'm with you,' Taavi said. From above there came the patter of heavy bolter fire starting again. Short, precise salvos. Conserving ammo.

The Demolisher's blunt snout appeared again. Rawlin threw himself down onto the ground, aimed, and fired. The air rippled as the super-charged beam raced out. Taavi felt the heat on his cheeks. It melted a small, neat hole in the armour plates, throwing molten slag into the cramped interior.

The explosion blew the wall down on top of them. Something slammed into Taavi's leg. It felt like he'd been hit by a sledgehammer. Throne! He tried to pull free.

There were footsteps, struggling through the rubble.

Volscani. Taavi scrabbled for his lasrifle. Of all the ways to die, he thought. Pinned to the ground.

The hunter stood over him. 'You staying there?' a voice said.

'Rath? Where did you come from?'

'I couldn't let you leave this, could I?' Rath held up the meltagun.

'Rawlin?'

'Dead. Can you get out?'

'If you move this,' Taavi said.

Rath put his shoulder under the metal spar and lifted. Taavi dragged his leg free.

'Broken?'

'I don't think so,' Taavi said.

'Good,' Rath said. 'Here, take my shoulder.'

Rath's company fell back across the square as best they could. Some of them picked their way through the side streets, others tried to use the avenues of blackened tree stumps for cover.

Sergeant Taavi limped back. He took shelter halfway across the square with about fifteen other troopers, in the ruins of a public latrine. He kicked a loop-hole through the wall to give him a view up to the south-east corner of Statue Square. Volscani were picking their way through shell holes and barbed wire, over dead bodies and blackened, half-buried tanks and transports, sand-bagged windows, doorways and sewer outlets. Taavi fired a brief salvo of shots as the Volscani started to charge across the square.

They let the Volscani come on into the killing zone then opened fire with everything they had. For a few hundred fighters, the firepower they put out was devastating. Statue Square was alight with las-bolts, autocannon shells, heavy bolter shots and grenades.

The combined firepower ripped through the Volscani, mowing them down in heaps.

The Volscani foot-sloggers came on twice more, and each time they were punished. Rath's company had known that they would be driven back across the square and had prepared for just that eventuality, so as the Volscani tanks pushed into Statue Square they were ready. The lead tanks were ripped apart with lascannons and demo charges, and after a furious firefight the armoured columns ground to a halt.

Next morning the front lines had been shunted up to the north side of Statue Square.

Medicae Rone had laid out his equipment and was sweeping the dirt from his new field hospital as Taavi entered. It looked as if the medic had aged ten years.

'Sergeant,' he said by way of greeting. 'How do you like my new facility?'

Taavi took in the line of dirty mattresses, salvaged from the ruins, laid out on the grey marble floor. Rone gestured to a padded velvet armchair. Taavi sat. His hands cupped the polished ends of the chair's arms.

'So,' Rone said, seeing the blood and the wound. 'Your leg.'

'Yeah. A wall fell on me. I didn't realise that some-one had shot me until I saw the hole.' The las-round had burned a neat round hole, a generous thumb-size in diameter, into the fabric of his trousers. 'No idea when,' Taavi said.

He unbuckled his trousers and slid them down as far as his knees. His own skin looked pale against the dark of the crusted blood and scorched wound mark.

Rone sucked a breath in between his teeth. 'Looks clean,' he said at last. 'Just missed the femoral artery.'

Taavi nodded. 'Think I'll live?'

Rone looked up and laughed. 'Well, you won't die from this.'

The medic didn't have much to bind the wound up with, but he gave it a dusting with counterseptic powder and then bound it up with a strip of boiled cloth cut from a Cadian greatcoat. 'There,' Rone said as Taavi pulled his trousers back up. 'Good as new. Now get back out there.'

Taavi picked his way out into the street. Exhausted survivors crept through the ruins as grey light spread over the city.

Rath's company had made their new front line along the north side of the square, where a rockcrete revetment lifted the foundations of the fine hab-blocks twenty feet above the floor. The captain had made his command post in the cellar of a retired general's oak-lined drawing room. The walls were hung with ancient portraits of military figures, a broken mirror hung over an ornate brass fireplace, and the leather sofa had been torn open, pale hair stuffing strewn across the floor.

Taavi found Rath on the front line, as the captain looked out across the square. The Volscani were now dug into the buildings that had been home twenty-four hours earlier. One half of the museum had collapsed. The Volscani had torn the aquila from the facade of the Veterans' Hall and the marching figures on the museum pediment had been prised from the wall and lay smashed on the broad stairs.

Taavi could see the red figures. There were hundreds of them. 'Why don't they attack again?'

Rath didn't know. 'The forces of Chaos are easily distracted.'

There was a long pause. Taavi's eyes were wide and staring. 'How many did we lose?'

'A hundred and forty-six.'

Taavi had feared they'd lost more.

Rath listed the missing squads. 'Rendal and his men got crushed in the museum. Childe's squad were trapped in

the Veterans' Hall. They came on us faster than I'd feared.'
He paused. 'How's the leg?'

'I'll live, apparently.'

Rath laughed. 'Have you eaten?'

Taavi shook his head. He hadn't even thought about it,
but now his stomach rang empty.

Rath turned to him. 'Go eat.'

Minka could smell the food as Gunnel and Malfred got
a pot of slab-stew to the boil.

They had set up the canteen next door, in the panelled
library, the tomes of military history making a ready supply of fuel. Gunnel had lost a hand. The stump ended
halfway to his elbow. It had been bandaged, and he was
clearly still getting used to the missing limb, swearing pro-
fusely as he tried to work one-handed.

Olivet was setting the vox up in Rath's HQ. He was
a young lad, and like her had started the war as a
Whiteshield. Olivet looked up, saw Minka, and seemed
at a loss as to what to say. 'So,' he started. 'Yegor died?'

Minka nodded.

Olivet pulled a face. 'I'm sorry.'

Minka looked down. Yegor's death felt like an age ago.
She couldn't understand why he was still talking about it,
then realised it was less than a day since she'd been picking her way through the ruined schola.

She shook herself. Olivet was tuning the vox into the
Lord Castellan's channel.

'How long?' she said.

Olivet checked his chronometer. 'Five minutes.'

She nodded. 'I'll just sit down here.' She crouched down
and leaned against the wall.

A shadow passed over her. Rath tapped her on the helmet. 'Cheer up,' he said.

Minka pulled her helmet down low over her face. *Flower of Cadia* began to play over the vox.

'Turn it up,' Rath said as the notes of *Flower of Cadia* fell away and Creed's voice filled the silence.

'People of Cadia. Brothers in arms, warriors all of you. You ask me what I want from you. I shall tell you. But first, good news. Our forces are moving across many fronts. We are driving the enemy back...' Creed listed units and battles and little victories, reports of enemy retreats, brigades destroyed, objectives reached. *'But brothers and sisters, I need your help.*

'We face a monstrous evil with resolve, with courage, with the faith of the unconquerable Imperium of Mankind! We have trapped the enemy upon our barbs – let us hold him here, while the Imperium prepares the counter-strike that will destroy him utterly!'

At the end of the broadcast, Creed spoke with rousing defiance. *'I ask of you this. I ask you to defy the enemy with all your might. Fight them to the last. Do not give ground, unless you can inflict more pain upon our foes. Do not hope, for in hope lies despair!'*

At the end his gravelly voice ground out two words: *'Cadia stands!'*

Minka mouthed with him. But if the forces of Cadia were driving the enemy back, why, then, were the defenders of Kasr Myrak fighting without support?

It didn't make sense. To Minka, it felt like they were losing. Badly.

She looked up to see Rath staring at her. His augmetic eye glowed with a dull red light, as baleful as the Eye of Terror.

* * *

The Elysion Fields

Zufur the Hermetic did not care that the rest of his war-band were fighting about the walls of Kasr Kraf. Their anger and fury washed off him, like oil, or another man's blood. At least that was what he told himself, but through his helmet he heard their shouts and curses, their blood-curdling oaths, the bark of their bolt shells, and he felt his hearts quicken, his pulse begin to pound, the bestial anger rising within him like a flooding well.

'Where are you, Zufur?' Sikai the Thriceborn hailed him over the vox.

It had taken Sikai six hours to realise that Zufur's warriors were not there, on the battlefield.

Zufur could have taken offence at the length of time it took the Black Legion captain to notice Zufur's warband were not slaughtering their way through the ruins of Kasr Kraf's third ramparts. He heard the moan and throb of Sikai's chainaxe, the momentary slowing of the blade as it snagged on bone.

'Am I needed?' Zufur responded.

'We never need you, Hermetic!' Sikai laughed, and there was the sound of his blade chopping again and again into dead or dying meat.

Zufur ignored the insult. 'I will leave the killing to you.'

Sikai laughed once more. *'You always do.'*

In his mind's eye, Zufur could see Sikai's fanged mouth open in a smile. Fighting on Cadia was pleasurable in a way that none of them had appreciated beforehand. It was joyful. Exultant. Victorious. Zufur felt his fist clench. Killing was an itch that had been growing in intensity. He swatted the thought away. Zufur the Hermetic had deeper desires he had come to Cadia to fulfil. The culmination of a lifetime's study. 'I have more important business.'

'What can be more important than killing?' Sikai demanded. Through the vox, Zufur heard the other warrior's chain-blade roar its approval.

'You kill with an axe, I work with subtler weapons. I think, if you counted, I have murdered millions more than you.'

'You are always talking, Zufur. Put an axe in your hand. Wade through the blood of your foes.'

Zufur was irritated with himself. 'You wade. I will swim through their blood.'

As he spoke he saw the forest appear. 'There,' he said.

The thing that piloted his craft had been human once. Zufur had forgotten the man's name, but he had been perfect for Zufur's needs. All he'd needed were a few mod-ifications. Silence was one of them.

The pilot had not willingly consented to the alterations. But that did not matter. Zufur did not like his slaves to speak. Now ribbed pink tubes ran from the pilot's mouth and eyes, his legs had been removed, his hands ended in fleshy tendrils that disappeared into the flight deck consoles.

'Bring us down.'

The lander shuddered as it made its descent. 'There,' Zufur pointed.

The pilot's tendrils tensed. There was a wet slosh of fluids moving through his body and the tubes of his mouth rattled. Sometimes Zufur imagined that there were words in the wet sounds. He should have had the man's larynx removed too, he thought.

The lander settled. The wet gurgles from the pilot went on, even though there was no one to hear them.

Zufur's warband was already securing the area. He climbed down the cockpit ladders. He had waited ten thousand years for this.

Zufur the Hermetic jumped the last ten feet and landed with a thud on the thin grass. He had lost count of the number of planets he had set boot upon. Each world had its own texture underfoot, but none was quite as satisfying as Cadia. It was hard, but not brittle. Soft enough to allow humans to live.

He strode forward. The soil seemed to shrink at his touch. Its horror was as satisfying as the struggles of his pilot. Zufur paused for a moment and looked up. There, above him, amid the purple-and-green stain of the Eye of Terror, was his home. Standing in this place was a delicious transgression. He felt like an imprisoned slave who finds the door of his cell left open, walks out and looks back on the hole where he has been shut up for so long.

And it was not just being on Cadia that counted. He was here, in this particular place. The very keyhole, as it were, for it was not the planet of Cadia that had held the warp back, but these stones.

He turned to gaze on them. The structures rose before him like a forest: each one unique, sublime, perfect. Things of beauty, yes, but torment also, for these were Abaddon's shackles.

Zufur of the Black Legion had studied the pylons for ten thousand years, but he had never had the chance to touch one – until now. He strode down the ramp of his lander, the tubes in his nose filling his lungs with a sweet and sickly stimulant.

The pylon was pale grey, like marble. It stretched up before him, a four-sided spike, a hundred yards tall. Just one of thousands that filled the vast plains about him. But this one was cracked, and a piece had sheared away from the spire.

Zufur strode forward, looking for the one.

At last, he found it: untouched, unscarred, perfect.

Zufur removed the gauntlet of his suit of power armour. These pylons had held the warp back since long before the Heresy of Horus. Fools like Sikai tried to win the war against the Imperium of Man by killing Guardsmen one by one. It was as hopeless as trying to hold the sea back with your open hands.

Humanity bred as quickly as men like Sikai could kill them. Zufur was not so foolish. He had been one of the first to throw in his lot with Abaddon, one of the first to join the Black Legion. Abaddon had seen what needed to be done. He had an understanding – a vision – that none of the others possessed. Zufur flattered himself that he had a vague sense of what Abaddon saw clearly. When they aimed it was not at the throat of a human, or a Space Marine. It was at a city, a world, an empire.

Zufur had no doubt about the success of Abaddon's Thirteenth Black Crusade. But the Chaos gods were fickle. Just in case, he would bring a pylon back to his archo-smithy and learn the secrets of the pylons of Cadia.

He looked up at the perfect pylon and pressed his hand against it. Through his bare skin, a thrill of warmth and energy rushed into him. The pylon throbbed with life, like a slow, persistent heartbeat. It was strong, healthy, vibrant; a fine specimen. He felt relief, hatred and the sweet taste of vengeance. It was the one he wanted.

Behind him, from the landing ramps, his slave gang was descending.

He turned to the gang leader, an augmented tech-priest that Zufur had taken from Agripinaa, the priest's hood thrown back off his tattooed scalp. He bowed and spoke through sharp steel teeth. 'This one, master?'

'Yes,' Zufur exhaled. He watched as the excavators began to reverse off the lander. Teams of mind-slaved ogryn stumped down after it and stood in an uncertain pack, their arms slack at their sides, waiting for orders.

'Careful,' Zufur told the priest. 'I do not want a scratch upon it.'

It took a day for the excavator teams to locate the roots of the pylon. Spider-leg cranes unfolded. Cables were secured about it. Black gantries rose, and a pair of crane heads, like the legs of a praying mantis, slowly unfolded and lifted the pylon straight from the ground.

The next step was critical. It was now, as the weight was taken along the length of the pylon, that any hidden fractures or imperfections could shatter Zufur's prize.

He stood to watch as the lifter slowly lowered the vast pylon onto the back of the tracked carrier.

Gang leaders hurried back and forth, shouting, pointing, as the mind-slaved ogryn moved slowly and stiffly to tighten or loosen the cables or adjust the padding.

At last, the pylon lay supine and Zufur felt the pulses of his hearts slow once more.

He had supervised the entire process, not needing to sleep. All the time the angry noise of battle had been fed through his helmet vox. It was only now that he noticed it, like a vaguely buzzing insect veering towards the ear.

The shouts, the screams, bolters, chainswords, the thunder of ordnance blasting through armour.

'Sikai. How many have you killed?' Zufur asked.

'Eight thousand, seven hundred and forty-six,' Sikai voxed.

'Have you taken the city yet?'

There was a moment's pause, during which Zufur could hear the faint sound of slaughter over the vox. *'It cannot be long,'* Sikai eventually replied.

Zufur laughed to himself. Hand-to-hand combat was such a slow way of winning a war. Sikai and his ilk were nothing more than distractions to keep the attention of the defenders away from the real danger.

Ahead, the land was pocked and broken by the passage of war, and all along the edge of the pylon fields the vast stone structures were cracked and broken.

It was over the ruins that the grey Land Raider ploughed. Wolf heads were emblazoned on both sides, and on the assault ramps the craft bore crossed axes: the personal badge of the White Wolves.

The Land Raider led the hunt. It turned into the pylon forest, and the rest of the pack followed: bounding shapes of great Fenrisian wolves, and behind them the Wulfen, some running, others loping along like half-apes, with their hands on the ground like paws.

The company of the White Wolves was dwarfed by the vast pylon forest. They plunged down into a deep crater, a hundred yards wide, over the shattered rocks from a broken pylon, and then they saw the foe.

Mounted on a snarling thunderwolf, Ottar the White was chief. He led the pack, his great axe, Lightbringer, shining with its own inner white light. Before him, between the avenues of pylons, he could see the brass and black of the enemy lander.

The heretics had pulled a pylon from the ground. It lay like a fang wrenched from its socket. Ottar sneered at the enemy. 'Look at them! They want to remove the pylons one by one! Fools! That will not help them! Forward, brothers. Forward!'

Behind him, his company howled with battle-joy.

The black power-armoured heretics reacted quickly. Precise bolter fire flared towards him. Bolt-rounds ricocheted off the pylon edges. Ottar felt them impact against his chest-plate, but the Black Legion fell back as the ogryn guards stumped forward.

The first to meet him had a crude gun in one hand, buzz-sword in the other. The solid shells punched against Ottar's grey chest-plate. Warning runes lit within Ottar's helmet, but he was wild with the joy of the hunt, and he bared his fangs, letting out a wordless snarl of anger and fury.

If the ogryn thought to slow the Space Wolf's charge, he had not met the Sons of Fenris before. Ottar's wolf closed its giant maw on the massively muscled forearm of the ogryn guard, snapping through arm and fist and firearm, ripping them clean off.

The ogryn's moment of horror was cut short as Light-bringer came down on his thick-skulled head. There was an ice-flash of white energy, the crude rivets of his helm bursting open as the axe crashed through steel, skull and brain matter.

The ogryn guards came forward. A wall of bodies and ripper guns and buzz-saws.

Ottar led the charge, limbs and heads and grisly lumps of torso flying off to either side as he cut his way through them, his wolf riders close behind him, their chainswords buzzing furiously as they protected his back. The charge punched deep into the guts of the enemy.

Even as Ottar's thunderwolf was killed beneath him, the assault ramp of the Land Raider *Ghost of Fenris* slammed down and Terminator-armoured figures charged out, war cries ringing out under the hellish sky. Moments after they hit, the Wulfen caught up and drove all before them, howling and tearing ogryn, heretics and Chaos Space Marines apart.

Ottar leaped free of his slain wolf, the joints of his power armour grating as he accelerated to a sprint. Light-bringer flashed over and over as he drove through the enemy. Mind-slaved labourers flung themselves at him in an insane wave. He killed them just as quickly. They fell one on top of the other, the bodies mounding about him as he slowed almost to a halt.

The Black Legionnaires of Zufur's warband had waited for this moment. Now the Space Wolf leader had been brought to a halt, they charged, cutting him off from the warriors behind him.

The two-headed axe held them at bay, but the damage had been done.

As the Space Wolf charged a meltagun flared. The shot punched a hole through the warrior's armour, and came out the other side with a hissing steam of super-heated blood and viscera.

The bearded Space Wolf staggered for a moment as if his axe weighed him down, but he would not fall. Not until he was dead.

Zufur strode forward.

His warband had done their job. The melta shot would

have killed most warriors, but the Space Wolves fought harder than any others he had known. The suit of warplate was scratched and dented, there were oily fluids leaking from its joints, and the warrior's left leg was slowing as the power armour began to fail.

The Space Wolf removed his helmet. Zufur was not so foolish as to return the honour.

'You can't take every pylon from the planet!' the ancient warrior shouted. 'I am Ottar the White, and I will rip out your throat! I will tear your guts out and tie you to the pylon with them!'

Zufur let the Space Wolf swing at him. Each time he stepped aside, leading the Space Wolf on. Then, quite suddenly, he stepped within the arc of the giant axe and plunged his sword through the grey chest-plate. The move was sudden, unexpected and deadly. The blade he carried tore through the Space Wolf's ceramite armour as if cutting through cloth. It rattled in his hand, like the mouth-tubes of his pilot, as it feasted on his enemy's insides.

The look on Ottar the White's face was one of pain and hatred as Zufur's sword sucked his soul from him. At last Zufur pulled the blade free and Ottar the White fell dead.

FIVE

OBSERVATION POST 9983

The kasrkin burst into the room. There was black snow on their carapace armour. They moved with tough, precise, well-drilled movements, fingers poised on triggers.

The men of the 101st kept well back. The kasrkin colour sergeant wore a Cadian-issue power fist; it crackled with wandering threads of blue light as he ran a stern eye about the room. He wore a vox-bead on his chest. 'Safe,' he announced.

Five more kasrkin swept in, power swords drawn. There were staff officers and adjutants. And then *he* entered.

Creed appeared not to have shaved for weeks. He seemed both smaller and harder. It was as if the weight of command had compressed him. His handshake was firm, his gaze intense. 'Major Bendikt, much has happened since we stood on the observation platform of the *Fidelitas Vector*.'

'Lord Castellan!' Bendikt said. He was lost for words.

'There's been a monumental cock-up. We've been stuck up here...'

Creed listened with a careworn and weary air, then put up his hand. 'Don't worry. There is a plan. Mine, in fact.'

Bendikt stammered. 'But the war. We have sat here and we've done nothing!'

'Yes, I know,' Creed said. He patted the back of Bendikt's hand. 'Don't worry, we are about to change that.'

Creed filled any room he was in. All eyes were on him as he paced up and down. He was more than their commander. He was everything to Cadia: leadership, inspiration, hope. For Bendikt, he was also the prophet.

'You knew that something was afoot,' the commander of the 101st said.

Creed paused. His eyes were bloodshot. The skin beneath was heavy and baggy, but within them a fierce light shone. 'Yes. But even then I did not foresee the manner or the method of attack. Tyrok Fields... Well, we were all surprised. For a while. But plans had been made, against the unforeseen. Even so, the battle has been...' Creed paused as he looked for the word he wanted. 'Hard,' he said at last.

'We heard,' Bendikt said. 'But all this time we were here, helpless. We could not do anything but listen. We've been listening to the vox traffic dying off... We feared that all were lost.'

Creed nodded slowly. He put his cigar stub to his mouth. It appeared to have gone out, but he puffed on it anyway. 'It is not lost. In fact, things have not looked so good for a long time.' Bendikt looked surprised, and Creed smiled briefly. 'We have weathered the storm. The enemy has nothing left to throw at us. It is time for us to counter-attack. The swing is in motion – Cadia is readying her counter-punch. The 101st are part of that.'

'How?'

'You're at full strength?'

Bendikt nodded. They had taken on a company of Whiteshields three months before embarkation back to Cadia. 'Pretty much.'

'Good,' Creed said. He was clearly preoccupied with something.

Bendikt spoke quickly. 'Excuse me, sir. But I don't understand. We have been waiting here, without word or command. How can we help you? We have no tanks.'

There was an amused light in Creed's eyes. 'You don't know what this place is, do you?'

'No,' Bendikt said. He took a guess. 'It's not an observation post?'

Creed shook his head. 'No. It is not an observation post. This is Salvation 9983.'

'What does that mean?'

Creed puffed on his cigar. 'Let me show you, Major Bendikt, and then I think you will understand.'

They found the old man praying at the shrine. Rivald stood and took in the squad of kasrkin about Creed. He made the sign of the aquila and bowed. It was a simple and elegant gesture. 'We thank you, Lord Castellan, for all you have done for our planet,' the old man said.

Creed nodded but kept moving briskly forward to where the great doors stood in darkness.

The name 'Salvation 9983' was dimly visible from the distant lights at the stairwell.

'Kell,' Creed said. The colour sergeant looked up. 'Hand me the master key.'

Creed took a long brass wafer from his colour sergeant and walked towards the locking panel. His fingers found the opening and he slid the wafer into place. The effect was instantaneous.

All about them, sleeping machine-spirits woke from their amniotic and engine-oil dreams. The mountain began to hum as long-dormant maintenance engines came back to life. There was the distant sound of clangs and wheezing machinery; the sound of lift shafts rattling behind the quarried stone; the muffled automated speech of servitor-lifts; slow winding cog-wheels; the slow and steady hum of immense generators starting up.

At the far end of the vaulted hall, strip lumes blinked back to life. Creed's office staff looked up and about in wonder as the chamber's cathedral-painted ceiling, which had lain in darkness for an age, was revealed.

The view was sublime. Murals showed the years of Cadia's founding before the kasr were built, with open cities of wide boulevards. A place of peace and safety. A picture of a different age and a distant mind-set.

They stood in wide-mouthed wonder. 'What is this place?' Bendikt asked, and as if in answer the door mechanisms before them unlocked with a dull clunk. An alarm rang, the ground beneath their feet started to tremble, then the vast ceramite doors began to move. The word 'Salvation' split slowly and inevitably apart as each panel slid into mountain recesses. Light shone through the toothed intersection, throwing a slab of widening light onto Creed, Bendikt and the others.

There was a gasp of air on their faces, like that of a

long-sleeping man coming suddenly awake. Warm yellow light spilled through the widening gap. The sight within took Bendikt's breath away.

Creed grinned. 'I give you tanks!'

Bendikt walked through the opening and saw row upon row of Leman Russ battle tanks. They were painted in Cadian drab, unused, apparently fresh off some ancient production line.

He looked about. Most were main-line variants, but there were many rarer Executioners and Vanquishers.

Colour Sergeant Daal walked around the side and knocked the promethium drums at the back with his knuckle. 'The fuel tanks are full,' he called. One by one they went along the line. 'They're all full,' Daal said in wonder.

Bendikt did not quite believe it. He pulled himself up onto one machine and found the cabin hatch open. He peered inside, half expecting to see a crew, but the Leman Russ was empty, though the systems were alive. He gave Daal a look, then slipped inside and tried the controls. Fuel tank full, batteries charged. He leaned back from the driver's seat to the cabins at the back of the cramped space inside.

The magazine door slid back, and there each shell lay in its tube. Frag on one side, krak on the other. All through the room tank crews were selecting vehicles and climbing in. The noise of their laughter echoed with the roar of promethium engines being started.

He pulled himself up, slid down the side, landed on the floor and spun around in astonishment. There was everything an armoured company could want, or dream of: support Salamanders, Trojans, Atlas recovery tanks,

Samaritan-pattern Chimeras, fuel transports. Ancient suits of carapace armour hung in rows against the wall. Vast stacks of neatly ordered lasrifles. Battery packs, winter camo suits, boots, belts, webbing, dry rations, backpacks stuffed full of musty-smelling medicae supplies: sutures, bandages, phials of pale blue liquid, syringes.

Creed slapped him on the back. 'Happy?'

'Speechless,' Bendikt told him. 'But how do we get them out of here?'

'Don't worry,' Creed said. 'It's all taken care of.'

'We're not flying them out?'

'No. You're not flying out.'

Colour Sergeant Kell stood by the door. He was getting impatient. At that moment he put his hand to the vox receiver in his ear. 'General Creed. They're calling for you.'

Creed checked his chronometer and pulled a face. 'Sorry. I'm needed,' he said to Bendikt, and started walking towards the stairs that led to the landing pad. He talked all the way about the battle, the war-fronts, commanders whom they both knew.

Bendikt took it all in. In less than a minute the lift had brought them back to the parapet level. The door to the outside was open. Flecks of black snow were blowing inside. Valkyrie engines were warming up. Bendikt followed Creed and Kell up the steps to the doorway.

Bendikt could no longer hold himself back from asking: 'But what is this place?'

Creed paused. 'In the early days of the Imperium of Man, great minds foresaw a moment such as this when we would be alone and fighting the full might of the enemy. They ensured Cadia should always have a second force that could be hidden away, fully supplied, until their strength was needed. This is one such facility. Cadia is seeded with them.

'You and the 101st are part of a reserve army. We have taken all that the enemy can throw at us, and now I am about to unleash you on our foes.'

With those words, Creed ducked outside, and Bendikt followed him out onto the parapet.

There was nothing distinctive about Creed's Valkyrie. It was painted with plain Cadian drab, a standard pattern armed with multi-laser and two yellow-tipped Hellstrike missiles slung under each wing. The black hose lay on the landing pad, with a small puddle of promethium dribbling out onto the floor.

It had just been refuelled. The masked faces of the two crewmen were uplit by the green dashboard as they looked down to the consoles before them. They were running through the last instrument checks. Colour Sergeant Kell led them along the narrow parapet to the landing pad. The gusts of wind were gale force. Bendikt put his hand to his head to keep the wind from blowing his helmet off. The Valkyrie's side doors were open. The sponson heavy bolters were covered with a simple tan tarpaulin. The gunners were standing waiting. An orderly in the plain green drab of the Cadian 8th placed a set of steps under the Valkyrie door. Creed ignored them and used the handle to pull himself up into it. He stood in the doorway and had to shout to be heard over the whine of the engines. 'I nearly forgot.' Creed pulled something from inside his jacket. 'Here!'

Bendikt grabbed the tightly bound cloth and pressed it against his chest.

'There's fifteen regiments who'll be joining you. Take command. Understand?'

'Yes–' Bendikt started.

'Strike south towards the Elysion Fields. Engage the enemy with *extreme* violence.' Creed grinned. 'I have other men that I am calling on. I had to come and see you in person. But fear not, we're going to deal them such a blow that their teeth will rattle!'

The whine of engines grew so loud Bendikt's words were almost drowned out. 'Thank you, sir. But why me?'

Creed paused. 'I saw you fight on Relion V!'

The Valkyrie door was thrown shut, and Bendikt stood alone for a moment as the flier lifted up from the landing pad. There were a few seconds as the pilot struggled against the winds, then he engaged the thrusters, turned the gunship's nose away from the mountain, and she fell into darkness.

The lights of Creed's Valkyrie quickly dwindled.

Bendikt threw the door closed behind him. In his hand was the bundle that Creed had given him. He held it up, wondering what it could be. Black cloth. He unwrapped it. Gold braid. He looked up. Only Mere was there, sitting by the vox and starting to power it down.

Mere saw the expression on Bendikt's face. 'What is it, sir?'

Bendikt showed him what he held in his hands.

Mere walked towards him. His eyes widened. 'Well. Congratulations, sir!'

'What does it mean?'

'Looks pretty plain to me. He's just promoted you.'

Creed had brought him hope. Bendikt held it in his cupped hands, protected from the storm. He started towards the stairs, but Mere said, 'You should put those on, General, sir.'

Bendikt felt foolish.

'Here, I'll do it,' Mere said. He removed the major's epau-lettes with due care and replaced them with those of the general. 'There,' he said, and held up the red sash to put it over Bendikt's shoulder, but Bendikt laughed. 'Let's waste no more time. There is work to be done.'

Within an hour the entire Cadian 101st Armoured Regi-ment had selected and named their vehicles, and each crew was loaded up and ready.

Bendikt's Executioner tank moved forward, down the vast ramps that zigzagged into the roots of the mountain, and behind him, in threes, the 101st Armoured Regiment moved towards their sally port.

General Bendikt stood in the cupola, red sash with gold band across his chest, and broadcast on all channels. Our enemies think they have knocked us down, he thought, but Cadia has stood back up again.

All fights are won by the man who refuses to lie down.

PART THREE

COUNTER-ATTACK

ONE

BASTION 8, 17TH ARMY HEADQUARTERS, MYRAK RIVER FRONT

There were few places on Cadia still under the direct control of Cadian High Command. Bastion 8, on the Myrak River Front, was one such. It was still resisting, even though half of the 17th Army Group were pinned down in the Myrak Salient, in danger of being cut off. For three weeks the neck of the salient had been drawing closed, like a noose. Now, it seemed to the fighters on this front that the moment of decision had come.

The man who had led the defence of this front was General Grüber. He was the kind of commander who built his name on the bones of his soldiers. He would spend the life of every Guardsman under him if it got him further up the command chain. He had held his front with a mixture of discipline, bloody-mindedness and a stubborn lack of imagination. Grüber's strategy was simple: defence in depth, and for him, that meant thirty miles of minefields, artillery kill zones, anti-tank strong points and trench upon trench, supported by hundreds of heavy weapon emplacements. For months, heretic assaults had stalled within this mire. The foremost units had lapped up against the Martyr Walls of Bastion 8, then flagged and stalled and been thrown back.

His bloody-mindedness had stood him in good stead in his hundred-and-fifty-year career within the Imperial Guard. But this was not necessarily a quality that allowed him to perform the task he now knew he had to achieve, which was to mount a dazzling series of attacks.

But Creed had issued his orders, and Grüber had to obey.

Now he stood in the command bunker and stared down from the raised dais, his aquila-tipped cane of office tucked neatly under his arm. There was a strained silence as the brigade commanders filed in. His units had been defending and retreating for so long they had a numb, beaten air to them. Grüber knew he had to pull off the speech of his life. He had no idea where he was going to start.

He waited for the doors to be closed before putting his hand to his mouth and effecting a brief cough. There was silence as he stepped forward, his smartly polished boots clip-clipping on the wooden planks of the dais.

'Fellow warriors,' he announced. 'The time we have been waiting for has come.'

His words were met with a dull silence.

Grüber paused, the metal fan shutter of his augmetic lens whining as it focused on prominent faces about the room. He felt he needed to say more. 'We have faced an assault from earth and sky. We have faced the wrath of the Archenemy, and we are still alive. We are still fighting. That is a victory in itself.' He took half a pace forward. 'We still have faith.'

Silence, again, the general noted, though he could tell that they were warming up a little. He took another pace to the side, clipped his heels together, removed the staff of office from under his arm, rested the silver aquila in his palm and paused, looking down at the faces of his commanders. He had the odd sensation, not for the first time, that his men were looking for something that he did not possess.

Creed was the problem. The young upstart had, in the short time that he had been Lord Castellan of Cadia, changed the way that Cadians expected to be led. Being authoritative, being professional, being stern – these things were no longer enough. Cadians wanted a commander to *inspire* them now, and Maximus Octavian Grüber III had never, ever, in his entire one hundred and eighty years of life, been accused of being an inspirational leader.

He reflected on this for a moment as he stood, staring down. 'We shall rock the enemy back. We shall hit them so hard that their teeth rattle!' he said, shaking the aquila in the air, copying a painting he had once seen of Macharius, but even when he quoted Creed's own words he did not seem to have the knack of delivery that Creed most clearly had.

This was a sadness that Grüber had been struggling with in the past hundred days, when everything he had known, the solid ground that he had placed his booted feet upon, had proved transitory, ephemeral, uneven. His long career had been based on assumptions that were no longer relevant, and a young orphan upstart named Ursarkar E. Creed had risen to the height of military power.

Grüber stiffened and drew himself up a little higher. He took in a deep breath.

'This morning, I spoke to Lord Castellan Creed.'

Just the mention of Creed's name was like a magic charm that summoned his spirit.

In an instant, he felt the mood of the room change. Officers whose shoulders had started to slump – from exhaustion, or boredom, or a general war-weariness, ground down by death, lack of supplies, the constant pummelling from the enemy – sat a little straighter, their shoulders thrown back, their chins lifted high, eyes bright with hope and expectation.

The change rippled down the room. Grüber found, much to his own chagrin, that even he was standing a little straighter, if that was at all possible. He found strange emotions rising within him. He pursed his thin lips for a moment, then took another step to the centre of the stage.

He repeated Creed's name and changed the sentence to put himself at its core. 'Lord Castellan Creed called *me* this morning and asked me how your spirits were. I told him that you were eager to assault. That you were desperate to take the war back to the enemy. I told him, men of the Seventeenth Army, that you were ready to begin the long-awaited counter-attack.'

He could see their attention beginning to wane, and knew he had to return to Creed again. 'The Lord Castellan commanded me, commanded us all, to launch attacks upon the enemy.'

There was a ragged cheer that started at the back of the room and rippled forward. 'Today is that day!' he declared, and put his hand out for silence.

'Creed wanted me to relay his own words to you. His

very own words.' He paused as he looked down at the paper in his hand and began to read. '"The future of Cadia hangs in the balance. We are to make war upon the enemy. To bring destruction and death to each and every one of them." I am to lead the Seventeenth Army to the Elysion Fields.' He paused, his last words drowned out as the officers in the room all leaped to their feet.

The fight back had begun.

Bastion 8 lay a hundred and thirty miles from the first pylons of the Elysion Fields. In that gap, there were at least seven armies of the enemy, and yet Creed had demanded that he reach the Elysion Fields within three days.

'Get there with all haste,' Creed had told him.

Grüber liked to fight in a plodding, ponderous, unstoppable manner, typical of generals of the Astra Militarum. 'I cannot get there within a month.'

'I need you there in two days. Two days, Grüber, understand. Two days! That is an order.'

'I understand,' Grüber had said, even though he knew that with the troops he had, the supplies that they did not have, and the strength of the enemy before them, there was no way they could fulfil Creed's wishes.

Grüber looked down at his commanders and wondered if he should give them the timeline that Creed had given him. It was impossible, he knew, and he feared that asking the impossible of them might break their fragile courage.

The general wavered in a rare moment of indecision. He had promised, he reasoned, and so he should honour his word. He coughed to clear his voice. 'Lord Castellan Creed needs the strength of the Seventeenth Army at the Elysion Fields within nightfall, two days from now.'

They could never do it. He felt that their morale would

break as he asked this of them, but the reaction of the officers astonished him.

A thrill went through the room. They were being asked to achieve the impossible. They smiled and laughed and turned to each other with wry comments. If that was what Creed asked of them, they would do it.

Grüber took in a deep breath. 'Two days, men of Cadia. Two days and we shall be in the Elysion Fields!'

There was a roar as the commanders rose to their feet. 'Two days!' they shouted back. Grüber found himself swept up with the mood in the room. 'To the Elysion Fields!' And then shouts of 'For Creed! For Cadia!' and 'Cadia stands!' General Grüber breathed this moment in deep.

He had spoken to his commanders, and they were inspired.

TWO

THE MYRAK SALIENT, HIGHWAY 4

His orders were to move forward at all speed and engage the enemy with ferocity, but Colonel Lars Heni of the Cadian 662nd Mechanised Brigade was hours from his starting point and already his column was bogged down on Highway 4, ten miles short of Bastion 8.

He punched the cupola in fury, slid from the cabin – cursing the awkwardness of his augmetic leg – and marched up to the half-track in front of him. In the glare of torchlight, he saw a row of gap-toothed abhumans looking down on him, their eyes lit with a crude mix of frustration and animal intelligence. He threw open the driver's door. The air stank of musk and cheap gun lubricant but the driver's seat was empty. He shone his torch around to find someone to talk to. 'What the frekk is the hold-up?' Lars shouted up to the abhumans.

One of the ogryns roared back. If there were words there then Lars didn't understand them, but he could tell they felt as annoyed as he did. The pistons in his augmetic leg hissed as he limped forward. The queue of armour stretched before him as far as he could see, their shaded headlamps casting low spears of light in the gloom.

Twenty tanks up, there stood a young Cadian at a road-block, arguing with the driver of the front ogryn half-track. 'We've been stuck in this queue for three days,' he was saying. 'I've got ogryn here. I don't know how long I can keep them calm for.'

'No,' the officer said.

Lars pushed forward. 'I'm Major Lars, 662nd Mech Brigade.' The officer took Lars in, from his augmetic leg to his lean build and brass honour gorget. 'We're to be at Point Sixty-Seven in three hours' time. Creed's orders.'

The officer looked at him. 'Sorry,' he said. 'The way is blocked. I have my orders too.'

'It's imperative that we are let through.' Lars showed his rank but the warrior was unconcerned.

'The way is closed,' he said. 'Nothing I can do about it. Orders from Grüber himself.'

Lars cursed. 'Creed called me personally this morning. He insisted that I lead this attack.'

'Yeah, right,' the other man sneered.

Lars' fist caught him square on the chin. A sound, solid blow that felt exquisite to deliver. Any normal Guardsman would have gone down under a blow like that. The man Lars had just hit shook his head, put a hand to his lip and held it out to check if there was blood. 'I'll give you that shot free, colonel, but next time I'll forget your rank.'

Lars didn't like to do this, but it got things done. He pulled the gorget aside for a moment to show his medals. Medals worked better than shouts or threats. The officer took the line of honours in. The triple skull badge, the Merit of Terra and, lastly, the gold badge of a Ward of Cadia.

The other man's manner changed. 'I wish I could help,' he said. 'But look. You can see. Everyone is moving. The big attack is coming. I'll do the best I can.'

Lars gave the man a look. 'Thanks,' he said, but he was already looking for another way out of this mess. He didn't think the officer's best was going to be good enough for him.

Lars cursed as he climbed stiffly back up to his tank. 'We're not going to make it,' he said as he dropped into the commander's seat. 'At least not this way.'

His crew looked tired. Their eyes were rimmed with dust, their cheeks were dirty. 'The roads ahead are blocked.'

The driver, Hesk, took out two lho-sticks and offered one to Lars. He hadn't smoked for years, but sometimes nothing else quite worked. He pulled out a Munitorum-issue igniter, flicked it open and lit both. It was unlucky to light a third. The time it took to light a third lho-stick was all that a sniper needed to aim and fire. He blew out the flame, flicked the igniter closed and slipped it into his breast pocket.

'So,' Hesk said, puffing smoke from his mouth and nostrils. 'We'll have to go off-road.'

Lars sighed and nodded. The map was unfolded. It was too big for the cramped space inside the tank. Hesk positioned it under the light so that Lars could read it clearly.

Lars put his fingers to the map, marking out lines before him. Creed's orders were all in his head. Creed had insisted upon that. 'There are too many spies,' Creed had warned him. 'But be there,' he had said. 'Promise me.'

And Lars had promised.

'So which way?' Hesk said.

Lars checked the coordinates in his head. 'Here,' he said, pointing to the place. 'We're relieving Kasr Myrak.'

'I thought it had fallen.'

'Apparently not.'

'You're sure?'

Lars gave a short laugh. He wasn't sure of anything except that Creed had given him personal instructions and they were all in his head. Lars smoothed out the map and refolded it. 'If we go off-road we could go along the Myrak Valley.'

'As long as we don't run into the enemy.'

'The idea is that we *do* run into them.'

Hesk took the map and opened it up again. 'It's rough ground there.' He spoke with authority. 'I did my winter training there.'

'Got a better idea then?'

'Yes. If the land has not been broken up too badly. There's a line of dry land down here, in the valley bottom.'

Lars nodded. It was rough terrain but he didn't see that they had any choice. He climbed up into the cupola. His driver got the machine-spirit warmed up, and then slammed the Leman Russ into gear. 'Right,' he said. 'Here goes.'

Lars took his vox-control as they slewed off the road. 'All crews,' he called. He gave the coordinates and each of the squadron leaders confirmed, all the way down the line of tanks, supply vehicles, fuel carriers and ammo trucks.

The ground began to tremble as the entire brigade swung round and turned off the highway into the trackless wastes of Cadia Prime.

They headed north-east, bounding over the ploughed-up tracks of what could only be Leviathans and the distinctive mark of Warlord Titan footprints. It was exhilarating to be moving again, with the wind in their faces.

They passed burned-out tanks, the crater in which a Warlord had exploded, the scattered shapes of dead men, lying where they had fallen – in heaps at times, five or six deep. The bodies had been dead for months. As the tanks rolled over them they bobbed and bounced on the corrugated surface. The stench of old, burned human flesh was horrible. Only the cold kept the flies down. Who knew whether they were heretics or loyalists – the tanks ran straight over them, barely pausing: war had come to Cadia in all its scale and horror. Lars had seen it as bad as this before, but not many times. As the land levelled out, Hesk changed up the gears and pressed his foot on the accelerator.

Lars felt the engine begin to hum as they changed out of third gear for the first time in three days. Despite the stink, it was good to feel the wind through the windows. Good to be moving at speed once more. Good to be delivering the counter-blow, at last.

When they reached Point 67, Lars Heni brought his column to a halt.

'This is it,' he said.

Hesk opened his hatch and looked out. 'So what do we do now?'

Lars checked his chronometer. 'We wait,' he said.

Hesk sniffed. All of Cadia looked pretty much the same these days: a burned, barren wasteland. All that differed was the wrecks, which showed where battles had been fought.

'How long?'

'Two hours.'

'And then?'

'We attack.'

Hesk nodded. There was a long pause. 'What if you get killed? What do we do then?'

Lars gave his driver a stare. He patted his augmetic leg. 'They've tried killing me before,' he said. 'It didn't work.'

Hesk half smiled. 'No, really. What will happen?'

'Keep moving forward,' Lars told him.

Point 874, Trench System B, Myrak Salient

The sandbagged bunker had a well-stamped earth floor, a simple field chart-table, and a rack of lasrifles stacked in the far corner. Colonel Jan Vetter of the Cadian Earthshakers paced back and forth. He cursed better than anyone in the combined regiment of the Cadian 290th/340th Artillery and he was in full flow as he raged down the vox at the Munitorum clerk in charge of resupply.

'Where are my shells?' he shouted, and added a long line of expletives. 'We've had nothing for two days. My entire battery, silent!' He slammed his open palm down on the chart-table. There was a pause before he started again. 'You told me that yesterday! I need shells. The assault is supposed to start in ten minutes, and I still don't have my shells!'

One of his staff officers, Yastin, touched his elbow and pointed. Headlights were arcing through the gloom. It was a Chimera chassis, Salamander command vehicle. Vetter's staff looked hopeful. 'I think they've arrived,' Yastin said.

'They frekking better have,' Vetter cursed as he climbed

up out of his sandbagged bunker, standing up and raising a hand so he could be seen in the gloom.

The five-hundred-mile-long and three-hundred-mile-wide
Myrak Salient had been gradually shrinking back as Volscani
armoured divisions had thrown themselves against the base
of the salient, attempting to entrap the 17th Army within.

Six miles ahead, in the last lines of trenches, there was
a terrible slaughter going on.

You could smell smoke and cordite and rotting bodies even here.

Vetter's regiment had been pummelling the attacking
columns until their supplies of ordnance had run out.
High Command, as always, seemed oblivious. They had
issued new targeting coordinates and a strict deadline for
the bombardment to start, and Jan Vetter had been swearing ever since. On the vox, to his staff, and in a long and
one-sided conversation with General Grüber, which had
gone on mostly in his head.

'Maybe the rumour is true,' Vetter's adjutant, Yastin, said
as they waited for the Salamander to arrive. 'Maybe we're
going to attack.'

'Well, we need frekking Earthshaker shells first,' Vetter
said. 'We can't fire orders at the enemy. Throne take them
all! If Creed was here he wouldn't let such a shambles
go on.'

The thought of Creed made them all feel a little better.

The Centaur's lights cast long beams, illuminating the
swirling dirt and ash that swilled continuously up in
the breeze. 'Here!' Vetter shouted, though he could not
be heard. He waved his torch and the Centaur's tracks
slewed it towards him. Before it had even stopped a
comms officer was out, running low to the ground.

'Are you the–' the officer started, but Vetter shouted over him.

'Yes,' he called out. 'You're late, and this frekking bombardment is supposed to start in five minutes.'

The man's face showed a mixture of apology and resilient defiance. 'It was tough getting through,' he said. Vetter didn't look for an explanation, but the man gave it anyway. 'A maniple of Warhounds broke through.'

Vetter had seen the explosions and felt the earth tremors. He'd guessed something like that had happened, but that was someone else's problem, not his. 'Well, I've got an artillery barrage to send!'

The other man nodded. Fighting was starting up to the west. He could feel the tremors through his Cadian-issue leather boots. 'Right!' Vetter said. 'There's four hundred Basilisks along this line. They're three deep...' he started, but the comms officer knew his business as well as Vetter, and already his supply train of half-tracks and Trojans were peeling off and finding the dug-in Basilisks.

Within less than a minute the first ordnance trucks were reversing into position behind the dug-in Basilisk tanks. Neat lines of artillery shells were stacked five deep. The ammo carriages groaned under the weight of high explosives and cast metal. Crude clawed servitor arms slowly began to pile the Earthshaker shells onto the ground behind each gun. The whine of hydraulics seemed almost too loud.

'Come on!' Vetter urged, but the supply crews were already at work, lifting the wooden pallets of Earthshaker shells into position. 'Grüber's going on the offensive!'

'I thought he could only walk backwards,' a young gunner said between breaths as he slid an Earthshaker shell into the loading breech. Just the idea that they were going to go on the attack at last. It was intoxicating. There was giddy banter among the men. Vetter realised he hadn't heard anyone joke for... well... months.

'Yes indeed, Guardsman!' He grinned. 'Grüber wants us to move forward. We'll be in Kasr Kraf by midnight.'

His vividly violet eye ran over the activity as the empty ammo trucks pulled away and others reversed in to take their place. A whistle blew. Vetter checked his chronometer. There was less than a minute to go. 'Load!' he shouted, though the breeches were already loaded. He realised he'd been gripping the torch too tightly, and flexed his hand. The nerves were getting to him. He cursed himself. Human, but Cadian.

An air raid alarm sounded. At the end of the line, his anti-air turrets were swivelling to the west. Vetter couldn't see what was coming. The first Hydra started up, four lines of tracers streaked up into the sky. A direct hit into this mass of ordnance could blow them all to the Golden Throne. The fact didn't scare him. Vetter had seen death on thirty-seven planets and despite the steel plates in his femur and scapula, and the ache in his left shoulder, nothing had quite managed to finish him off.

Another alarm started. The other two Hydras opened up, the twelve light trails seeming almost to bend as the automatic targeting sensors traced something flying towards them hard and low and fast.

'Enemy fliers,' Yastin called out.

Vetter nodded. He was counting down to zero hour.

A fireball curved off towards the south and impacted in a dull orange blast, hazy through the smoke of war. Vetter lifted his chainsword, thumbed the stud to set the teeth spinning for a moment.

'Make ready!' he shouted.

The gun crews reacted with swift, effective, practised movements. Vetter had come from the 340th Regiment, but the two had been merged so long it was hard to remember which of the old crews was from which unit. The months of fighting had thinned their ranks drastically, but the new recruits were shaping up well.

Vetter held his arm aloft as another alarm sounded and this time the Hydras swung round to the south-east. Soon all their twenty anti-air platforms were engaged, fluid lines of tracer fire tracking the enemy.

'Make ready!' Vetter ordered.

He counted down the seconds.

Eight, seven, he counted as a long metallic neck of brass and wires appeared from the gloom before them, soot trailing from its nostrils like a dragon of old.

Between the counts of seven and five, the helldrake's sinuous body emerged. It had wings of steel, and when its snout opened, it gave a scream like tearing sheet metal.

Four! There was a ripple of movement as the gun crews stood to, signalling they were ready.

The vox officer, Dresk, was standing next to him. Vetter didn't even wait for the question. 'Yes,' he said, 'we're ready!'

Three.

Dresk turned to pass on the message.

Two.

Vetter allowed himself a deep breath in that tasted of ash and battle and smoke and death, put the whistle to his lips and raised an arm.

One.

The guns fired on time, four hundred Basilisks roaring as one.

It took five seconds before the next salvo rang out. Breeches were opened, cleared and re-armed, slammed shut, and fired again.

Not bad, Vetter thought, but his men could do better.

By the sixth round, his crews were warming up. The barrage became a constant roar of thunder and smoke and recoiling Earthshaker barrels. Inch by inch, gun crews adjusted the barrels, forcing the barrage forward at the pace a Leman Russ could drive. Suddenly Vetter remembered the flying daemon engine that had been beating towards his lines. He looked about and saw nothing.

Had it passed overhead? he thought, and looked up, where it had last been seen, flapping into the face of the guns.

Bits of metal were falling from the sky like feathers.

THREE

MYRAK SALIENT

In the shattered bunkers of Kasr Kraf, the South Polar Orbital Arrays, the island kasr of the Caducades Archipelago – all across Cadia, where defenders still lived and fought, Guardsmen sat waiting by their vox-units, their faces tense, their eyes downcast, as they ran through the upcoming assault, and their part within it.

At zero hour the vox-units crackled to life and Creed's voice ground out.

'The fight back has begun...' he told them. *'Have faith. Have courage. Have no mercy upon our foes.'*

Then whistles blew. The order was given. It was do or die.

Decimated regiments that had been fighting for months had been thrown together according to availability, logic and chance. Infantry were paired with tank brigades; drop-troops with armoured fist squads; scout regiments with artillery companies. The few massive line-busting

Baneblades and their ilk were pulled together into squadrons and companies.

There had been heated arguments and fights as regiments with proud and individual distinctions were merged with young regiments that lacked a long pedigree.

The lieutenant of the Cadian 3rd, who were one of the founding regiments of the Cadian Gate, had refused to serve under the command of a colonel of the Cadian 4002nd Rifles – a unit that was itself an amalgamation of three other regiments, one of which had been decimated by the Commissariat after it had broken in the battle for Gestal Heights, in the Scarus Sector.

A major of the Cadian 99th Lancers had resigned his commission rather than serve under the command of an infantry officer. He led his roughrider squad in the first charge on the Nexus Gate, had two mounts shot from under him, and was last seen leading the survivors up the ramparts towards the enemy.

But Cadian units followed the same professional codes of conduct and war. They all faced the same enemy.

Unknown to the enemy and the Cadians alike, Creed's hidden army were making their way out of the safety of the Salvation outposts. The scale of the counter-attack was vast.

On the far-flung continent of Cadia Tertius, servitors loaded squadrons of Thunderbolts and Marauder destroyers with Hellstrike missiles. Hidden launch-bay doors opened, and squadron after squadron soared out, to clear the skies of Cadia.

On the plains of Cadia Primus, infantry regiments lined up at the underground armouries as quartermasters unloaded hellguns and lasrifles, flamers, grenade launchers, demolition charges, heavy bolters, autocannons and lascannons with well-oiled tripods. The speeches of Creed rang out over the vox-relays and the fury of the warriors, who had chafed at their isolation, became as cold and merciless as a freshly whetted blade.

It took some rifle regiments two days to make the climb to the sally points. Under the hills of Cadia Secundus, armoured units were brought up from the depths by vast lift halls that carried a whole squadron of tanks at a time. The closer to the surface they came, the stronger the scent of ash and burning. Then, at last, they stood before the closed sally ports and the tramp of boots came to a halt.

For some of the troops waiting at the doors, it was hours of standing. Others arrived only moments before the scheduled opening of the Salvation gates. Generals, majors, colonels, lieutenants and sergeants all made their speeches – some long and erudite, others short and curse-filled and to the point.

Across Cadia Primus and Secundus, millions of elite Cadian Shock Troopers gripped their guns tighter, ground their teeth, cursed the enemies of the Imperium of Man and readied themselves for war.

That morning Cadia fought back.

In the trenches of the Myrak Salient, whistles blew and whole platoons moved up over the top into a hail of heavy stubbers and bolters. Armoured fist squads, loaded into their Chimeras, charged across no-man's-land in columns five wide, their turret-mounted autocannons and multi-lasers tracking for targets. Tank regiments with honour rolls that stretched back eight thousand years moved out, battle cannons smoking. Airborne units lifted off, packed into Valkyries that flew low to the ground, side gunners scanning for targets.

For some unlucky regiments the time arrived, the codes were tapped into the locking panels, and nothing happened. The earth had been so transformed by orbital bombardment that the doors of their bunkers would not open, and the units realised that they were trapped.

But most who charged out on Cadia Primus found a land devastated by war. The land they knew was now an unfamiliar maze of craters. Proud cities were burned and empty shells. Vast tank graveyards showed where battles had raged on the surface and the land had been turned black, as if a wildfire had crossed the entire planet and scorched everything in its path.

Each unit had coordinates to head to, objectives to seize, but for many of them the battles had already been lost, the kasr they were meant to be relieving already plundered.

'There has been a wildfire,' General Justus declared to his men. 'It is the Arch-heretic. It is Abaddon. He is responsible. It is him we hate. And all who follow him.'

On the burning plains of Cadia Primus, many units found themselves surrounded by Iron Warriors. The lead tanks of the Cadian 652nd Armoured Brigade suddenly erupted in flame, and as the rest of the company tried to move around them, they were also taken out with well-aimed lascannon shots. The column ground to a halt as tank commanders made desperate attempts to move the burning wrecks out of the way, while more and more of the column was torn apart by an enemy they could not see.

A few tank commanders attempted to fire back, but it was a hopeless task, and soon Iron Warriors ran amok through the parked columns until the whole bunker was a roiling mess of fumes and fire.

As the scale of slaughter on Cadia Primus grew in horror and violence, foul sorceries were unleashed and the bounds that held the immaterium back began to weaken. Amid the black and smoke, lurid and impossible shapes appeared. Red packs of vicious, horned monsters tore tanks apart with their claws and unholy swords. Vast winged shapes loomed up, with battle-axes the size of a Sentinel, snarling and gnashing and howling for blood. Men were struck dumb with terror. The immense daemons crushed tanks with a single blow of their axes, or a stamp of their red, hoofed feet. Although they were millions strong, the forces of Cadia found themselves outnumbered and overpowered. But despite everything, they resisted with all their strength.

Proud regiments, who had carried victory across the Imperium of Man, each found a hill or a mound, planted their banners in the burned earth, firing and bayoneting at the waves of heretics, inch by inch being slowly overwhelmed like an atoll being swallowed up by a rising sea.

The continent of Cadia Secundus had been hit less hard than those to the north, and here the forces of Cadia had fared better. There were many places such as Bastion 8 where command and control retained a firm grip. The defenders charged out, and many of them shared the same experience as Lars when he led his tank column forward.

'Contact!' he voxed. His guns were loaded. His targeter was already winding the barrel round.

'Tanks,' Lars voxed to his unit. He was going to say 'dozens' but he could see that he was wrong. There were a hundred tanks, at least. More and more streaming up from the ground before him. 'Holy Throne!' he said. 'Hold your fire. They're Cadian!'

The two columns came together, lead tank to lead tank.

Lars shook his head in amazement. 'Bendikt, is that you?'

From the Salvation outposts whole armies appeared, fresh and ready for battle.

The tide of war began to change, and across the continent, Cadian forces felt the sudden injection of fresh troops rock the heretic forces back, and many made swift progress.

At the Primus-Junction, the 79th Armoured Regiment crashed through a section of the line held by the Volscani Cataphracts, firing plasma guns from the back of the Chimera transports, killing the heretics in their thousands. The 992nd/328th/674th Scout Regiment had a combined force of over six hundred Sentinels armed with multi-lasers and autocannons, and fifty with lascannons. Under the cover of a short-range artillery barrage from the two hundred Medusas of the 1911th Artillery Regiment, the Scout Sentinels moved forward, led by the veteran Sentinel pilot Lieutenant Ester Vathe.

As they approached the trenches of the enemy, the phalanx of walkers accelerated into a loping run, heavily-armoured Sentinels screening the lighter units behind.

The Sentinels came under sustained enfilading fire from heavy bolters and lascannons, and lost over fifty walkers in a matter of minutes. For a moment it seemed that the charge would be thrown back, but then Ester Vathe charged the lines of the enemy, singing Imperial hymns.

The massed Sentinel column hit the trenches and the fury of the Volscani foot soldiers.

There was a brief and furious fight as the Sentinels kicked and stomped their way through the foe. They would have stalled, until a sudden white light appeared in the sky and drove the enemy back.

Some claimed to have seen a bright human shape in the sky. Some saw Creed. Either way, the momentary shock it inflicted on the enemy allowed the heavy flamer-armed Sentinels to rush up and bathe the heretic trenches with burning promethium. Dark shapes leaped about in the torrent of burning, and then they fell, submerged and overcome with smoke and fumes, and the Sentinel drivers stamped on any that made it out. There was a furious battle of man and machine, and then, in less than half an hour, they were through, into open ground, wreaking a heavy cost on the supply trucks of the enemy and widening the hole in their line.

In some parts of the battlefront, command and control had been hit so many times by Black Legion terror squads that even the famous Cadian discipline was starting to creak under the pressure. The effectiveness of the attacks was haphazard and, sometimes, counter-productive.

The Cadian 987th/23rd tank regiment set off three hours too early. Their sixty-three Leman Russes and two Hydra flak tanks smashed through the heretic cultists along Sublime Ridge, and ploughed on through six miles of hastily thrown-up defences, Hellhounds scouting ahead and to either side, filling the trenches with burning promethium and allowing the main battle tanks to keep on rolling towards their objective, the heights to the north of

Kasr Myrak. Their commander, a Cadian veteran of only thirty-five years, known as Bold Brasq, sighted an enemy tank formation coming towards them and destroyed it in a firefight that lasted less than two hours, leaving wrecks burning over fifteen miles of the Myrak foothills.

It seemed at first that the misstep would prove a bold and brilliant move, but their assault went too far, too fast, and it was not long before the enemy reacted and the tanks were set upon by a flock of metal carrion that covered the armour in flame and boiled the crews alive inside their vehicles.

The Hydra tanks put up a solid defence, but to no avail, and once one had been destroyed, the task before the other was too great. It was picked off by three of the creatures, which came at it from all sides, like carrion birds mobbing a wounded beast.

With their air defence destroyed the rest of the tank column was exposed and isolated. Bold Brasq's Exterminator-pattern Leman Russ battle tank had been winged by a lucky missile strike and was making slow speed towards the shelter of a charcoal forest of bare stumps when it was set on by seven of the flying machines.

Brasq was manning the turret autocannons. As soon as they were in range he started to fire. Spent shells rattled off the tank hull like a hailstorm, and the tracers made an almost continuous line of light.

'Have faith,' Brasq had told his crew, and they were Cadian: tough, remorseless, realistic. He hit a flying creature in the wing. It spiralled down to earth and hit the ground head first. Its back was broken in an instant. He hit another in the breast, a sustained volley that tore wing from body.

The third swirled up into the air for a moment, managing to stay just ahead of the autocannon rounds, as two more flew in from behind.

Bold Brasq had a moment's warning, as the roar of their coming was like the sound of a gale in the high veldt pines. A moment was all he needed. He dropped down into the tank and pulled the cupola down behind him, one half-turn locking it shut.

For a moment there was silence, and then another roar as the monsters breathed upon the sealed tank.

The heat inside rose alarmingly as the flame torrent continued. There was a clunk as one of the tracks came loose, a cough as the engine gave up, and still the flame torrent continued.

'Frekk,' Brasq cursed as the vision slits glowed with a bright blue light. Within seconds the temperature had risen even more alarmingly. Thinner patches of the ceramite amour began to glow a dull red and then orange.

'We're going to cook,' Corter screamed from the driver's seat as the inside of the cramped Leman Russ cabin went from frigid to scalding hot. He threw off his leather straps. Brasq tried to speak, but he found himself gasping for breath. The firestorm was sucking all the oxygen out of the air. The vision slits hissed as their temperature soared, and then something dripped onto Brasq's hand and he cried out in pain.

The black plastek knob that locked the top hatch had melted and was dripping. Burst relay pipes under the floor sent hot jets of steam and scalding water into the cabin. Brasq cursed as he tried to flick the dripping substance off his skin. The air stank of ozone. He used his gloved hand to open the top hatch. Another black drip fell onto his cheek. There was smoke in the cabin, and it caught in the back of his throat. He kicked as he pushed himself out of the Leman Russ and into the flames.

Colonel Valentin of the Cadian 47th 'Firedogs' had spent his months in Salvation 37A getting drunk on a ton of fine Scarus amasec that had somehow replaced a large section of their ration supply. When the time came for the lifts to the surface, the engine of his Hellhound assault tank was turning over nicely as he shared a last shot of amasec with his other commanders, then clambered unsteadily up into its cupola.

He was largely sober when he led his unit of Hellhounds and assorted assault tanks up to the surface, but was sporting the mother of all hangovers as he pulled his white silk scarf about his neck and waved his column forward into the grey smog that passed for day on Cadia.

'Forward, brothers!' he shouted, not even bothering to broadcast over the vox channels.

He didn't even check his coordinates. He didn't need to; it was clear where the enemy trench lines were from the tangle of razor wire and the dull shine of Aegis defence lines scoured of camo paint by the weight of fire that had been thrown against them. One minute before the attack was due to start, his whole company of five hundred assault tanks was in position at the head of a force of over two thousand tanks that were arranged in battalions behind him.

'Ready, sir?' his driver, Matto, called up.

Valentin's scarf flapped in the breeze. 'Can't frekking wait.'

The opening salvos of the bombardment drowned out his words. They made the earth shake and the sky tremble as the world filled with a roaring maelstrom of sound and fury. Valentin put the scopes to his eyes and watched the heretic lines erupting with fountains of earth and smoke. The precision of the barrage was awe inspiring. It hit the front line with almost clinical discipline, throwing up a line of mud as if a long underground charge had suddenly been ignited.

'Holy Throne!' Valentin laughed as his tank trembled. It felt to him that his vehicle was a living thing, eager to get at the foe. It was the heretics' turn now to taste hell.

'Who else is spearheading this attack?' Matto shouted up.

'Steel Punch and Cadian Stalwarts.' Valentin could see the other assault tank brigades moving into position on either side. He felt a sudden panic that they would start first, and steal his glory.

Valentin's head was still light with alcohol. Their attack details had been meticulously timed with the barrage, but Valentin could not wait. Half a minute before the bombardment was due to move on, he signalled his driver, and the Hellhound tank lurched forward, camo netting swirling in the draught of its own passing.

Behind him his whole column started to move forward, tracks spinning and dust rising in their wake. It was half a mile to the heretic lines. Valentin's scarf flew out almost straight behind him as his tank led the charge. Amid the ruin and the explosions, he could see shapes desperately trying to man guns, or falling back in confusion as the massed Hellhounds sped across the open ground, their tracks skidding as they kicked up the dirt.

The barrage crept forward as the Hellhounds closed the last few hundred yards. It was a race now for the assault company to cross the ground before the surviving heretics could man their anti-tank weapons.

Valentin was halfway across the open ground when the first shots began to flare out towards them. Tracer fire streaked the sky as heavy weapons opened up from pill-boxes and emplacements.

He laughed at the sudden light show whizzing past his ears. The firing was wild and disorganised. That any were managing to fire with the bombardment that was raining down on them seemed remarkable. He did not duck. He had never felt so alive as at that moment, with the fury of the heretic blasting out at him.

'Take fire to the enemy,' he called to his crews. 'Faith in the Emperor of Mankind.' At the end of his speech he cried, 'Cadia stands!' as autocannon shells rang out on the armour of the Hellhound.

The range finder spiralled down. At a hundred and fifty yards he tested the flame cannons. The nozzle of the Hell-hound cannon gave a brief spurt of liquid fire, a thin pressurised cone that fanned out into a swirl of flames. Hellhound-grade promethium filled his nostrils. It felt good, despite his hangover, helped his mind focus.

At a hundred yards Valentin slipped down into the firing position and began to pan the Aegis line on the left for a target. It was draped with the dead bodies of Guardsmen, used as sandbags. There was at least one heavy-weapons team in there, guessing from the lines of tracers.

A missile arched out and hit the tank to Valentin's right. The explosion underlit the clouds with red and yellow as its fuel tanks combusted.

Inches-thick ablative armour ripped open like paper. A torrent of fire gouted two hundred yards into the air, and then, long seconds later, bits of burning metal began to rain down.

Valentin barely noticed it. He tracked, aimed and fired, and the plume of fuel arced out, feathering with flames. His targeter flared green as the flames overloaded the sensors. He let the flames linger for a moment on the pillbox. The liquid fuel poured in through the narrow vents and filled the interior with an incandescent fire.

His tank was already moving on to the next. There was a thud as the Hellhound hit the wire. The barbed coils held for a moment, the tracks spinning. There was a screech of metal as the wire snapped and the Hellhound surged onwards. It hit the Aegis line with a judder that threw Valentin forward. Matto gunned the engine and the tank veered up, belly exposed for a terrifying moment, before they crashed back down again, slamming forward on the simple suspension.

Valentin swung around to pour fire into the enemy lines. The first gout filled the first trench like a canal of knee-high promethium, all aflame. The next arced towards the second Aegis line. The third hit a squad of heretics, rushing forward, bent low, demo charges in hand.

Valentin grinned as dark shapes tumbled out of the inferno.

Dance, heretics, dance!

Then the demo charges blew and there was the wet slap of body parts hitting the front of his tank. Matto tracked round. There was a dull thud of a human being knocked to the ground and crushed, not the note of a melta or krak charge. Behind him, Valentin's column was hitting the heretic lines, widening the hole that they'd punched through.

On Valentin's right, a Hellhound – it must have been

Kristen's – hit a mine and slewed sideways. It came to rest in a shell-hole, nozzle-flame still hissing menacingly. Another lifted up over the Aegis defence line and was hit in the belly with a close-range melta shot that ripped through the Hellhound and combusted the reinforced armoured fuel tanks. It was lifted twenty feet off the ground with the explosion and fired burning wreckage across the battlefield, a hundred yards in all directions.

He pressed his vox-stud to all channels. 'All tanks, proceed south,' Valentin ordered. 'Maximum speed. Maximum violence. Cadia stands!'

'Cadia stands!' was repeated in every tank.

They plunged forward, smashing into the second, third and fourth lines of defence, the pause in their momentum longer each time before they pushed through.

This was the crucial moment. They had to keep pressing forward, despite the losses, forever pushing through for open ground. Hauser's tank got snared in wire and came to a skidding halt. A missile arced out and hit it on the armoured flanks.

There was a pause, and then it started to burn. The driver's hatch slapped open, and flames began to rise from within. *Out, damn it!* Valentin willed, but whoever had managed to get the hatch open did not appear. Maybe they'd gone back to help someone, Valentin thought. *Out*, he willed, punching the cupola before him, but then the fires spread and the whole tank went up with a hiss of flames that built to a blowtorch roar.

Valentin drew his pistol, shot an axe-wielding heretic through the forehead.

'Forward!' he raged, as his inferno cannon blazed out once more.

FOUR

BASTION 8, MYRAK SALIENT

Bastion 8 was a rockcrete star, sunk into a dry moat fifty yards wide – the largest of the string of ancient defences that ringed the highlands – excavated with atomic bunkers, barracks, ration stores and munitions depots, and stoutly fortified in three stepped levels, each one offering enfilading fields of fire in all directions.

It was from there that General Grüber launched his counter-attack. He rode in a Baneblade named *High Lord*, a magnificent, brass-worked masterpiece, with four lascannon sponsons and a raised cupola throne. It trundled forward, Cadians raising their lasguns in salute. They passed over the trench systems and pushed forward through the detritus of war, chasing the front line as it pushed deeper and deeper into the guts of the heretic army.

The *High Lord* ripped through the trench systems of the foe, its main guns pummelling any armoured resistance, while sponsors tore the combat stimm-induced fighters apart with heavy bolt shells as long as a man's hand. The vast tracks barely noticed the tank traps and trench systems that had been worked with so much care by the enemy. The Baneblade crossed six lines of trenches. At midday on the first day of the assault, an improvised column of assorted Black Legion tanks was thrown against it. They came rumbling forward across the burned, open moorland, black banners flapping in the smoke-dark air.

The Baneblade smashed through craters and piles of wreckage. It took four gunners to man the Baneblade's main cannon. They assessed the danger, pinpointed a Vanquisher at the back of the column, and swung the turret round. It took them only a few seconds to line the tank up and fire. The Baneblade shell tore a hole in the armour of the Leman Russ wide enough for a man to climb through. Its explosion ripped the tank into shrapnel.

On the foredeck of the Baneblade the Demolisher cannon targeted the closest of the enemy tanks and fired a rocket-propelled siege round at it. When the smoke cleared there was nothing left of tank or shell but a smouldering crater and a few scraps of burning metal.

All units were pushing forward. It was as if a crack had opened in a vast dam. The torrent was too fast and too powerful, the head of water too great to be held back. The gap opened wider until Cadian units were pushing forward on a sixteen-mile front, with infantry and supply craft coming up behind them.

All the time their massed artillery regiments were hammering the enemy backlines, preventing them bringing up reinforcements or even mounting an effective response.

Grüber sat in the throne, sword drawn.

His attendants begged for him to come down and protect himself. Grüber was stern. 'Who dares to stand against us?'

Across much of the Myrak Salient the earth was pocked with craters, the vegetation scoured away or burned black with war. The prospect was one the Cadians were familiar with as they moved forward by foot, or in armoured transports.

Captain Lation's 114th Cadians made rapid progress, defeating three small tank forces that had been sent to halt him. The first two were units of heretic Guardsmen, manning captured tanks and armoured transports. They were easy prey for the elite Cadian units, their ruins left burning as the Cadians pushed on. But the third was a pair of Black Legion Predator tanks that fought a desperate and effective battle, sniping, falling back, and sniping once more.

Lation lost three Leman Russ tanks and sustained damage to two more before his gunner managed to catch a Predator as it sped between the ruins, hitting it with a battle cannon round to the weak side armour. The Predator was lifted up by the explosion and slammed back to the ground, a broken and burning shell. A second tried to retreat between the rocks, speeding backwards, trailing smoke into the air.

Lation had fought on the mist-bound moors of Maner and had a knack of guessing where a foe was heading. 'Krak,' he ordered as the gunner dragged an armour-piercing round from the magazine, turned and slid it onto the loading ramp.

'Loaded!' the driver said, throwing the gun door shut and locking it closed.

Lation elevated the gun barrel, adding another fifty feet to the shot. He made a quick prayer to the Golden Throne, then fired.

The round arced off, leaving a swirling track as it plunged through the ink-black smoke. There was a pause as the cloud wound in upon itself, and then there was a sudden flash of flame that shot straight up into the air like a furnace blast.

Lation led the column forward, checking that the second tank had been destroyed. The Predator had been hit on the turret, and the armour-piercing round had burned a neat hole through the reinforced plating and exploded within the tank, igniting the magazine.

It was a hit that would have instantaneously killed an Imperial Guard crew, but one of the Traitor Space Marines had survived, horribly wounded. Its legs had been blown away and half its face had been burned down to the bone. But it was still alive.

'Bring us close,' Lation ordered his driver.

Lation's tank stopped twenty feet away from the wounded Space Marine.

Goldburg, his gunner, spoke. 'What should I load, sir?'

Lation paused for a moment. 'Nothing.'

The thing was huge, malformed, inhuman. Its eyes were yellow, with vertical slits, like a snake's. When its ruined mouth moved Lation knew there were words there, though it was an accent he could not understand. He slid down from his tank and landed on both feet. 'I do not fear you!' he shouted. He felt courage from his words.

The thing snarled at him.

The size of the traitor before him only became apparent

as Lation drew closer. Its chest was as wide as some men were tall. It was massive, solid, though terribly wounded, and still moving as it struggled for breath.

Lation drew his service-issue laspistol. He set the charge to the max, lifted the gun and sighted the thing's forehead. This time he understood the accent. 'Fire true, captain.'

Lation felt sick at the sound of the thing's voice. His hand shook as it stared into him. The light of its eyes turned orange and then red, like a real fire burning.

'Shoot, captain!' the thing hissed.

Lation fired. The first shot hit the traitor on the side of the cheek. It scored a deep burn.

'Again!' it hissed at him.

Lation's hand was shaking now. The next shot missed. He stepped forward for the third and held the pistol with both hands. 'In the name of the God Emperor of Mankind,' he called out, and fired a third time.

Sally Ports, Salvation 9983

It felt good to be driving again. Bendikt stood in the turret of his tank and breathed the moment deep, but even as he led his column forward, he waited for his vox officer to connect to General Grüber.

Grüber's voice was tight and drawn. *'What is your strength?'* he demanded.

Bendikt knew the figure off by heart. He was leading one thousand five hundred Leman Russ tanks, assorted patterns. Fifty Hydra defence platforms. A squadron of assault tanks. Thirty-nine Knights Errant. A hundred thousand mechanised infantry. Ten thousand kasrkin. Bendikt allowed himself a smile. 'We make up the 207th Army.'

There was a long pause that Bendikt enjoyed.

'*You are sure of your numbers?*' Grüber's voice queried.

'All correct.'

'*What is your position?*'

Bendikt checked. 'Point Seventy-Three.'

'*207th Army is not on my list.*'

'We're new.'

There was another long pause. '*That is impossible.*'

Bendikt paused. 'Location confirmed. Point Seventy-Three.'

'*You cannot be.*'

'We are, General Grüber.'

Grüber's voice was curt. '*I said that is impossible. Please check and confirm immediately.*'

Bendikt paused for a moment. He did not bother checking but brought the vox-link back up to his mouth. 'Confirmed, sir.'

'*You're twenty miles behind enemy lines.*'

'Confirmed.'

'*Lead your forces to cut off hostile army units.*'

'I'm afraid I cannot.'

'*What do you mean?*'

'I have orders from the Lord Castellan, Ursarkar E. Creed.'

'*And what are those orders?*'

'I cannot tell you.'

Grüber put on his officious voice. '*Major Bendikt. You are addressing a general of the Astra Militarum.*'

Bendikt let the moment hang, and engaged the vox-stud. 'Yes, General Grüber. I am also a general. I have my own orders. I will be following those. Good hunting!'

* * *

A battalion of Volscani defended the pontoon bridges over the Myrak River. Behind them, in the far distance, the pylons of the Elysion Fields rose up against the horizon.

Bendikt used a scope to assess their position. Three Leman Russes and a Destroyer tank dug into the river-banks. The heretic unit put up a commendable defence. Their infantry squads were dug into foxholes. Missiles arced out from them as the tanks fired at a furious rate.

The 89th Army Group demolished them in less than ten minutes, and Bendikt led his army out over the Myrak River and past their burning wrecks, the Volscani troops lying dead.

In two hours his army had crossed to the other side. They paused to refuel, re-arm and regroup, and then they were off again, batting away three heretic forces that were flung at them. It was not until nightfall that they met serious opposition: a Black Legion column that had been diverted to impede their progress. The Traitor Space Marines brought Bendikt's army to a halt for nearly two hours, as outflanking units enveloped them, and they slowly ground the Black Legion down.

The battlefield was littered with burning wrecks. They belched black smoke into the gathering gloom.

Bendikt's tank was pushing cautiously through when Mere called up to him. 'Lord General,' Mere said. 'It's the Lord Castellan.'

Bendikt nodded as he took the vox-link and started to speak, but Creed cut him off.

'Bendikt,' he said. *'Where are you?'*

'We've crossed the Myrak River.'

'Good,' Creed said. *'Well done. But I need more. Can you reach the Elysion Fields by dawn?'*

It was fifty miles. 'Confirmed,' Bendikt said. 'We'll be there.'

Creed's voice sounded strained and weary. Bendikt could imagine him putting his fingers to his temples and rubbing them before he spoke. *'Thank you. Do all you can. Please. You're the closest troops. Please, do your best. Cadia depends on it.'*

FIVE

17TH ARMY GROUP, MYRAK FRONT

War lit Cadia. It was as if the planet burned.

On the surface raging firestorms lit up miles and miles of battlefront, while overhead lightning storms in the high atmosphere illuminated the night sky, punctuated by blinding flashes as warships died in cataclysmic explosions, their plasma reactors going nuclear and the burning wrecks falling towards the planet like vast flares hanging in the darkness.

All was war, and gleaming above it the Eye of Terror pulsed and bulged as arcane sorceries were invoked. The vast globe swirled with vivid purple and yellow, blotches of unholy light pulsing and fading in sickening patterns.

Under the hell-flames General Grüber's army hammered relentlessly at the armies before them, slaughtering heretics as they howled and shrieked forward. The forces they faced were high on frenzon. For a day they battled through the endless tide of screaming bodies.

Lina was on the left wing, with one of the surviving

armoured units of the Cadian 8th, 'Lord Castellan's Own'. She'd been a sponson gunner at Tyrok Fields, but with war and field promotions she had risen to main gunner on the Ryza-pattern Demolisher, *Hammer of Tyrok*.

The *Hammer* was a temperamental beast of a tank, and on the second day of the assault her engine started to clang dangerously, then she ground to a halt.

In the absence of a tech-priest, it fell to Lina. She was the best at coaxing unhappy machine-spirits.

'It's your soft hands,' Ibsic said.

'Frekk you,' Lina told him as she lay under the tank, trying to unscrew the drive-shaft panels.

Tanks filed past on either side. Commanders had cloths tied over their faces. Some waved. All stared.

A Titan-hunting squadron of three Shadowswords trundled past, their service tanks skittering about them. It was a magnificent sight, with Scout Sentinels, a brigade of Hydras and a complement of ancillary support vehicles and tanks. In the centre of the great convoy were the three Shadowswords, their fixed volcano cannons still smoking. Lina let out a long, low whistle. It was only when you compared the size of a Shadowsword to a Leman Russ that you got a sense of the scale of these things. The immense tank crested the rise, the fixed gun swinging towards her as it descended.

'Look at those,' she said, and started laughing as a second and third behemoth crested the ridge. Just behind the sponson-weapon cabins, the side hatches squeaked as they swung open. Her crew spilled out and stood beside their tank to watch.

'Holy Throne!' one said.

'Frekk,' said another.

It took half an hour for the Titan Hunter squadron to

make their way across the veldt. The sight of a pair of tech-priest Chimeras frustrated Ibsic. It wouldn't take one of them long to fix *Hammer*. But with each minute their unit was racing farther and farther ahead.

Lina was down there for more than an hour. She finally slid herself out from under the tank, sat up and rubbed lubricants from her hands.

'Got it fixed?'

'I think so.'

She was climbing up when there was a sudden flash of light, and then a rolling boom.

Lina ducked. 'What was that?'

Ibsic had his scopes out. 'I think they just nailed a Titan,' he told her. 'Seventy degrees west.'

Lina grabbed the scopes. The landscape before her was flat, marked only with wreckage from the sky battle, which stood up from the ground like tufts of burning grass. 'I don't see it,' she said.

Two hours later they reached the place where the Titan attack had been stalled. A dead Warhound lay on its back, like a drunken man in a down-hive bar: legs wide, and head tilted back in a posture of utter debasement. Smoke rose from the hole in its chest cavity, a thick, noxious blend of promethium, lubricants and human flesh, all burned to ignition by the heat of the impacts.

'Look at that!' Ibsic said. Their tank slowed to a crawl. Lina pushed her way up out of the cupola. The size of the dead machine was breathtaking. The paintwork of the Titan was chipped and worn. The barrels of the turbo laser were blackened and heat-stained. The ammo feed of its Vulkan mega-bolter had broken open and spilt bolt shells across the ground. She took in the size of the shells. 'Frekk.'

The fight was still going on. The flashes strobed Lina's face as she looked out.

'Keep the gun loaded,' Ibsic warned her.

'Done,' she said.

There was good hunting that morning. In the ferocious battles, the heretic counter-attacks were held and thrown back. They came across three more dead Renegade Titans in the next five miles. The last was a Jackal class. It had been knocked out perhaps half an hour earlier and had not yet been isolated by the tech-priests. As Lina's tank approached, a Mechanicus Chimera pulled up alongside the stricken Titan. Lina watched as a tech-priest glided out, octopus-like, on a bed of coiling mechadendrites.

It reached the head of the Scout Titan. Mechadendrites touched the Titan's head and a shudder went through the great construct, and then the head lolled limply to the side.

It was like watching a farmer put a bolt into the brain of a grox. Lina looked away.

'Let's get out of here,' she said, but kasrkin were holding the lines of armour back as a Shadowsword drove up.

The super-heavy tank came to a halt, a thin wisp of smoke still rising from the volcano cannon. The battery fans were still blasting cold air through the cooling systems. Behind the cannon, a hatch opened and a slim, hawkish man climbed up, put his hand to the side of the mammoth tank and slid down the side of the fixed-gun mounting.

The tank commander walked along the Shadowsword's decking, one hand to the gun barrel to steady himself. He wore the markings of a tank ace. But it was his poise that Lina found instantly intriguing. It was like watching a peacock. He came down one of the metal ladders, jumped the last ten feet and landed squarely.

When he turned towards her, Lina saw the handsomely scarred mouth and silver gorget.

She knew straight away who he was and nudged Ibsic. 'It's Pask!' she hissed, but Ibsic had seen at the same time.

Pask pushed up his peaked cap and strolled over to the dead Titan. He put a hand against one of its vast three-jointed toes. He struck the pose of a big-game hunter on a death world. 'Seven in two days. Not bad.'

Lina didn't know what to say.

'Think we've broken them?' Ibsic called out.

Pask looked up. 'Hmm. Yes.' He pointed up to the sky. They glimpsed the lightning flashes of a Naval battle. 'Terra has answered our call.'

Lina didn't know what he meant.

'The Imperial Fists Chapter have come to our aid. They have brought the *Phalanx*.'

Lina nodded, but she didn't really know what he was talking about.

'We've got them beaten.' Pask gave a short, weary smile. 'Now we need to punish them. Make sure they never forget it.' He turned his back and returned to his Shadowsword. 'We have to make sure they never dare attack us again.'

For the rest of the day Grüber's 17th Army plunged through the heretic armies like a stiletto blade. He was fearless when they stormed the enemy strongpoints, his Baneblade lending its weight to the attack whenever it appeared to stall.

He made an obvious target, and his armour saved him from sniper fire a number of times. He took a shot to his leg, but refused to step down, and insisted that the medicae dress his wound there, on top of the Baneblade.

Lina was involved in two battles: one against a column of Chimeras, the other against a tank brigade dug into the slopes of a low rise above the river valley.

That day Creed's broadcast did not come, but there was so much to do the attacks pushed on regardless. Creed did not broadcast the next day, either.

It was night when the vox-box spluttered into life, an hour before the dawn. Lina was curled up in the bottom of the tank. Her head was pressed up against the hard metal of the magazine door. *Flower of Cadia* started to play and she felt a prickle of fear go through her.

'Ibsic!' she called. He was sleeping in a hammock slung above her. She had to poke him with a finger to wake him. 'It's Creed.'

Ibsic flicked a light on.

'Turn it up,' she told him.

He turned the vox-set up but as the tune came to its end Creed's voice did not come. There was nothing but the crackle of static. Lina felt her heart begin to beat faster. Something was wrong, but then a woman's voice started to speak.

'The Emperor asks only that you obey. Intolerance is a blessing. The Faithful Dead watch over you. The Martyr's grave is the foundation of the Imperium. The only crime is cowardice...'

Lina had to shake Ibsic. 'What's wrong with it? Delanty!'

Delanty, the driver, had the best touch with the vox. He crawled back and fiddled at the controls. The military music came in and out. He gave up. 'It's working,' he said.

'It can't be.' Lina slammed a hand onto the top of the machine. 'She's just reading from the *Tome of Uplifting Thoughts*. Something's wrong. I can feel it. Something is terribly wrong.'

SIX

GUILD QUARTER, KASR MYRAK

In Kasr Myrak the buildings along the north side of Statue Square were burning. Rath's company had lost their vox when they'd fallen back. Volscani kill teams had come up behind them. The jaws had snapped about them, and too many of them had been caught.

Yelena's squad had been taken alive. Somehow Minka had slipped out. But not until she'd found the bodies.

'They were all dead,' Minka told them. She looked at her hands. 'They were skinned.'

Rath was still covered in dust. He stood up. He squeezed her shoulder with his hand. She waited for him to say something, but he had no words. No encouragement. Nothing.

There were only thirty-odd left. They had their backs to the river. They had taken a beating. There was more to come. Minka closed her eyes, but all she could see was Yelena's squad, each wet corpse hanging like meat from the lampposts along Munitorum Street.

She shook herself.

'Now there's just us,' Taavi said.

Rath nodded. He had his back to them.

'When will they come for us?'

Rath turned. His look was fierce. It rekindled Minka's flagging defiance. 'I don't care,' he said. 'Whenever they come, we'll be ready.'

Rath had no answers. 'In the last supply drop, they sent us these.' From his pack, he pulled a rattling cloth bag. He lifted up a handful of small glass phials.

Zask looked grim. 'Frenzon?'

Rath took one from his palm and held it up.

Taavi gave him a hard look. 'You think we're done for?'

'No. But if there is nothing left…'

'I won't take it,' Taavi said. 'I'm a Cadian. I'm no penal legionnaire that has to be drugged into battle.'

Rath looked about. He was looking for takers.

'Maybe we'll take more of them out,' Zask started. He was finding it hard to get his thought out. 'I mean. If we kill more of them. Does it matter, how we go?'

Minka remembered the hanging bodies. Maybe it would be better to go into the long night mad.

'Give me one,' she said. Rath put the phial in her palm.

'How do I take it?'

'Bite it,' he said.

'What happens when it runs out?'

Rath gave her a hard look. 'Don't worry. When it runs out, you'll be dead.'

That evening Rath's company sheltered in a cratered building, half of them awake, staring into the darkness, looking for whatever might come.

Minka faced south across the ruins. They stood up like

broken teeth. She thought she saw shadows, but nothing came, nothing moved, and she heard nothing, except the heavy breathing of Olivet, who was watching the street with her.

'Did you take any?' she said.

Olivet shook his pocket; it rattled with phials.

Minka had her phial, but she couldn't imagine going mad into the darkness. It was too much like the Unnamed. 'Think you'll take it?'

He shrugged. 'Not until the end.'

She nodded and felt for the phial through the thick cloth of her jacket. It was small, hard, faceted. 'I don't think I'll take it.'

'So why did you take one?'

'Just in case. I want to go sane and disciplined.'

'Like a Shock Trooper?' Olivet said.

'Yes. It's all I ever wanted to be.'

There was a long pause. 'Think we're still Whiteshields?'

She looked up. 'Well, you still have the stripe on your helmet.'

He laughed. In normal times they'd have been promoted from Whiteshield to Shock Trooper after they'd killed their first enemy. But these times were anything but normal.

'I won't take mine,' Minka said. 'I don't want to end my life like a mad dog.'

After the first watch was over, Minka woke Taavi.

He jumped awake, and she had to whisper to him to calm him down.

'Just me,' she said.

He nodded, and blinked and pushed himself up.

Minka took her turn resting, but she found it hard to

sleep with the baleful purple-and-green light of the Eye of Terror throbbing in the night above her. It was so bright that it cast a shadow on the ground.

Even when she closed her eyes she could see it. She tossed and turned, pulled an old greatcloak over her head and dreamt that she was flying above Kasr Myrak and that beneath her the city was as bright as a summer day, before the war. She was safe, she understood, and that was a feeling she could almost not remember. She was light, she was radiant, and she was safe.

Two hours before dawn Minka was wrenched awake to cold and dark, and the shouts of frightened men. She did not need to be told it was the Volscani.

'Where?' she hissed.

Taavi was crouched next to her. His face was smeared with dirt and ash and sweat, and half lit by distant gouts of promethium. He gave her a quick brief: a two-pronged attack through the second floor of the hab-blocks overlooking Munitorum Street. There were shouts, the bright flash of lasrifles, and then the crump of grenades going off and suddenly a flamer firing into the night.

Rath was already moving, slapping his chief fighters awake. 'Quick!' he hissed. 'Come!'

Taavi was up. Minka followed.

They used the sewers and basements to come up at the Volscani from below, firing through the broken floorboards, while other teams came at them from above, pinning the Volscani down, like an animal caught in the upper and lower fangs of its hunter.

The fight took nearly two hours of desperate hand-to-hand combat. Rath dispatched the last Volscani with his knife and the survivors picked their separate ways back to the riverbank ruins. Minka was beyond exhaustion. Her feet dragged. Her body ached. She was parched. Her mouth was full of dust and ash.

'All right?' Rath asked.

Minka shook herself and nodded. She had drifted off. 'Yeah.'

'Sure?'

She nodded, then realised that her shoulder was bleeding. She pulled her jacket back. It was difficult to see clearly.

Rath took her arm. His face was expressionless. 'Looks clean,' he said. 'Make sure it gets bound up.'

Minka nodded. She couldn't find any words.

'Taavi!' Rath called. 'Get her patched up.'

Minka slumped down. She closed her eyes. She fell asleep for a second, and jerked awake when the needle pricked her skin.

'We should be dead,' she said.

Taavi nodded.

'Are they teasing us?'

Taavi didn't know.

'There's less of them. See the lights?' He pointed vaguely northwards with his chin. The flicker of battle was drawing slowly closer. She thought she could hear its distant rumble. It was all she'd yearned for. All she'd dreamt of for months, but now it was here it seemed as distant and unreal as a desert mirage. Taavi sounded cheerful. 'I think the relief is coming. I think the enemy are taking a pounding out there.'

Minka paused. 'So Kasr Myrak will be relieved after all. Does Rath know, you think?'

'He knows. But even if they're coming, how many of us are left? I don't think we can hold out.'

For a moment despair filled Minka. She teetered on the edge of it, and knew it was the exhaustion. Knew it was what her enemies wanted: to break her spirit. To crush her soul.

She felt the presence of the Archenemy, like a clawed fist crushing at her heart. And then, a memory. Of being lifted into the sky and being told the sacred duty of every Cadian. To fight. To resist. To never give in.

She swallowed back the dust in her mouth. Said a prayer to the Golden Throne, and there, like a wavering light in the distant darkness, she felt hope. It ran through her bones like a slug of amasec. She took the phial of frenzon from her pocket and let it drop onto the ground.

She stamped down, cracked it open with the heel of her boot. It smelled of liquorice and spice. It was good to let it go. To take frenzon was to be like one of them: the enemy.

She was human. She was a Cadian. She was a fighter. There was faith in her bones. 'I think we can hold out,' she said. Exhilaration ran through her like stimms. She gripped his hand. 'You must believe, Taavi.' She held him by the shoulders. 'Believe!' she told him. 'We can do it. Do you believe?'

He stared at her and she could see that he did not. His eyes glistened with tears as he pursed his lips and shook his head. He did not feel it. He was dead tired, exhausted, fearful, but there was a fierce belief within her. She shook him and he swallowed and nodded. At last, he croaked the words out. 'Stop, Minka. Please. You believe for me. That will be enough.'

* * *

That evening Minka woke with a start, from a dream where she had been buried under rubble and was drowning in dust and gasping for breath until a golden light shone and she floated up from the rubble, like a feather caught in a gust of air.

The elation woke her suddenly, and she saw her fellows standing about her. She was sleeping on a shelf of rubble. Her greatcoat was thrown over her shoulders, her legs hugged to her chest. Her limbs were sore as she straightened them out. She wanted to see what they were all looking at.

As she stood she saw to the north the flashes and fires of fighting closer to the city.

'They're coming for us,' Rath said.

In the distance there was a sudden bolt of red light. It shone out and then there was a rumble of an explosion. It seemed much closer than before.

Taavi stood up. 'How far is that?'

Rath shook his head. 'Twenty miles.'

'Might as well be a hundred,' Taavi said.

The lights dimmed, and the fighting seemed to have died down. It was as if a long dark room had been momentarily illuminated, and when the shadows returned they seemed deeper than ever.

No one said anything for a long moment. They were too tired. Too battle-weary. Their hope had flickered for a moment.

Only Minka stood staring north. Her sleep had been brief and fitful, but her exhausted body no longer needed anything but belief. Her faith became stronger as their strength grew less. It filled her now, almost like a light. It made her pale face radiant in the darkness.

'They will come for us,' she said.

She looked down. They were all staring up at her like a prayer-day congregation, and she felt her devotion to the Golden Throne surge through her. 'They will come,' she said. 'It will not be long. Victory shall be ours. All we have to do is hold out. We must never give in. Understand? Never!'

Their pale moon faces stared up at her, wanting to share her confidence. Her gaze went from face to face, and her smile spread. At the last, she looked across the seated men and women and saw the dull red light of Rath's augmetic eye.

The captain said nothing. He did not believe in hope.

SEVEN

ELYSION FIELDS

There was nothing the Space Wolf, Skarp-Hedin, hated more than these twisted, malformed parodies of the Adeptus Astartes. They were not just abhorrent, they were dangerous. Their ability to grow weapons from their infected flesh repulsed him. Killing them was not a pleasure; it was a primal need. It was a duty. As war swept across the pylon forest of the Elysion Fields, Skarp-Hedin was feeding that need.

The Chaos Space Marine had two malformed mouths. They both snarled as it tried to form another arm. Skarp-Hedin's sword crackled blue flame as it cut the budding limb off. The mouths moaned with pain and Skarp-Hedin's boot crashed down onto the creature's chest.

There was a crunch of power armour, bone and flesh.

Brother.

A voice spoke in Skarp-Hedin's ear, but the Space Wolf

was too intent on killing to pay it any heed. He'd lopped off the monstrous traitor's limbs, as children would pick off the legs of beetles. And now he was going in for the kill. As he reached down one mouth mewled in incoherent agony and suffering, but the other spoke to him.

'You can kill me, but victory is within our grasp.'

'You will not see it,' Skarp-Hedin snarled.

'You are as lost as I.'

Skarp-Hedin was beyond words. He put his weight behind the sword's hilt and drove it through the neck of the thing beneath him. It died with a shudder and Skarp-Hedin breathed the stink of blood deep, and looked about for another enemy to kill.

Brother.

The voice spoke again. Skarp-Hedin spun on his heel and stared about him, looking for foes. The Eye of Terror filled the sky with purple, and on the plain around him were heaps of bodies.

Moments came back to him. While human armies met in vast battles, two elite warbands of Space Marines and their Chaotic brothers had met each other in an exultant duel of sword and axe. Skarp-Hedin had followed his master, Ottar the White, as a hound follows the pack leader. The melee had attracted more and more ancient warriors, like carrion to a dying beast. Now, as Skarp-Hedin spun about, it seemed that no one else lived. Nothing moved.

His nostrils flared. He could tell the blood of his gene-brothers apart from that of their foes. He could smell their gene-seed, despite the distortions that Chaos had wrought.

He sniffed for warm blood. He smelled for life among the piles of dead. He stood at the top of a hill of bodies in the grey and black power armour of the Space Wolves and the Black Legion. Heads had been severed. Gore puddled about the fallen bodies, each showing the excessive trauma that it took to kill a member of the Adeptus Astartes.

Brother.

Skarp-Hedin spun about, crouching low, ready to fight. They had been surrounded. There had been hundreds of the Black Legionnaires, but now they had all gone. He had not killed them all. He was sure. His mind scrolled back through the vid relays in his helmet.

No. He had not killed them. They had fled before his fury, climbing back into dreadclaws and landing craft and blasting off from the planet.

Skarp-Hedin laughed, great fangs bared in his supreme confidence. He had been outnumbered, he had fought them, and he had destroyed them. He beat his chest with berserk fury and exultation.

Traitors and cowards!

Something moved at Skarp-Hedin's feet. He put a bolt-round into the thing's skull. It had once been a member of the Emperor's Children. Now it was dead, its last lungful of air coming out in a tide of red bubbles. He looked down and saw that he was standing on a pile of the dead, fifty bodies deep.

His grey armour was flecked with blood, some of it his. He snarled as he spun about looking for another opponent, but the land was empty except for the dead. And all knew the dead did not rise again.

Brother.

From the top of the corpse mound, Skarp-Hedin looked out on a hell of battle. In the far distance ruined tanks still burned, like foothills to the vast wrecks of Titans and Leviathans that rose over them all, their empty hulks now dark and flame-stained and silent. Closer to him, where his warband had been brought to ground, hills of the dead rose up, crags of heads and torsos and boots, covered with the grotesque covering of reaching hands and fingers, like the wretched flora of a daemon world. The hills marked where each of his fellow brothers had stood and fought as they tried to cut their way through the enemy and had been brought low. The air stank of death and blood, and from deep down in the bottom layer of bodies, the unholy reek of decay.

And there, at his feet, beneath the headless stump of the Obliterator, he saw the shrivelled skull of his chieftain: Ottar the White.

It all came back to him as he stared down at the body before him. His chieftain surrounded by foes, setting about him with his axe and calling on his retainers for help. Skarp-Hedin had ripped through human and trans-human. The air was thick with the stink of super-heated blood. His sword still sizzled as if it wanted more.

'Lord!' he hissed.

Brother.

'Lord! I failed you, lord.'

Brother.

The ancient Space Wolf chieftain had taken wounds to his arms, legs and torso, but it was the final melta shot that had seared a hole through his grey-and-gold-worked power armour that had done for the ancient warrior. It had taken out one of his hearts and had overwhelmed a body already wounded, already weakened. Already dying.

'I failed you,' he said through fanged teeth that snarled in fury. 'We have failed this world.'

Brother. The planet is lost.

The words had no meaning for him. Above him, the Eye of Terror filled the sky with lurid patterns of purple. They cast a baleful light.

Skarp-Hedin had to force Ottar's dead fingers open to get the blade free. Even in death, the Space Wolf would not let go.

The planet is lost, brother.

Skarp-Hedin's fingers lifted the great double-headed axe. The weapon balanced in his hand, light only for a Space Wolf. Skarp-Hedin's fangs drew back as far off an artillery duel reached a crescendo.

Lightbringer was as old as Fenris itself, a beautifully crafted weapon, haft and blade all forged from a single block of meteoric iron. It felt warm in his hand, the blade still crackling with nascent energy. The blade glimmered darkly and Skarp-Hedin grinned. He knew that the deal had been struck.

Brother. The planet is doomed.

Skarp-Hedin's nostrils flared as he sucked in the Cadian air. Far-off strobes of lance fire stabbed down through roiling clouds of smoke and ash. In the flickering darkness, he saw the wild light of packs of daemons, blinking through the Immaterium.

More enemies to kill.

With great loping strides, and limbs that did not tire, the Space Wolf began to move south. He was the last now. The last of his warband, the only one to carry the names of the dead and their great tales back to Fenris. This alone was responsibility enough. He could not let the feats of his brothers go unrecorded.

'Brother. The planet is doomed. We need to get you off the planet. Confirm position'

The voice was insistent inside his helmet. But Skarp-Hedin was lost to the joy of hunt and battle. A star appeared in the distant sky and above the thunder of battle he heard the distant howl of Wulfen, and in answer, Skarp-Hedin put his head back and howled.

Zufur the Hermetic was dead, with all his cursed warriors about him.

They made a fitting cairn for Ottar the White. No Space Wolf could wish for more.

EIGHT

POINT 395, MYRAK FRONT

Valentin's Hellhound squadron was still half a day away
from the Elysion Fields when the Marauder destroyer
swept low over the ground. Four more followed and the
last one gave them a simple salute as it waggled its wings
and swept on southwards, weapon mounts fully loaded
with hunter-killer missiles. Valentin couldn't remember
the last time he'd seen air support. 'Just look at that,' he
said. 'Where the hell did they come from?'

'I don't care,' his driver said. 'As long as they put those
weapons to use.'

As the roar of the Marauders diminished, they could
hear the vox playing *Flower of Cadia*. 'Hush!' Valentin said,
and turned the volume up.

It was Creed's voice, at last.

'People of Cadia.'

'Shut up!' Valentin punched his gunner and the Hellhound slammed to a halt.

'You have done all that I have asked, and more. You have driven the enemy back. You have won the battle for Cadia.'

There was a pause. 'You have won, but it is my duty, my heavy duty to tell you all that Cadia, our home, is doomed. Not for lack of courage and strength on your part. You have won the battle. Your honour is unblemished.

'You might think that this is a defeat for us. But it is not. I assure you. Preparations are being made now. After this message, there will follow a broadcast announcing the evacuation zones where landers will come to lift you all from the planet. I repeat. This is not defeat. The fight will go on. We shall carry the flame of Cadia back to the Imperium. We shall fight to defend Holy Terra itself.'

At the end of the broadcast a different voice – strained with emotion – recounted a list of evacuation sites. Valentin's crew listened in numb silence.

The list started at the beginning again. It repeated three times before anyone spoke.

'Frekk,' Valentin said.

He looked up and the others nodded. Frekk.

Myrak Front, 17th Army Group

Lina's *Hammer of Tyrok* was spearheading an assault on a Volscani redoubt. She was stripped down to her undershirt. Her back was slick with sweat, her forearms slick with lubricants and soot, her vox-bead hanging about her neck. She fitted the chains around the krak shell, pulled it across the tank and lowered it carefully into place.

'Loaded!' she shouted, but instead of firing, there was a pause.

'Loaded!' she shouted again over the salvo of heavy bolter rounds, fired by the front gunner.

The bolt feed jammed. The gunner pulled at the bolt-rounds, and the loading mechanisms clicked as the bolts fed in.

They were so busy fighting they didn't have time to pause as *Flower of Cadia* began to play. But when Creed began to speak Ibsic turned the volume up and they worked a little harder and faster. But then the evacuation order was issued.

'What did he just say?' Ibsic said.

Lina paused, but then a round pinged off the front of the tank and she slammed the breech closed. 'Loaded,' she said.

Ibsic cursed as the turret swivelled round.

'Loaded?' he called.

'Loaded,' Lina called back. She caught the driver's eye and lay back against the magazine panels. 'What the frekk did they just say?'

The tank rocked back as the main gun fired. 'Confirmed kill,' he said, and dropped down from the firing seat into the tank. 'Did they just say evacuation?'

His crew stared at him. None of them moved. They'd all heard it, and now the vox was listing evacuation points.

Lina's immediate reaction was that she was not evacuating. She was *not* evacuating her home. She would fight and die with her home.

But the list of extraction points kept repeating.

Lina kicked out.

'I don't frekking believe it,' she said.

NINE

RENAULT TRACT, CADIA SECUNDUS

The Drookian Fenguard was what the Munitorum classed as light infantry: tough tribesmen used to privations and working independently with little support or equipment. Movement was something they excelled at, but for the last two months they had been fighting a losing battle as the fens cover they had been relying on had been gradually eroded by fire, or simply swarmed with enemy troops.

Iasen Kwayn was Widluos of the Kern Clan of Drook VI, who were known to the scribes of the Munitorum as the 53rd Drookian Fenguard. He took his role of counsellor, law-giver and rememberer seriously, especially now, when it seemed that the existence of the Kern Clan was at risk. They were like the Drookian fangfish whose pools had been drained, and who were left flopping back and forth on their sides.

The Drookians were deep in the frozen marshes of the Renault Tract, where miles of rattling, dry sorghum were draped with trailing mist, fighting an army made up of cultists from a number of hive worlds who still bore their ganger tattoos.

The sorghum was thick as bamboo. It made the perfect environment for the light Drookian troops, and despite their small numbers they'd been fighting for months half hidden within the trackless miles.

The Chaos troops had resorted to clearing whole tracts of land with flame. The Fenguard warriors were putting up a stubborn resistance as they retreated deeper into the marsh, but the numbers of dead were gathering pace all the time, and mile by mile the enemy were finally hemming the Drookians in. The end could not be far off.

As he waded through the stagnant water Iasen knew that there was no more point in running. It was time to call on their father, the Emperor, and to make their last stand.

A grenade exploded about fifty feet before Iasen. There was an outbreak of firing – a short and vicious cross-stitch of las-rounds in the tight confines of the marsh. Iasen crouched as he saw a squad of Fenguard retreating at an oblique angle to the battle. They were wearing their rebreathers. Their eyes met his and they signed to him to keep moving back. It was all they had been doing for days.

Iasen slipped back, leaving a brief ripple, the marsh-sorghum barely rustling.

Look! one of the others signed to him, and he looked up. There had been many stars in the months that they had been fighting. Bright explosions in high orbit, as fleets of vast cruisers pummelled each other with ferocious broadsides. But this one was unlike the others. It seemed distant at first, and not quite like a plasma reactor overloading. It was too small, too yellow. It grew in intensity at a steadily accelerating rate.

Iasen nodded. A hand touched his shoulder.

'Chief wants you,' said the Drookian. 'You must come now.'

Iasen found the Drookian chief standing with his retainers in a small, dark pool, slick with an oily film of promethium. The chief's elite attendants were dressed in all kinds of shabby Imperial cast-offs, all now the same drab and faded grey. Their faces were obscured by their crude rebreathers; tubes wound around their necks and shoulders, their skin was blue with tribal tattoos, and all wore their clan knife slung from a plaid sash.

The chief's face was pale yellow with the light of the Eye of Terror. 'We are nearly surrounded, Widluos.'

'Yes, lord.'

'I have decided that I will die here, on this mound.'

Iasen nodded. 'Then I am glad to stand here with you.'

The chief's face was stern. 'You cannot.'

'But–' Iasen started.

His chief spoke over him. 'You know all the old stories of our clan. One of us must escape Cadia, and bring news of how the Kern Clan died.'

Iasen looked around the others. They were all staring at him over their rebreather masks. He understood. 'Not me!'

'It is my order.'

Iasen looked at the faces of the other retainers. Behind their rebreathers, their eyes were hard and set. They had determined it. This was the moment for them to die. He would not be with them.

Iasen felt betrayed. 'I cannot leave you, lord. You are

my clan chief. What is out there but a hostile world? Men will look down on me with contempt, and say that I lived when my lord did not. I could not live with the shame.'

'It is my order, Iasen,' the chief said. 'One of us must escape to tell the tale of how we fought and died.'

Another firefight broke out, even closer this time. As Iasen looked at their faces, he saw their eyes grow bright. They shone with a yellow light.

One of the retainers saw it first. He signed and pointed. There was a star in the sky. It was growing brighter. Iasen turned. They all followed his gaze. The star lit the sky like a second sun. After a few moments, it was too bright to look at. It cast a shadow on the ground. They could hear its roar, like an earthquake rolling towards them.

Iasen cried out as it passed overhead, filling the sky.

The sonic shock threw him flat. He found himself on his hands and knees, staring at the silhouette of his head against a burning sky, and he remembered the prophecy about the end of the world. That doomsday would come with a bright star, too bright to look upon.

As he lay there he saw flames.

The whole marsh was burning. The story of his clan would never be told. The fens of Drook would never learn how her sons had fought, and won, and died.

The star that lit the skies of Cadia was a fragment of an ancient object of xenos technology known as a Blackstone fortress.

The Archenemy had propelled it towards the planet, and despite all the combined firepower of the remaining shreds of Battlefleet Cadia and the Adeptus Astartes strike cruisers, they could do little more than blow chunks off its edges, like chips from a piece of flint. Desperate captains flew their defence monitors into the Blackstone, hoping to deflect its course, but the ancient hulk had been propelled forward at such a speed that there was no way it could be stopped or hindered.

The smaller pieces hit the planet like shooting stars, burning up in high orbit. The main fragment was as large as a moon. It hit the stratosphere and its edges started to burn. It plunged down, an incandescent missile, tearing across the atmosphere above Cadia Tertius and Secundus and whipping up whirlwinds behind it.

The vacuum it created caused a sonic shock that crushed tanks. The impact caused a crater two hundred miles wide and the shockwave sent gales and tremors that levelled everything for a thousand miles. Millions of tons of earth were thrown up into the atmosphere, creating a mushroom cloud that filled the mesosphere with enough dust and debris to cause a millennia-long ice age. Concepts like day and night no longer had meaning. Huge cracks rippled through Cadia's crust. The tectonic plates of Cadia Prime began to break and blister as shockwaves thundered out, like ripples from a brick hitting a pool of still water. Tsunamis of magma broke the mantle of the planet.

Rockcrete bastions were thrown to the ground, ancient kasr were levelled, but worst of all, the forests of Cadian pylons, which had held back the warp for so many millennia, were thrown down in ruin.

At this the Eye of Terror began to reach out for Cadia and seize it. The Cadian Gate was not just breached. It had ceased to be.

The cess pool of the warp now rushed through the gap, swamping all in its path.

The Dark Gods laughed.

As storms wrapped Cadia, the last Black Legion kill squads fled the planet, chasing their flagship, the *Vengeful Spirit*, as the ancient battlecruiser retreated. They left the heretics and cultists to their fate: the populations of entire hives, entire worlds that had fallen to the despair and treachery of the Dark Gods. What did they care if the millions of slaves died? The Imperium of Man could supply many more.

Without their Black Legion masters to guide them, the cultists fell upon each other in berserk blood rites, ritual slaughter, or scenes of debauched cruelty. They made easy targets for the disciplined Cadians, and surviving units mounted fighting withdrawals as they made their way to the nearest evacuation stations and left the planet.

The few remaining astral choirs tried to pierce the warp to alert Holy Terra. Their screams died as Black Legion death squads homed in on their positions and murdered them in the inner sanctums.

Cadia's evacuation plans had first been drawn up in the aftermath of the Second Black Crusade. As the order worked its way through the surviving servitor networks, embedded protocols took over the programmed functions of cyber-organic creatures. Cogitators that had been devoted to maintenance systems or planetary defence networks switched their focus to calling in landers from orbit, assessing unit strengths on the ground and directing loyal forces to the best evacuation point. Mind-slaved servitors stopped working and stood in slack-jawed silence, trying to mouth the word: *evacuate*.

But much had changed in the generations since the plans had been set down. The caution of Cadia's forebears was viewed with mistrust and suspicion, as if even the contemplation of evacuation was treachery. Over the generations, the evacuation protocols had been updated occasionally and haphazardly. The effects were sporadic and ill-conceived. Confusion reigned across Cadia, made only worse by the terrible ruin that had been made of the northern hemisphere of the planet.

Units of the elite Cadian 4th, who had been fighting guerrilla campaigns in the polar snows of Cadia Secundus, found their nearest evacuation station was on the far side of an Iron Warriors plunder camp. With no choice, they launched a full-frontal assault on the trench defences, and found them abandoned, except for a handful of enslaved feral warriors.

The 103rd Mechanised endured the tempest and earthquakes from within their Chimera armoured personnel carriers. Once the evacuation order came, they were confident of making it to their extraction point, which was only twenty miles away. But the land between had been so broken and reformed that it was impassable to tanks, and they were forced to abandon their vehicles and foot-slog it through the crazed patterns of the lava fields, only to find, when they reached the evacuation point, that it had been swallowed in vast pools of bubbling red magma.

The 46th Rifles were over a hundred miles from their evacuation point. They force-marched through the night, abandoning any who were unable to keep moving, only to find that their evacuation point no longer existed, but had been flooded by the collapse of the Ukulov Dam.

Other regiments found their extraction points located within massive warzones, or firmly held by units of the enemy, or that they were the victims of a cruel glitch within the system and they had been given erroneous details.

Some found their evacuation sites in good order with a clear command structure, ordered queues waiting for their landers to arrive. The truth dawned on them, as the hours and days wound on, that no one was coming to take them to safety.

For them, the long war was over.

Any attempts to resolve the confusion through the planet's vox networks fell largely on increasingly hysterical ears as commanders who had kept their men alive over the last three months finally gave vent to their fury and frustration and impotence – voxing it out into the ether, for any who might hear.

But the ears of the galaxy were closed.

Even those who arrived at the extraction points understood that they were far from safe as the warp reached out to embrace Cadia. The walls of the Immaterium had begun to shred, the laws of physics and order and reality no longer held, and the world began to fill with shapes and sounds and colours that defied human categorisation. And the Dark Gods laughed.

TEN

CADIA SECUNDUS

Point 29.443 had once been part of a ridge of round-topped hills, with rocky crags falling down towards the plain, but Administratum landscapers had long since flattened the hills and spread the displaced earth out to create a wide, level place for planetary landers to pick up troops. Now it had been designated as Evacuation Point 57B.

It lay in the middle highlands of Cadia Secundus: a broad level area, two miles square, sealed with thick slabs of rockcrete. Before the War for Cadia, the edges of the slabs had been marked out by tufts of grass and old grox-droppings. It had long mystified local grox herders, or bands of frozen Whiteshields, stumbling lost through night exercises in the Mewlip Hills and finding their feet on level ground.

But now it offered the only hope of salvation to all the loyalists within fifty miles.

First to arrive was Sister Heloise, Mistress of Repentance

of the Sisters of our Martyred Lady. She had seven surviving Sisters Repentia with her. They had been scouring their sins away in battle with a warband of Black Legionnaires, but the Adeptus Astartes had disengaged an hour before the impact and left the Sisters hurling curses in their wake.

They had struggled through the gales, hacking at packs of mewling daemons. And now they had to secure this place.

'Minister to the wounded,' Heloise ordered her Sisters Repentia.

Repentia Beatrice refused to move. One eye was covered by a black patch, the stubble of her scalp was sore and flaking, there were splatters of gore up her arms and thighs, and her eviscerator was resting on her shoulder. She looked out from the high plateau, saw the war and flames in the distance, and stuck out her chin. She had to shout over the roar of the gale. 'We're warriors, not wet-nurses. There is war out there!'

Heloise's pain-lash caught Beatrice across the shoulder and her knees gave way. 'Why are you being punished?' Heloise demanded.

Beatrice's pale cheeks flushed. 'For disobedience, mistress.'

Heloise's face thrust forward. 'Exactly. The war here is almost done. It is our duty to serve, Repentia. And we are needed here. When the Cadian warriors have been taken safely off the planet, then we can remain and continue the fight.' Heloise pulled the mask from her head, and her black bob fell free, sweat-soaked and streaked with grey. Her face was drawn. 'But I am the one who decides that. Understand?'

She cracked her whip and caught Beatrice a second time.

Repentia Beatrice ground the words out. 'Yes,' she said, reluctantly. 'I will minister.'

She used her eviscerator to push herself up again and slung the great weapon across her back.

Beatrice was a warrior; ministrations were not natural to her. The first band of survivors was staggering up the hill. It was a band of thirty Cadians, some bootless and limping, others bandaged, striding through the storms. Their faces were pale and drawn.

Beatrice clenched her hands into fists as she stared at them. In her heart, she saw them as failures. They were all failures, but she remembered her orders.

'Welcome, brothers,' she called as they came forward, but her words were clumsy and unpractised. She was better at singing war hymns, not offering consolation. 'You have reached Evacuation Point Fifty-Seven-B.'

The men stared, eyes numb, minds pushed beyond their limits. Beatrice stepped forward and offered a hand to them, but her manner was as stiff as a block of wood. The men shuffled forward, taking up their position, but at the back two men lingered – one with his arm draped over the other.

'Move along,' she told them, and pointed which way they should go, but as she did so the man being helped along by the other staggered and fell. Beatrice stood over him. 'Get up!' she commanded, but the man groaned and half-rolled to the side.

If she'd had a pain-lash with her she would have used it on the Guardsman, but she looked up and saw the harsh gaze of her Mistress Repentia on her. She moved forward and put a hand under the man's armpit.

'Up!' she told him, but he did not move. 'What is wrong

with you?' She knelt next to him, her black knee-greaves grating on the rockcrete surface, and prodded the body with her gauntlet. 'He's dead,' she said.

She stood and faced the man who had carried his friend. His eyes were rimmed with dirt, his lips were chapped; it looked like he had not slept for days. She saw a refusal to believe, and from somewhere, from deep within her, and from long ago, she felt a brief spark of pity.

'What is your name, Guardsman?'

'Nazar,' he said.

There was almost a touch of gentleness as she put a hand to his arm. 'Nazar. You have reached safety. Have faith in the Emperor.'

As the hours wore on, surviving units trickled in and were assigned one rockcrete block to each regiment. It helped to organise the scattered units.

Some of the rockcrete squares were half full of surviving troops, others had only a handful. All the time the skies grew darker and darker. The howl of daemons rang out. Men's fingers began to tremble. The hearts of veteran Guardsmen began to beat faster.

Repentia Beatrice pulled her eviscerator from her shoulder. Mistress Heloise cracked her whip and brought all the Guardsmen together. She started to sing a hymn named *Be Thou My Armour.*

The Sisters Repentia sang with her, their voices high and beautiful. 'Sing!' she ordered the Guardsmen. One of them wasn't singing. She slapped him across the back of the head. 'Sing!' she shouted, and as she patrolled up and down, the discordant voices of the Guardsmen joined in.

* * *

Evacuation Point 88A, near Bastion 8

In the foothills behind Bastion 8 Lord Commissar Grake took command of Evacuation Point 88A. He arrived with the remains of the Cadian 77th Airborne, who had covered over eight miles from where they had been managing a fighting retreat. His men were fearless in their dedication and so far he had only shot three men in the entire hundred-day campaign.

As daemon-light began to flicker in the skies above them, he knew that only the most severe discipline would keep them alive. When the next company of men arrived, nearly a hundred Cadians, they looked dead on their feet.

'Halt!' Grake shouted. His black leather jacket flapped in the cold breeze as he paced towards them. 'Attention!' he ordered, and despite their exhaustion, the men straightened up as they realised that they were being inspected. They straightened their tri-dome helmets, holstered their lasrifles. Some even rubbed their boots on the back of their calves as Grake stalked along the line.

He stopped before a man with a bandage on his head.

'You!' the commissar said. 'What is your name?'

The small man stepped to attention. He had a thin moustache, and a week's stubble on his cheeks. 'Guardsman Pape!' the man said, and saluted.

'Where is your rifle?' Grake demanded.

Pape looked about him. 'I dropped it, sir.'

Commissar Grake pulled out his pistol. One of the men in the second rank stepped forward to speak for him. From his uniform, he was the major.

'Sir!' he said. 'The lasrifle was broken. We had wounded men to carry. I commanded him to drop his weapon.'

Commissar Grake turned on him and shot the major in the head.

He went down like a grox, the bolt-round throwing him backwards against the men behind him, who were splattered with bits of skull and brain and gore. Grake swung round to where Guardsman Pape stood, and fired again. Pape fell against the men behind him.

Commissar Grake holstered his pistol. 'Now, who is in command of this shambles?'

The Guardsmen looked about for the highest-surviving ranking officer. Two men exchanged glances, trying to work out which was the senior officer. Eventually the older of the two stepped forward, his augmetic leg wheezing.

'Major Luka,' the old man said, and saluted. 'Retired, twice. Now serving as commanding officer of the Fifty-Sixth Rifles.'

Commissar Grake looked at the old man. 'This unit is a shambles. Bring them into proper order. Understand?'

Major Luka saluted. 'Yes,' he said, with an insolent pause, 'sir.'

The black figure of Commissar Grake strode out to meet each squad of arriving Guardsmen, bolt pistol holstered at his side, one hand to his peaked hat, his black leather coat flapping wildly in the wind. Within the space of half an hour, he had shot over thirty men.

The mood of the 56th Rifles was already aggrieved, but with each retort of the bolt pistol, their resentment turned to hatred. 'Someone should shoot him,' one muttered.

Major Luka caught the man's eyes and gave him a warning look. 'Hush,' he said. Accidents could happen, but it was better not to talk about them first.

* * *

Homing beacons marked out the landing zone but the skies were ominously dark.

The troops huddled close as the gales whipped dust and soot into their eyes. The sky was growing constantly darker. Sudden gusts of rain lashed their faces, then changed to bouncing, stinging black balls of hail. Their home was a graveyard. Now it was turning into hell. They willed a lander to appear, to lift them safely off-planet – and when the flashing yellow lights of a transport finally did appear in the air above them they stood as one, arms raised as the white bar of a searchlight stabbed down towards them.

The whipping clouds gave brief glimpses of the lander's pale belly, its cruciform shape, sponson weapons panning for enemy contacts. The landing gear was down. One of the ramps was already half open, and the men could see figures silhouetted against the inner light.

The Cadian refugees stood and rushed forward. Some of the younger troops waved.

'Back!' Commissar Grake ordered them. 'Back!'

The lander settled fifty yards from Major Luka. It was a standard ground-to-void shuttle: a broad, squat body, and two pairs of short, back-flung wings. The dark upper surface was scarred with the bare blisters of autocannon rounds, but the craft looked sound. Smaller landing ramps lowered from both sides.

The rear ramp came down in a series of three irregular jerks. A Navy rating ran forward, head low against the thrust of the lander's jets, the gales buffeting him sideways.

'Who is in command here?' he shouted, one hand on his hat.

'I am,' Grake said. The Lord Commissar stepped forward, his black leather coat flapping in the wind.

The rating turned to him. 'We only have fifteen minutes, sir. Enemy fighters inbound.'

'Queue!' Grake ordered them, waving his pistol. He stood on the landing ramps as the troops filed on. 'In regimental order. Leave equipment behind! Hurry. Ten minutes until we leave.'

Half of Major Luka's 56th Rifles made it onto the lander, just as Grake signalled to the Navy rating. The ramp began to rise.

'You cannot leave them!' Luka shouted, but Grake turned on him.

'You dare to tell me my business, major?'

'Sir, I just want to say that these men should not be left behind. There is space on the lander. Let them on.' Luka stared back at the faces of the men they were leaving behind.

It seemed that Grake was about to relent, but then a daring Guardsman caught the lip of the ramp and started to haul himself up. Grake put a bolt through his forehead. He shot two more who tried to clamber aboard. Major Luka turned away. He felt sick. They should have killed this commissar.

The ramp closed with three jerks, slowing for the last few feet as the door seals engaged. Major Luka stared out as the view of his home narrowed to a handspan, and then bare inches. The last image he saw of Cadia was through the whipping gales, thousands of pale faces looking up, their expressions vivid in the white flash of the searchlight.

Then the ramps closed with a hollow clang, a hiss of air and the clunk of the void-seals engaging, and the noises of the storm were stilled.

The lander was three-quarters empty.

'We should have taken more,' Major Luka said.

Commissar Grake had holstered his pistol. 'We should all have done more,' he said, and then turned on his heel and strode up the vast landing ramp, his footsteps ringing out in the hollow metal shell.

Myrak River

General Bendikt's evacuation point was at a levelled plateau named Old Man's Hill. His tanks were parked in neat lines, dust hissing through the gaps, the tank crews peering skywards.

The lander touched down a hundred yards away. Navy ratings waved the tanks forward. The troops quickly filed aboard. Twenty minutes in, the engines started.

Bendikt was standing at the side of the main loading ramp. 'What's happening?' Bendikt demanded as the ramps started to close.

No one listened to him.

'Hey!' he shouted.

The Navy rating managing the controls was a small, underfed-looking man, with a baggy uniform two sizes too big for him. 'We have to leave,' he shouted. He waved towards the cockpit as explanation.

General Bendikt looked back at the queues of men. 'That's impossible,' he shouted. 'Look!'

There had to be thirty thousand men waiting to load. The rating shrugged. It was all beyond him. He was just following orders.

'Give me five minutes,' he told the rating.

'Orders,' the other man said.

Damn orders, Bendikt thought. He pulled Tyson close enough to hear. 'Do not let this man close the ramps until I say so. Understand?'

Tyson pulled his laspistol from its holster and flipped off the safety. 'Understood,' he said.

The rating's gaze went from one to the other, and then to the laspistol. He looked sick. 'You'll have to talk to the captain,' he said.

'I shall,' Bendikt said, and gathered twenty men.

Bendikt led his men to the front of the lander. The cockpit door was unlocked. He stepped inside. The snub-nosed chamber was cramped; the control panels were lit with buttons, levers and green info screens.

Bendikt stooped. The pilots were strapped into their seats. To the right, by the door, three mind-slaved servitors were already starting the departure protocols.

'This lander is not leaving,' he announced.

The pilot did not turn around. 'Sorry. We have to, or we won't get off the planet at all.'

Bendikt put his hand on the pilot's shoulder. 'I said, this lander is not leaving. I have an army here. You will stay until all of them are loaded. Is that clear?'

The pilot turned. He was not used to being spoken to like this. 'I have my orders,' he said.

Bendikt did not flinch. 'You have your orders, but I have a laspistol. And if you do not do what I command then none of us will leave this planet alive.'

Lina and Ibsic managed to board the third lander that arrived at their evacuation point, along the banks of the Myrak River. They had driven their tank aboard, and now they crouched by the tracks of *Hammer of Tyrok*, nauseous with the buffeting turbulence of the higher atmosphere. The craft lurched again and there was a cry of fear through the cramped deck. Even the tanks slid dangerously, and the chains that held them down creaked.

'I hate landers,' Lina said as she wiped the vomit onto her sleeve. 'Put me back on Cadia!'

There were tens of thousands of warriors like them, penned up inside the vast hangars of the landers without any idea of what was happening.

'We'll never make it,' Lina said as the lander rattled dangerously.

Ibsic kept his head down, his eyes closed. The last sight of Cadia had made him sick. All he could see was that vast column of smoke and ash, volcanic fires fountaining into the sky, and all he could taste was the dirt of Cadia in his mouth.

Across Cadia scenes of panic and order were taking place as fleets of landers descended from orbit, straight to the prescribed extraction points. At some places, troops rushed the landing site and the landers refused to set down. At others, fighting broke out, and half-empty transports lifted free, only to be brought down by a tank shell or melta charge.

In places, it was Marauder bombers who landed, gunner crews pulling desperate Guardsmen aboard. Some pilots stayed well beyond their allotted time. Others touched down at entirely deserted extraction points, the Navy ratings squinting out into the soot and ash storms and seeing no one to extract.

Where the fighting had been fiercest, running battles took place with cultists who tried to scramble aboard.

The lander crews took as many soldiers as time, orders or opportunity would allow, and lifted off, struggling to rise with the weight of the men and women aboard.

Once the carriers had lifted off, they had to face the hunter-packs of Chaos fighters and killers. Some had flights of Thunderbolts and Marauders that drove the enemy off, while some were undefended, and the enemy fell on them like hyenas on stray wildebeests, dragging the landers to the ground.

Some of the evacuation craft reached high orbit, where fleet-based fighters and assault boats were still engaged in a furious battle for the skies of Cadia, and where they had to avoid the deadly impact of Black Legion assault torpedoes and dreadclaws.

When they were boarded, some Cadians mounted furious defences, cutting down the Black Legion Space Marines with incandescent lasrifle salvos. Others had been ordered to leave their weapons behind. They fought with whatever they had to hand, overwhelming individual warriors with their fists, clubs and bayonets.

Once they had unloaded, some brave lander crews returned to Cadia, honouring promises they had made to men left behind, and some of them were successful, carrying another load of veterans from the dying world. But increasingly, as daemons began to manifest all over the planet, fewer and fewer landing craft made it off the planet. And soon the flow of escaping men ceased completely.

General Grüber was on board the last evacuation craft. He had personally supervised the loading of most of his army, and once the window for flight was almost closed he finally agreed to leave the planet.

He moved along the lander, hand to the walls to steady himself as the craft lurched upwards through the howling storms.

By the time he had reached the cockpit there were armed ratings standing by the door.

'Sorry, sir,' the nearest said. 'It's locked.'

He was a tall, dishevelled-looking man, with a slight stoop and thick lips, which made his speech indistinct.

Grüber articulated crisp, aristocratic words in contrast. 'I would like to speak to the captain. Let me inside.'

The man touched his hand to his hat in a Navy salute. 'Sorry, general. The bridge is locked.'

Grüber bristled visibly. 'Then unlock it.'

The man laughed. 'It's locked so you and we cannot get in.'

'I am General Grüber, of the Cadian High Command,' Grüber said.

'Well,' the sergeant said, with a wry laugh, 'looks like you failed.'

Grüber barely understood what had happened until he felt the hands of the ratings on his shoulders, and realised that he had the sergeant by the throat, pinned against the metal sheeting wall.

'How dare you?' he was hissing, and the sergeant was gasping for breath as Grüber's thumbs crushed his windpipe. There was a moment's satisfaction, then behind him he had a brief glimpse of one of the Navy ratings lifting the butt of his shotgun, and it all went dark.

Grüber's head still hurt when the lander docked with their warp-capable craft. The air on the ship smelled of oils and the stale, damp scent of purifiers in need of a good scrub.

But it didn't smell of smoke. The absence was as noticeable as the stillness. The only sounds were the muffled groans of the ship's superstructure: the dull clangs of enginarium shafts, the low hum of atmosphere pumps.

There were no explosions, no gale, no tearing groan of a planet coming apart. The ship felt almost normal. The Navy ratings worked the airlock, briskly clamping the lander into place. Grüber took in a deep breath as the final doors opened.

He had lost none of his dignity as he led the Cadians onto the ship.

It was a tub of a craft that had been carrying foodstuffs in its vast hangar bellies and still smelled of slab and fermented protein slop. Grüber had arrived back on Cadia in the personal quarters of Warmaster Ryse and his staff from the Deucalion Crusade. It had been a jolly trip, with axel-wood dining chambers, long tables and the best Arcady Pride from the personal cellars of the Warmaster. It was the kind of transport that Grüber had become used to. He faced this slab hangar with ill-disguised disappointment and took in a deep breath.

The Imperium had failed them, and this was what the heroes of Cadia were reduced to: being ferried from the ruins of their home in a third-rate food carrier.

ELEVEN

KASR MYRAK

Without their vox the fighters of Kasr Myrak had no idea that the planet was doomed. There were twenty-five of them left in a guild hall, with their backs to the river. The Volscani were coming at them from all three directions.

Minka had just shot a flamer-armed Volscani. She was waiting for his partner to show himself round the corner of the building opposite when there was a sudden flash and a roar of noise. She thought for a moment that it was another flight of Marauders passing just overhead. The collapsing buildings did nothing to dispel this idea. It was a Marauder on a bombing run.

But the roar got louder, and buildings about her began to fall, and then the earth started to shake. Minka pushed herself up. She thought she could stay on her feet, but the tremors were so violent that she was thrown to her face.

The roof above her crashed down. The wall she was sheltering behind fell outwards into the street. The whole earth was shaking and Minka howled in terror, her voice lost in the tumult.

The quake went on for an age.

At last Minka pushed herself shakily to her feet.

Her city was gone. Statue Square, Divination Street, the Illium Block, even the high crags of Myrak Cathedral, where they had camped for the first week of fighting, were all gone. Everything they had fought for, inch by inch, block by block.

There was nothing. Not a single brick or block of rockcrete was left standing. All about her was a field of broken rock. Only the city walls still stood, but the hundred-yard-thick rockcrete defences had been broken into sections and scattered miles from where they'd once stood.

Minka spun around. She looked about in stunned silence. Nothing moved. No one. Only the Myrak River, swollen and full, still flowed east.

An aftershock passed and a gale began to grow. Then something moved. It was an arm. She picked her way across.

It was Taavi. He was covered in dust. 'Throne,' he swore as she pulled him free. 'Minka – is that you?'

'Yes,' she said.

'What happened?'

'I don't know.'

'Where's Rath?'

Minka looked around. She tried to guess where the rest of the company were. She picked her way along the top of the ruins. The ground beneath her was rubble and dust. Minka set her foot on a slab the size of a Leman Russ. It shifted under her feet. She paused for a moment, trying to overcome her fear.

'Rath!' she shouted. 'Rath!'

There was movement in the rubble. Minka used her hands to pull the debris away. Fingers were grasping for her.

'Help,' a muffled voice was saying.

Minka scrabbled at the rubble, grabbed the hand and pulled. The debris fell away, and in a terrible moment she saw the shoulder plate. It was a Volscani trooper.

She let go of the hand, pulled out her knife and drove it into the place where shoulder and neck connected. She felt the body tense in pain as she moved the knife around, looking for the artery. Warm blood bubbled up over her hand.

She pulled her knife free.

The gusts knocked her sideways, whipped dust storms of grit and rubble low across the ruins. 'Anyone?' she shouted to Taavi.

He shook his head.

Minka put a hand up to protect her eyes. She'd fought for these ruins for over a hundred days, and now it seemed that a kind of victory had come, with the irony that the city itself had been flattened.

Taavi's footing was uncertain as he made his way towards her. He took hold of her arm to steady himself. There was movement beneath them.

They knelt down and started to pull the bricks back.

Someone was in there. Minka could hear a voice. 'It's Rath!' she said, and scrabbled till her fingers were raw. 'Taavi, it's Rath!'

The two of them worked furiously. Rath cursed as they lifted the last rocks from his chest. He was grey with dust. He winced as they pulled him up. It was like helping an old man to stand. 'Throne,' he said again, and fell back. They draped his arms over their shoulders and Rath hung on them like a dying man. He straightened his limbs slowly, groaning with each movement.

They carried him to the side of the river and set him down. Minka felt under his arm. He winced as she moved her fingers along his ribs.

'They're broken,' she said.

She knew how to bind his arm to his side, but she had nothing to strap it with. She hunted about for a scrap of cloth. A vast column of black was rising in the northern sky. None of them knew what this all meant.

'What the hell has happened?' Rath said.

Taavi looked to Minka.

'I don't know,' she said.

Rath sat up. He blinked as if there was something wrong with his vision. 'What happened to the river?'

Minka turned. The water was rising at an alarming rate.

'Something has blocked it,' Taavi said.

Within a few minutes, the river overflowed its banks. The rising water started to lap across the wharves towards them, dark and thick with sediment. Minka and Taavi dragged Rath a little way up the bank of rubble. They sat as the waters rose, Rath with his arm bound to his side, his face grey with dust and pain.

Aftershocks kept rippling across the ground. On the hills above Kasr Myrak, fires were starting to grow. They were the red, baleful light of magma pushing its way up through the crust of Cadia. Rivers of fire were starting to flow down towards them.

They sat waiting, but there were no enemies to shoot, no reinforcements.

Minka tried to find her way back to Statue Square in the hope of locating their vox, but it was useless. Her city was unrecognisable, the ruin heaps unstable, and she could not tell where Statue Square was... or had been.

When she got back, Rath was where she had left him, propped up against a piece of rockcrete. Taavi was standing over him.

Volcanic eruptions were reaching higher and higher into the sky. They cast the only light.

'So,' Minka said. 'What now?'

'We hold the city and await reinforcement.'

Minka gestured towards the strange flatness that had once been Kasr Myrak. 'What city?'

She was sitting, staring out over the ruins, when she thought she heard laughter on the wind.

It came again, from a different direction, then again, streaking across the sky. It was a wild, insane sound.

Minka looked up into the darkening sky. The temperature began to drop, and Taavi caught Minka and pulled her to her feet.

Laughter came from a thousand voices, all around them. Minka felt the rubble beneath her shift. She ignored it at first, but then it moved again.

She stood. 'There's someone moving,' she said.

They looked down as the rubble shifted again. Someone was clawing their way up.

Taavi and Minka pulled the stones away. They saw a hand, bloody and raw, reaching up for them.

'Cadian!' Minka shouted as she saw the cuff.

Within moments they found an arm, a shoulder, a head of dust-grey hair, and a dusted face was staring up at them. It was Olivet. He thrashed and kicked against the weight holding him back. 'It's all right,' she said as she pulled his arm. 'You're free.'

Olivet pulled at her. He pulled so hard he dragged her towards him. Minka fell forward. He embraced her and turned his face towards her. She thought he was going to kiss her in gratitude, but then there was pain, and he was gripping her so hard that even when she had both hands pressed against him she could not push him off.

She could hear the shouts of Rath and Taavi, and she screamed when she felt Olivet's teeth grind down on her ear and tear it.

There was blood on her hand. He'd ripped half her ear off.

'Calm down!' she said, and Rath grunted with pain as he pulled her away. Olivet kept thrashing, his body pinned down at the legs.

He was not kicking against the weight of the rubble, but to get *at* her, Minka realised. The sight was chilling. 'Shoot him,' she said.

Taavi strode forward. He lifted his lasrifle. 'Stop, or I'll shoot,' he said as Olivet thrashed about, waist-deep in rubble.

'Just shoot him,' Rath shouted.

'In the name of the Emperor,' Taavi said, then fired. The shot hit Olivet in the head. But it had no effect. He fired again, and again, pumping the Cadian with las-rounds.

Half of Olivet's head had gone by the time he fell back.

'What was wrong with him?' Minka gasped.

'He was driven mad from being buried,' Taavi said. 'He didn't know what he was doing.'

Minka pulled her legs away. Yes, she thought. He was driven mad. Throne, they'd all been through enough to be driven insane. Mad, was what they all agreed.

But then, she felt something move beneath her. Another hand appeared a yard to her side. Then another, twenty feet away. 'Look!'

Humps of rubble were starting to rise from the ruins of Kasr Myrak. A Volscani pulled himself up, dragging his foot free, and then charged. Taavi hit him with the butt of his rifle. There was a crack as bones shattered. The blow slammed the Volscani sideways, but he barely paused. He hit the ground and then pushed himself up and came at them once more.

Taavi fired. The las-bolts hit the Volscani in the thigh, chest and shoulder before he went down. But then another Volscani rose. Then two, then five.

A Cadian appeared, loping over the ruins. Half his head was missing, but he stood shakily and turned towards them.

'Gunnel?' Minka called.

The thing that was Gunnel snarled like a beast and started forward. A hand caught Minka's boot. Its nails raked the leather, catching for a moment on the heavy steel buckle. She stamped down hard and felt the crunch of bone. The fingers were broken and misshapen but they still clutched for her. 'Rath!' she shouted. 'We have to get out of here.'

Rath was fumbling with his knife.

Minka pushed her knife back into its sheath. 'They're dead,' she said. 'They're all dead.'

She pulled Rath up and they half fell down the slope towards the river.

Taavi covered them. Another torso burst out from the rubble slope in a shower of rockcrete and dust. 'Taavi!' Minka shouted. She grabbed a piece of wood and swung.

It crunched into the thing's skull and knocked it from its feet.

Suddenly they were all shouting and firing. Rath found a gun and tossed it to Minka. She caught it and fired two shots into the back of the thing clawing upwards. In the corner of her eye, she saw something right itself and turn towards her, low and hunched like an animal.

It might have been Naul. She couldn't tell. He'd died a while ago. His corpse was swollen with death, rags of guts hanging through the torn uniform. The stench made her eyes water. Minka fired. The putrid flesh burst as each round struck it, like a pustule popping.

A living man would be dead three times over, but the cadaver kept coming towards her, mouth hanging open, eyes rolled up into its head.

'Taavi!' she shouted. Another Cadian, like the first, head bandaged and bloodied, the stump of one arm waving as it struggled to come towards her. Minka fired. The second blasted part of the thing's skull, but it did not stop. Then two more figures appeared. They had been dead for months. The flesh was dark, bones showing through where the guts had rotted away, the hollows of their eyes empty.

One was a civilian woman, and the other a child, weeping pox-marks on its dust-grey face, dark eyes glittering with malevolent intent. Minka fell back. All she could hear was her own panicked breath and the thunder of her heart beating loudly as another two cadavers appeared before her.

Minka fired into each of them at point-blank range, even though she knew it was useless. Las-bolts burned holes into the rotting flesh, but the corpses' bodies did not flinch. Her foot skidded on rubble and blood. She saw the flash of steel. She and Rath were back to back.

'We have to get out of here,' she hissed.

'Taavi!' Rath shouted, but Taavi was down and unmoving.

Rath cursed as he decapitated one of the dead, kicked another over with the flat of his boot, swung wildly at the one with the bandaged head. His knife opened it up from sternum to navel. There was a dull pop as the skin and muscles of its front parted and the grey snakes of intestines flopped out. A man would have screamed, but this thing came on regardless, its booted feet trampling on its own grey and bloated entrails. It slowed for a moment, then toppled forward, its legs hopelessly entangled, and fell onto its face.

Minka was too terrified to scream. Rath had her by the shoulder and was pulling her back. 'To the river!'

Rath hacked through the arm of one, took the head off another, and heel-kicked a third out of the way. They skidded down a scree slope and hit the bottom as rocks tumbled down upon them. Minka's jacket caught on barbed wire. It tore as she pulled it free.

As more undead crested the slope behind them, one fell forward and skidded face-down after them, arms reaching over its head.

It was carrying an auto-pistol. Rath bent to rip it from the dead hand. 'Here!' he said, and tossed it to Minka.

'Come!' he said, and took Minka's hand and pulled her down towards the river.

The water was foul with scum and oil. They pulled each other into the shallows. The river banks were choked with flotsam that lapped the ruined banks. Minka grabbed a piece of wood and threw herself on it, as Rath caught a floating drop-canister and held onto the end. The dead splashed down to reach them, but they kicked out into the middle of the river.

Rath was having difficulty keeping his head above the water. The cool water soothed the burn on Minka's palm. She used her belt to tie him to the canister, and then lashed herself to it as well and put her hand back into the water.

'There,' she said, as they bobbed out into the middle of the river and started to drift downstream. The current swept them around the exposed wing of a crashed Marauder. The wing had caught trailers of barbed wire and wood. Where the city wall crossed the river there was a black tunnel.

They were carried swiftly towards it by the flood. 'Look!' Rath said.

Minka turned. Behind them, shambling figures were throwing themselves into the water.

'They're following,' she said, and looked ahead. Figures were coming down to the water before them. She saw a child standing on the wall above the tunnel entrance. It hit the water with a splash. She cursed as she felt a hand grasping at her foot and she kicked out wildly.

She closed her eyes and prayed as the black hole of the river tunnel swallowed them.

TWELVE

LORD-LIEUTENANT BERWICKE

Naval Subaltern Grannus had had little personal experience of the Astra Militarum, but from what he had heard from other Naval officers in the amasec bars of Port Maw Cypra Mundi, the average Guardsman was only one rank above the feral world savages.

On the eighteenth upper deck of the Claymore-class corvette *Lord-Lieutenant Berwicke*, Grannus clipped his ceremonial carapace breastplate into place and drew in a deep breath. Before *this* had all started, he'd spent the last twenty years touring the wilder reaches of the Scarus Sector, collecting tithes of meat and furs and grain from feral worlds whose unkempt populations needed to be cowed into submission with a show of force and ceremony.

Six months earlier he'd been enjoying amasec on the agri world of Black Lake. They'd spent three weeks loading their hull full of grox-slab and were supposed to be moving on to the next planet of Connat's Guard, but received new orders to make all haste to the Cadian System.

The *Lord-Lieutenant Berwicke* had barely begun to deliver its load of grox-slab to the planet when the augury scanners showed a solid mass of contacts reaching from Vigiliantum to Solar Macharius. Enemy hunters. The rumour had gone through the ships, and the air on the bridge was tense.

There had been three days of urgent unloading before they'd been forced to disengage from orbit and seek shelter in the solar flares around Prosan, a bare and blasted rock close to the Cadian sun. The solar radiation had wreaked havoc with their systems and three machine-spirits had given up the battle, plunging large sections of the ship into darkness as the maintenance engines spluttered and failed. But that failure had probably saved them from detection by the sleek Black Legion Idolator-class raiders, whose precision targeting systems were even able to pinpoint ships that were sheltering closer to the solar flares.

For the last three months, they'd been playing a deadly game of hide and seek. The stress of being hunted had taken its toll on all the Naval crews. They'd been surviving on a mix of stimms and slab. Grannus himself had not slept well for weeks.

And then the *Phalanx* had arrived, and under cover of the vast warship, Imperial ships began to shelter. It was commonplace craft such as these that answered the call when the evacuation of Cadia came. Third-rate officers, like Grannus, who found themselves involved in a deadly military operation.

There was a knot in Naval Subaltern Grannus' shoulder. It had been getting tighter all morning.

The last time he'd taken on Imperial Guardsmen was fifteen years ago, and he'd never quite forgotten the experience. The Catachans had broken every rule in the book. They had lit fires in their hangar, killed seventeen canteen servitors and beaten Subaltern Reln and his fire-suppressant teams to within an inch of their lives.

He adjusted his ceremonial cravat, lifted his shoulders to his ears, and then rolled them back. He remembered the consternation the Guardsmen had caused.

There was a time when embarked troops who killed members of a ship's crew would have been quietly vented in the outer reaches of a planetary system, but the intercession of a three-hundred-year-old Mordian general with an unusual sense of humour had persuaded their captain to impose 'lock-down' instead. The Catachans had been given bare rations and water, and then they had been sealed within their hab-hangars for the whole month of warp travel.

It was Grannus who had drawn the short straw that trip and was sent to see if any were still alive, to tell them to prepare for embarkation. He still bore the scars of that encounter, both physical and mental, and they weighed on him now as he paused for a moment before the full-length mirror on the back of his polished nalwood door, drew himself up to his full six foot three and tilted his hat to a severe angle that exaggerated his long, hooked nose.

Savages, he reminded himself. Cowed by a smart dress uniform and a polished breastplate.

He adjusted the angle of his tricorn hat, lifted the duelling sword off its peg and checked the straps of his father's brass-hilted hot-shot laspistol. He flicked off the safety catch, set the charge to full and puffed out his cheeks.

He was ready.

Grüber's left leg was bandaged above the knee, but otherwise the hundred-and-eighty-year-old warrior was unharmed as he awaited the arrival of the ship's captain with an honour guard of majors. He saw the doors to the crew-lift grind slowly open and took in the movements of the shotgun-wielding Naval ratings with ill-concealed dislike.

He had not forgotten the indignity of his treatment on the lander. He would never get over the shame of losing his planet to the enemy.

As the Naval officer walked towards him, Grüber drew himself up to his full six feet. He had spent long enough on board ships of Battlefleet Cadia to know the many ranks that the Navy kept, and how they were indicated, and he took in the red tricorn hat, the gold-worked duelling sword and the epaulettes of this officer, and knew that the man was no captain. He did not wait for the customary greeting from the Naval officer but took a painful step forward.

The Navy ratings lifted their shotguns. Grüber refused to be cowed. 'I am General Grüber, of the Cadian Shock Troopers. I must complain about the way that we have been treated! We have received neither food nor medicine. You must rectify this at once!'

The subaltern smiled apologetically. 'General Grüber. My name is Grannus. I am subaltern on this craft. I apologise. My only excuse is that this is a time of war.' He paused and collected himself. 'First, I should welcome you aboard the *Lord-Lieutenant Berwicke*. But I must remind you that our ship has not been used as a troop transport for over fifteen years. We do not have the rations to feed you all.'

Grüber took another step forward. 'I have thousands of wounded and hungry men. Heroes, each and every one of them.'

Grannus flustered for a moment, bearing himself up. 'I repeat, general. What you ask is impossible. We are doing the best we can. I repeat, the *Lord-Lieutenant Berwicke* was not provisioned for troop transport. We are making arrangements now to have you moved to another ship.'

Grüber stepped forward. 'Why has your captain not come to greet us?'

Grannus fumbled clumsily for an answer. Grüber cut him short. 'I demand that you allow me up to the bridge. I have to make contact with the forces of the Imperium that have escaped from Cadia. It is imperative that some-one takes command. Is that understood?'

Anyone who had lived as long as General Grüber knew how to blend rank, gesture and threat into one heady mix-ture. Grannus had spent too long intimidating feral-world savages. There was nothing about him that Grüber found anything but comical.

Five minutes later, the bridge doors of the *Lord-Lieutenant Berwicke* opened, and Grüber entered with thirty of his Cadians.

On the bridge of the *Lord-Lieutenant Berwicke* there was a hush.

All eyes were on the green sweep of the augury scanners. The blips of the *Phalanx* flashed brightest, and about it the small pinpricks of Battlefleet Cadia and the evacuation fleet. But it was the empty spaces around them that everyone was concentrating on. They all knew that the Black Fleet was out there. None of them doubted that the enemy ships would make another attempt on the fleet – the massive guns of the *Phalanx* would deter the enemy – but the lure of bait would prove too strong. Not even the *Phalanx* would keep them off.

The augury flared green as it swept round with a low beep at each circuit.

Captain Zabuzkho was concentrating so hard he had quite forgotten about Subaltern Grannus.

When the bridge doors opened he looked up, his expression turning to surprise as he saw an Imperial Guardsman enter. The man shouldered past the astonished ratings and came to a halt just inches from the ship's captain. Zabuzkho could not remember the last time a Guardsman had stood on his bridge. The image was strangely incongruous. It was typical of these times. Things were falling apart.

'What is this?' Zabuzkho demanded. 'Grannus, what is happening?'

'Captain,' the Guardsman said, addressing him directly.

Zabuzkho took in the other man's bearing. He was tall, fit, lean. 'I am General Grüber,' the man said, and put out a hand. He had clearly been through rejuvenate treatment, perhaps thirty or more Terran years ago. His skin was slackening, and the pinched scars gave his mouth a slight sneer, but nothing could take away from his grim black eyes. 'I am General Grüber, Cadian High Command. I am commandeering this ship.'

Zabuzkho stiffened. 'I beg your pardon, sir.' He turned to face the man before him. The dais he was standing on gave him a good five inches on the other man.

'You are still within the Cadian Sector. This is a state of war. As a surviving member of Cadian High Command I am taking over control of your ship,' Grüber said. 'I shall return command to you when I am done. But in the meantime, you will obey me. Is that understood?'

Captain Zabuzkho did not answer. He took in the thirty Cadian Shock Troopers who had followed Grüber out of the lift, and he gave Grannus a withering look.

At last, he said, 'My ship is yours, sir.'

'Good,' Grüber said. 'My men need feeding. Please arrange whatever food you have to be distributed among them. And bring the vox officer. We need to find the Lord Castellan.'

A staircase wound down from the bridge to the communication chamber of the *Lord-Lieutenant Berwicke*. The vox servitors on the *Berwicke* were a trio of mind-slaved torsos, set into a seat of wires with tubes running from their eye sockets and mouths, their servo-hands leaving a scrawl of minuscule Gothic on the pink vox sheets.

'Grannus,' the captain said, and the subaltern escorted Grüber and his command staff down. They took in the wires, the servitors and the long sheets of Naval communications that fell in folds to the floor. Lalinc, one of Grüber's aides, lifted the vox feed and scrolled through it. It listed Naval engagements, ships lost, page upon page of Battlefleet Scarus communications.

On the planet, he'd heard little of the Naval battles, but now he took in the list of lost and missing ships of Battlefleet Cadia, the scale of the fighting seemed overwhelming.

'Any mention of Creed?'

Lalinc stirred himself. 'No, sir.'

It had been a long time since Grüber had been so hands-on. He looked at the crude communication array. 'How do we work these things... Grannus!'

The subaltern stepped forward. 'Let me know what you want, sir.'

Grüber looked at the servitors. They were almost skeletal, and they had a mouldy scent.

'I want a message sent out. I need to find Creed.'

Grannus had the orders relayed to the other ships in the fleet. Answers came back over the next four hours. Each ship's captain had their own peculiar manner. Some of them offered condolences in formulaic phrases, congratulated Grüber on the courage of his warriors or – from the battleships – sent offers to have Grüber transferred to their craft.

But as to Grüber's question, each of them replied in the negative. They had interrogated the soldiers in their care, asked for rumours of Creed's presence. No one had seen the Lord Castellan. As far as anyone knew, Ursarkar E. Creed had not escaped the planet.

For years before this moment, Grüber had been just the sort of old guard to have opposed Creed's rise. Creed had snubbed him a number of times, and Grüber had complained many times to Warmaster Ryse about him.

But now, as Lalinc read out each message starting with a negative, Grüber found his spirits flagging. He did not want command. He had been part of defeated army groups before and knew what was required. The troops needed rousing. They needed their broken spirits restored. The scale of the defeat was such that it needed a master to reforge the Cadian spirit.

Grüber knew that he was not up to the task. If ever there

was a need for a maverick like Creed, it was now. It was typical of Creed, he thought, to disappear at a moment like this.

He turned his back and felt all the eyes of his men upon him. Servitors scratched on the slow-ravelling message scrolls. Grüber closed his eyes. 'Well, until he can be traced – or until another member of Cadian High Command can be found – relay the message that I shall take command of the forces of Cadia.'

The evacuation fleet was scoured for all the surviving staff officers of Cadia's High Command. On the *Lord-Lieutenant Berwicke*, Grüber gathered officers from seventeen different regiments, different uniforms, wounded, dirty, bandaged. Tenders shuttled back and forth as Grüber set up the Cadian Command-in-exile. Surviving generals, adjutants and orderlies shuttled to the bays of the *Lord-Lieutenant Berwicke*.

'Bring them through the food hangars,' Grüber said. 'Let them see how low we have sunk. Let them see the cost of our pride.'

The officers were all grateful to be given a task, a purpose. But there were no officers from the Cadian 8th, 'Lord Castellan's Own'. Their absence was noticeable.

Their first task was to collect data. To find out which units had been salvaged, what was their number, what equipment they had managed to carry off the planet. The communication array started to overheat with the rate of dispatches and reports that were coming in. The scent of cooking flesh filled the room as the vox servitors' plug sockets started to steam. If they felt pain, they did not show it.

Hour by hour General Grüber established command structures over the Cadians. It was like taking rags and stitching them back into a recognisable garment.

'This is General Grüber,' he broadcast to the other ships of Battlefleet Cadia, 'of Cadian High Command. I am seeking Lord Castellan Creed.'

Over and over the response came back. 'Not on this ship.'

'Have they checked the wounded?' Grüber asked, and again the response came back.

'Yes, sir.'

'Anything?'

'Negative, sir.'

The final sightings agreed. Creed was last seen fighting on the Elysion Fields. The 8th were with him. None of the evacuees knew what had happened to him.

It was a fact that they would have to accept. Creed had been lost with Cadia. The captain had gone down with his ship. They would have to continue the fight without him.

All the time the fleet was being set upon by Black Fleet fighters. Ships and interplanetary landers gathered together. They were like a flock of sheep when the wolves were howling. For two days there were hit-and-run attacks on any vessel that fell too far behind. Cadians who had survived the fall of their planet were lost as their craft were ripped apart by Black Legion broadsides. Throughout the fleet there was an atmosphere of tense fear. And then the attacks ended.

They were still days from the closest viable Mandeville Point, but the Black Fleet had pulled back. No one knew where they had gone, or when, or if, they would return.

Relations between the Navy and Astra Militarum

commanders had become tense. Grüber had a vox-link raised to the Admiral d'Armitage of Battlefleet Cadia. 'Admiral, any trace of the enemy?' Grüber demanded.

'None, sir.'

'I know our foe. They will be back. Have your crews stand at the ready. Is that understood?'

There was a long, icy silence before the admiral spoke. 'I know my business, General Grüber.'

'I am sure you do,' Grüber told him. 'And I know mine.'

'Then do not lecture me.'

Grüber paused for a moment to collect himself. 'Admiral. We both faced the Black Legion. You in space, my men on the ground. I would like you to note that the soldiers of the Cadian Shock Troops are undefeated. After a hundred days of fighting, we were finally winning the battle on Cadia. Your fleet, however, failed to defend the skies.'

'A hundred days. And who kept your troops alive? Who kept them supplied? Who evacuated your troops from the planet, at much risk to themselves?'

'Your fleet, admiral. The service of the Imperial Navy has been exemplary. Accept my apologies. But please do make sure that the fleet stands ready.'

'I shall.'

Grüber did not argue any further; he had made his point. But the admiral clearly had something else to discuss. 'Any news of the Lord Castellan?'

'None,' Grüber said.

'Does that mean you are the sole surviving member of Cadian High Command?'

'I am the most senior officer, yes.'

'Then I would like to invite you to relocate aboard my flagship, the *Grand Alliance*,' d'Armitage said.

'Thank you, admiral. Is there space upon your ship for my soldiers?'

'How many do you have?'

'There's forty thousand upon the *Lord-Lieutenant Berwicke*.'

'General, my ship is a beast of war, it is not a transport. I'm afraid that many troops would affect the performance of my crew. I regret to say that I could not take so many on board unless direst need compelled me.'

Grüber nodded. 'Then I thank you. But I cannot accept. It was on this craft that I found shelter, and I will not leave them. If the *Lord-Lieutenant Berwicke* is good enough for them, then it is good enough for me.'

Grüber's presence on the ship meant that it was deemed necessary for the *Lord-Lieutenant Berwicke* to be shepherded to the middle of the Imperial Fleet. It was a small, ungainly shape amongst the lean silhouettes of battle-cruisers and escorts.

Day and night Grüber worked with the passion of a convert. Despite his bluster with the admiral, he knew that he had failed Cadia. All the high command had. Creed had told them that a Black Crusade was in the offing years before, and men like Grüber had wasted that time in pompous and self-congratulatory banquets, where they toasted their own achievements and mocked the upstart worrywart, who saw nothing before them but doom and darkness.

'You should rest, sir,' Lalinc told him, but Grüber refused. Lalinc pointed. 'Sir. Look. Your leg.'

Grüber looked down. Fresh red stains had leaked through the dressing on his leg. He had forgotten, and now he was too busy to stop.

'Fetch the medicae. He must be quick. There is so much to do.'

The medicae was an old man with soft hands who cleaned the wound. As he pulled a fresh, clean bandage from his sack, Grüber paused and the medicae looked down. 'Yes,' he said. 'I have requisitioned the ship's medical supplies. Clean dressings.'

It was a wonder that only someone who had been on Cadia all this time would appreciate.

Grüber drew in a deep breath and felt a wave of emotion rise within him. He put his hand to the medicae's shoulder. 'We fought hard,' he said. 'Didn't we?'

'Yes, sir. We fought beyond the last clean bandage.' The medicae put his hand on top of Grüber's own. 'We won,' the old man said, his soft hands warm on the general's own. 'We defended Cadia. We drove the enemy back. We won the battle.'

General Bendikt was among the officers summoned to the *Lord-Lieutenant Berwicke*. He stood in the lift as it brought him up from the slab-freezers. He was a little apprehensive as he waited to be shown through to Grüber's command post.

The loss of Cadia meant a strange new reality had come upon his world. He drew in a deep breath, put his shoulders back and stretched out the ache in his neck. There was an odd smell, he thought, like cooking slab.

An aide stepped into the room. He wore winter camo. It was not unusual to see men dressed in all kinds of uniform. The soldiers were wearing whatever they had been evacuated in. 'General Grüber will see you now,' he said, and saluted.

* * *

Bendikt took the steps down into the communication chamber. There were three servitors, their styluses gently scratching as the message scrolls wound onto the floor.

Grüber had one of the scrolls in his hand. He looked up as Bendikt entered, let the paper fall in folds to the floor. He held out a hand.

'General Bendikt,' he said. 'I am glad you could join me here.'

Bendikt looked about. 'It is a long way from the *Fidelitas Vector*.'

Grüber gave him a long look. 'You are right. It is. I wonder what happened to Warmaster Ryse?'

'I do not know.'

'No.' There was a gentle ping as another message came in. Grüber read the scroll for a moment and then looked up. 'General Bendikt. I hear you saw Creed in the last days of Cadia. Can you tell me anything of that?'

'I did,' Bendikt said. 'He came in a single Valkyrie to a bunker. It was named Salvation 9983.'

'Ah. Were you part of the Salvation? Do you know where he went?'

Bendikt shook his head. 'No idea, I'm afraid. He said he had many places to go. Something like that. We were standing on the edge of a mountain. A parapet, three thousand yards high. It was blowing a gale at the time. It was clear that something was afoot.' Bendikt paused. 'I heard that he was last seen fighting on the Elysion Fields. He ordered my troops there. We were within ten miles of his position when the evacuation order came. It got very messy. I assumed he had got off the planet.'

'Thank you,' Grüber said. He seemed distracted, and

then drew himself up. 'Your account supports others. It appears that Creed was lost on Elysion Fields.'

There was a long silence as they assessed the weight of that statement. 'Can I be of help, sir?'

'Yes. We need new command structures. Decimated units must be brought up to strength. I want army commands, divisions, battalions. I want a functioning army by the time...' He paused, and the question hung in the air. 'Well, wherever we end up.'

Bendikt put voice to the question many of them had been thinking. 'Where do we go?'

Grüber swallowed. There was only one place they could go. The place that would need defending, once the Cadian Gate had fallen. 'There is only one place. Holy Terra.'

THIRTEEN

MYRAK RIVER

The forces that had held the Immaterium at bay burst like a rotting carcass. Red, weeping wounds ripped across the sky, and through the tear in the fabric of sanity, warp beasts feasted on the millions of cultists the Black Legion had brought to Cadia.

In their crazed minds the heretics lifted their arms to the daemons as if welcoming salvation, and the warp beasts fell on them like rabid hounds, tearing flesh and bone in an orgy of killing and cruelty, and sucking out their screaming souls as a hound sucks out the marrow.

In this hell, Minka and Rath struggled along. They had left the river two miles behind, dragged themselves up from the ruined banks, their route driven by the safest-looking one before them.

Daemon hounds were baying behind them and Rath was flagging, supporting his weight on Minka's shoulder as he limped along.

She refused to give up yet. 'Just a little further,' she said, though it wasn't clear that there was anywhere for them to head to. 'Keep moving.'

'We're done,' Rath said. 'Stop. Let us die here.'

'No,' she told him. 'Just a little further.'

Daemon hounds were baying around them. If the beasts caught their scent then their end would be swift. Minka dragged him forward. She was heading she did not know where. She just knew that she could not stop, but at last Rath said, 'I cannot.'

His face was pale with pain. He winced as he put a knee to the ground, like a man giving feudal homage to his lord, but Minka grabbed him by his shoulders and tried to haul him up. There was a thunderclap in the sky above them. The red light was bright enough to cast shadows on the earth, and then there were excited howls. The hounds had caught their trail. She could hear their bloodthirsty baying. It was a horrific sound, like the scream of a million insane voices.

Rath was not moving. She shook him by his shoulders. She did not care if she hurt him.

'Get up, damn you!'

He groaned and she spun around, looking for somewhere to head towards. She could not give up. Her training kicked in. Find a defensible location. Keep fighting.

'Look!' she hissed. 'See that!'

Rath looked up. Through the ash clouds, there was a white shape, about half a mile before them. It was hard trying to see in the ruddy light.

'It looks like a lander,' she said.

They staggered forward. The hounds were all about them now, baying and laughing. 'It's crashed,' he said as they drew closer, but as they approached it Minka could see that he was wrong.

It was a planetary lander. The landing gears were down, and there were lights inside the cabin. 'Come on!' she hissed, feeling almost giddy. 'Maybe we're going to make it off this planet after all.'

It was hard to appreciate the size of the craft until they got close.

It was much bigger than Minka had thought. The ramps were closed, the engines dead, but the cockpit lights shone out. It was so big they could walk underneath the thing without bending over, and there was no way up. Even if she stood on Rath's shoulders, she did not think she could reach the access ladders.

Minka stared up at the thing, put her hands to her mouth and shouted, 'Hey!'

The hounds were getting closer.

She tried climbing up the landing gear, but there was no access. She stood under the ladder and jumped, but fell back, not even coming close to catching it. She jumped again but fell even shorter this time. They were so close. But there was no way aboard.

Rath's voice was low and warning. 'They're coming,' he said.

Minka turned. In the darkness, glowing red hounds were bounding towards them. The howls seemed to ring out all around them. Minka only had the autopistol she had salvaged from Kasr Myrak.

She pulled Rath next to her, their backs to the landing gear.

If this was it, she, like Cadia, was going to go down fighting.

* * *

The *Lord-Lieutenant Berwicke*

When he was told the destination was Holy Terra, Admiral d'Armitage communicated his concerns. 'Lord General, I do not know if we can make any translation at all. The warp is in tumult.'

'Well, it is death to stay here.'

'You're right.'

'So. What are the other options?'

D'Armitage paused. 'We could sail out into deep space. Power down. Wait for the Black Fleet to pass on. Warp storms pass.'

Grüber listened to the admiral's plan. It was an option if time was not a priority. At the end, Grüber said, 'That is not a route that is open to us, admiral. You have ten million of the Imperium's finest fighters stowed away in the hulls of Battlefleet Cadia. They need to be used. To be put into the war. To take revenge.'

D'Armitage was silent. It was Grüber who spoke again. 'Who is the best Navigator in your fleet?'

D'Armitage paused. 'Hyppolytus Fremm.'

'Good. Send him to me. We will find a way, Lord Admiral. I promise you that.'

Hyppolytus Fremm was locked away in his chambers, but his twinned pair of ratling attendants had been fretting about the empty, sterile chamber for hours.

Grüber found it hard to tell whether they were genetic twins or had been through intensive augmentation. The similarity of their movements made him think they were blood kin, but they had a disconcerting habit of moving and speaking in synchronisation. They seemed almost reflections of each other, as they stood in embroidered jackets of black velvet. After an interminable wait, there was a low chime and the two ratlings bent their heads towards each other and began to speak in low, hushed voices.

'Is anything wrong?' Grüber demanded.

They turned to face him, their movements synchronised, like man and reflection. They spoke together. 'The ways of the warp are tumultuous,' they said.

Grüber nodded.

According to d'Armitage, Hyppolytus Fremm was the finest surviving Navigator in the Battlefleet Cadian system. He had come aboard the *Lord-Lieutenant Berwicke* that morning, and had been sequestered in the astral chamber for nearly a Terran day.

'If there is a way to Terra, then he will find it,' the ratlings said, but it seemed from the delay that their master had not yet found a route.

Grüber nodded. He couldn't tell if the abhumans were male or female. They had a strangely androgynous look to them. He found his gaze lingering on their fingers, not narrow and thin, as their height might imply, but thick and stumpy. Despite all the strangeness about them, the ratlings were humans. All of them – ogryn, Navigator, ratling – the abhumans would share the same fate as the rest of the Imperium of Man.

General Grüber paced up and down outside, his staff in attendance. The two ratlings continued to speak to each other in hushed voices. At last, there was another chime, and then a bell rang high up in the chamber, and the two ratlings hurried to the sealed doorway.

Something, it seemed, was about to happen. Grüber

turned and drew himself upright, shoulders back, chest puffed. There was a long pause before the sealed doors opened, and Grüber had a brief glimpse of a shadowed staircase, reaching upwards to a dark chamber.

Down the broad steps a figure descended, slowly and unsteadily, his weight resting on his cane. The ratlings waited by the doorway, with an eager and expectant look to them, like a pair of hunting dogs.

When Hyppolytus Fremm stepped out of the observatory on the *Lord-Lieutenant Berwicke*, a silk scarf was tied about his forehead, covering his third eye. The strain of his search was clear to see. His face was drawn with deep lines. His eyes were red, and purple bags weighed heavily on his cheeks. He was leaning on a walking stick made from the exotic long nose-horn of the Ophelian narwhale, chased with gold and jewels.

The ratling attendants hurried to help Hyppolytus stand. He turned towards Grüber, took in a deep breath and was wracked by coughs. Grüber's face drew pale and drawn as he waited. As he did one of the Navigator's legs started to give way, and the ratlings looked to the general, as if for permission.

'Yes,' Grüber said. 'Please sit.'

A carved wooden stool was brought from the corner of the room. One ratling set it down with both hands, while the other helped the Navigator sit. A bottle was brought, and the Navigator took a long sip of thick, dark syrup.

'So,' Grüber said. 'What news? How long until we can make the translation?'

The Navigator's shoulders sagged for a moment. 'General Grüber, the fall of Cadia has set off a tsunami through the Immaterium. I have never seen such tumult. To make the translation to Holy Terra would be death. The warp storms there are terrible. I have never seen such…' He paused, and then said, with a deliberate look, 'chaos.'

General Grüber stiffened. 'There has to be a way.'

The Navigator put his hand on the shoulder of one of the ratlings. 'I cannot see one.'

Grüber snapped. 'Do I need another Navigator?'

'They will tell you the same. Or they will fail.'

There was silence as Grüber paced up and down, punching one fist into his other palm. After a long pause, he started again. 'Lord Navigator Fremm. It is death to stay. If the Black Fleet does not kill us, then the creatures of the warp will.' He paused to collect his thoughts. 'I have millions of fighting men that must reach Terra. They must get there before the enemy does. The future of the Imperium of Man depends on this. We *have* to reach Terra.'

The Navigator nodded. His sunken eyes were shot with blood. He appeared genuinely sorry, the bags under his eyes heavy with fluid. 'I must rest, General Grüber. I promise you this. I will look again. But I have to warn you that I do not hold out much hope. The Immaterium is breaking. There are warp creatures following us. I have seen them. They are but pale reflections of what awaits us in the warp. While a Geller field might hold them off, I do not know how long it would last under a sustained attack.'

FOURTEEN

PAX IMPERIALIS

Captain Berger banked, turning his Fury void fighter sunwards. It was a standard patrol, six fighters of squadron zeta doing a sunwards sweep.

The blue plasma of the engines of the evacuation fleet powering out of the system drifted through his viewport as his fighter turned. Far beyond them, the golden light of the *Phalanx* shone out, like a distant moon.

Squadron zeta kept banking sunwards till the Cadian sun filled their vision.

The star was now a dull glow in a miasma of red, like a bloodshot eye. Berger accelerated, sixty thousand pounds of thrust pinning his hands to the controls, the pressure of his void suit responding, the constant pulse of the blood-pump flushing his system through with oxygen-rich blood starting to strain against the effort. As he pulled out of the turn he felt the pressure lessening.

'Arming weapons,' his gunnery officer, Bettan, reported.

JUSTIN D HILL

She sat in the nose turret, beneath his feet. They'd been in the same crew for six years. She was one of the best gunners he'd flown with. Small, efficient, calm under pressure – and when there was no pressure, she liked to joke.

It made her good company. Helped the long hours of patrol tick by.

There was a brief pause as Bettan powered up the battery banks for the craft's impressive linked array of fixed-wing and turret Cypra Mundi-pattern lascannons. Power runes lit up inside Berger's helmet array as the systems went live. She even engaged the pair of Stalker anti-Starfighter missiles and fired off a brief salvo of red las-bolts to double-check the targeting matrixes. 'All weapon systems armed and ready.'

'Not taking any chances?'

'Nope,' Bettan said. She sounded cheerful.

How long, he wondered, till she told her first joke.

The last time they'd had contact was a week earlier, at the height of the battle over Cadia. Their flagship, the Emperor-class battleship *Pax Imperialis*, had followed the *Phalanx* on its relief mission to Cadia. The planet was ringed with Black Fleet craft, like a corpse covered with the black carapaces of carrion beetles – so thick that the planet could barely be seen. What could they do, he had wondered, against such weight of numbers and hatred?

There had been twenty Furies in their squadron that day, on escort duty to a similar number of Starhawk bombers. While the *Phalanx* went after the Blackstone, Navy captains picked their own targets, and the crews of the *Pax Imperialis* had a personal vendetta with the Exorcist-class grand cruiser formerly named *Kingmaker*.

The *Kingmaker* had a proud eight-thousand-year history of service with Battlefleet Scarus, but had gone missing on patrol around Agripinaa five years earlier. It had been presumed lost until a year ago, when a ship matching its description had been spotted as part of a Black Fleet force that wiped out a convoy between Cadia and Belis Corona.

The *Pax Imperialis* had been sent to hunt it down and destroy it, and after a two-month pursuit, they'd brought the ancient craft to ground around the asteroid belts of the Crinan System.

On paper, there was no match. An Emperor-class battleship outmatched the Exorcist in all respects. She was bigger, faster, out-ranged the enemy, and carried twice as many void craft. But the grand cruiser had been changed. The Exorcist was no longer just a vessel. It was a thing alive, and after a brief and inconclusive firefight, the captain of the *Pax Imperialis*, Vice-Admiral Chanke, had brought her in close, so that his flights of bombers could deliver the coup de grâce.

It was only as they reached visual range that the true extent of the changes to the *Kingmaker* was apparent. Her metal skin was bulged and pock-marked. Along her underbelly a row of red tentacles searched, like the arms of an anemone. The chill of heresy had sobered them all and prayers were broadcast over the vox-systems. The first wave of bombers was halfway to the craft when the auguries had suddenly lit up as six other Chaos cruisers powered up.

The *Pax Imperialis* had been hopelessly out of position and surrounded. All she could do was disengage and make for the nearest possible Mandeville Point. It had been a tough decision that involved abandoning the crews of the entire first wave to their fate.

Void-death was something they all feared.

Berger, Bettan, all of them had friends in that first wave. So, when they'd met again in the space above Cadia, that attack had been personal. Berger had volunteered to be in the first wave. Almost all the *Pax Imperialis'* crew had. The destruction of that turncoat was personal. They were determined to finish the job they had started in the asteroid fields of Crinan.

It had been a furious dogfight, punctuated by the exultant shouts of the bomber crews as they delivered their torpedoes at close range, the tense conversations of fighter pilots and the death screams as they were picked off. Berger's crew had taken out six of the enemy craft, but the bombing run had proved unsuccessful: the *Kingmaker* had retreated, limping and burning, into the safety of the Black Fleet, and again, it seemed that the pride of the *Pax Imperialis* had been their undoing, as the vast ruins of the Blackstone had drifted towards Cadia.

All this played through Berger's mind as he brought his fighter round, letting the monotone voices of the engine and gun servitors, intoning their mind-slaved procedures, wash over him.

When they were far enough away from the *Pax Imperialis* he diverted power to the scanning systems, and he could hear the tap-tap-tap as the course-planner, Federi, started to key in the scanning protocols. 'Sweep coordinates set,' Federi reported, and then, 'Augury on full power.'

Berger felt the pressure of his suit lessen as the Fury straightened up. Behind him his squadron fanned out in close formation, each craft a mile apart.

One by one squadron pilots reported in. Every minute there was a bleep as the scanner completed its full scan of the space around them. The Black Fleet was out there, somewhere.

It couldn't be long until they showed themselves. Of that, Berger was sure.

The scout patrols ran elliptical flights around the evacuation fleet. It was a constant rotation. Berger's crew were sleeping for six hours then flying again. Behind them there was a wall of swirling red clouds, and from that, tendrils reaching towards them. Each time Berger went out it seemed the fingers of the warp were drawing closer.

On the third scouting flight, Berger ordered his squadron to fly within a hundred miles of the foremost warp-cloud. The dull red light of Cadia's sun gave a ruddy sheen to a pair of old wrecked Gothic-class cruisers, floating in a gas cloud of their own vented atmospheres.

There was a blip. Federi's voice was controlled but urgent. 'Contacts. Sunwards, bearings 889-384.'

Berger conveyed the directions to the rest of his squadron. He voxed back to the *Pax Imperialis*. 'Contacts. Squadron zeta going to investigate.'

He powered forward, looking for visuals. 'Ready, Bettan?'

She ran a check on the weapon systems. 'Ready to burn.' There was a long pause. Space could be so empty, Berger thought as he scanned back and forth through his viewport.

'I think I feel sick,' Bettan said.

Berger had felt the same. 'Don't look into the clouds,' Berger told her.

'I'm trying not to,' Bettan said.

'Federi. Anything?'

'There was,' he said. 'The scanners have lost the contact.' There was a long moment of silence, then Federi corrected himself. 'Wait. I think there's something. Can you get closer?'

Berger turned the craft sunwards once more, getting as close to the growing warpstorm as he could. 'Got a visual?'

Berger stared forward. All he could hear was the swish of the blood-pump flooding oxygen-rich fluid through their systems.

'Nothing,' he said. Then, 'There's a light.'

Bettan flipped her systems to live. 'Engaging weapons.'

'It's small,' Federi said. 'Could be a tender or a light cruiser. Might be one of ours.'

Berger saw the yellow light and brought the Fury in at speed, skimming through the red light-clouds of the warp. 'Contact,' he said, and then swore. What he saw was not a tender or a light cruiser, but a man, impossibly large, standing in the warp. The man was reaching out towards him. He had a beard of snakes that melted into flames.

Berger blinked. The man had gone. 'What the frekk?' he hissed, as the targeting matrixes fixed upon a swirling cloud of purple eels.

Bettan was firing wildly at something.

Federi was groaning. 'Get us out of here,' he hissed through clenched teeth.

Berger did not know which way was back. He banked sharply and tried to turn. Something hit his viewport. It was like flying through a flock of avians, but these were more slug-like, and they splattered against the glass, leaving an image of snapping jaws.

Berger felt his fingers stretch. He looked down, and his fingers were now vines, reaching into the fighter. The blood pump was sloshing green fluid through his system. Suddenly the cockpit was full of lashing tendrils. He and

Bettan and Federi were now one entity. They were one with the Fury.

As the warp swallowed them, the blind thing that had once been Berger opened a fanged maw and screamed.

Fortress World of Kasr Holn

The evacuation fleet was reaching the smoking ruins of the fortress world of Kasr Holn when the ambush was sprung. From the warp-clouds demonic craft reached out a swirl of tentacles and impossibly fanged mouths that seized the rearmost ships and dragged them into oblivion. One of the daemons was so vast its suckered tentacle wrapped about Kasr Holn and the world began to come apart under the stresses of gravity.

The ships of Battlefleet Scarus could do nothing but accelerate to full speed. And then, before them, the augury scanners suddenly lit up with contacts, and the massed ships of the Black Fleet appeared, weapon batteries loaded to fire.

They were lost.

But then, in the darkness, a golden light shone as the *Phalanx* appeared.

It engaged Abaddon's flagship and threw the enemy fleet off balance.

There was a brief moment's opening. Admiral d'Armitage sent the *Delos*, the *Marquez* and the *Indomitable* forward into the heretic lines. Their decks were packed with incendiary explosives, their skeleton crews steering them on ramming trajectories with the largest heretic craft, before abandoning them to their fate. The *Delos* hit the Chaos cruiser *Mother of Hell* in the aft and she detonated seconds after impact. Her plasma reactors went critical and the secondary explosion tore the neighbouring *Scion of Hell* in two, her decks voiding a nebula of smoke, oxygen and bodies.

The captain of the *Eagle of Terror*, through a series of brilliant manoeuvres, managed to avoid the flight path of the *Marquez*, but she hit one of the escorts, a small pirate vessel of the Crimson Claws, and tore the smaller ship apart with her explosion.

The *Indomitable* was on a trajectory towards the *Vengeful Spirit*, and her pilot, Captain Gregor Knox III, a Cadian of over three hundred years' service in Battlefleet Cadia, insisted on remaining aboard his bridge to steer the fire-ship home.

Defence turrets on the *Vengeful Spirit* pounded the small craft, but nothing could dislodge the *Indomitable* from her relentless approach towards the enemy flagship. Interceptors raked her flanks, and she was burning from a dozen wounds as she approached within fifty miles of Abaddon's flagship, and Captain Knox stared in wonder and horror at the size of it.

He knew enough of Naval history to recognise its core as one of the fabled Gloriana-class battleships, but thousands of years of heresy and mutation had twisted its shape, and bent it to an evil purpose. Where its turrets and buttresses and cathedral windows had once been a testament to gold and pride and honour of the Imperial Truth, it was now twisted, malevolent, and dark with arcane energies, the window ports glaring out with a dull, intense, furnace-red light.

Captain Knox felt his hands shake as he steered his small frigate towards it. That his life was going to end,

FIFTEEN

LORD-LIEUTENANT BERWICKE

The Naval battle was just green dots within the holo-sphere display, with red runes flashing when a craft was destroyed. General Grüber watched the battle from the bridge of the *Lord-Lieutenant Berwicke*. The courage and skill of Battlefleet Cadia was demonstrable. Crew for crew, they out-fought the ships of the Black Fleet, but the Black Fleet outnumbered them almost two to one.

It was only the *Phalanx* that saved them, drawing the Black Fleet onto its monstrous guns.

As the evacuation fleet fled towards the outer system, they fought running battles with the pursing Chaos ships. And the longer this went on, the greater the toll. Battlefleet Cadia had been punished for the last hundred days. Her crews were exhausted. Her craft were damaged. One by one they threw themselves into the jaws of Abaddon's wolves so that the troop transports could escape.

It was a terrifying pursuit through the ruins of the

Cadian System. The orbital defence arrays at Kasr Partox were silent, their vast bastions and power generators ripped open with melta bombs, their crews slaughtered and the systems left inoperable. The docking yards of Vigiliantum were a graveyard of Navy hulks, sitting like cold stars within the nebula of their own destruction: gas clouds of frozen oxygen and promethium, a pale green in the light of the distant sun. From the hive world of Macharia, a comet tail of destruction trailed behind it as its death spiral, which would see it impact the Cadian sun, began. And where the prison world of St Josmane's Hope had once kept watch on the outer rim of the system, there was nothing now except asteroids – and a dark, bloated, pox-ridden daemon ship, the *Terminus Est*.

Waiting for them, as patient, poisonous and deadly as a spider.

Grüber made his way to the top of the craft, where Navigator Hyppolytus had his chambers. The door was locked, and his twinned ratlings bowed to welcome the general, but would not let him in. Grüber ran a finger around his collar. 'I need to speak to him, urgently,' he told them.

'You cannot enter,' the ratlings said in unison.

Grüber could not accept their answer. 'We need to make the warp jump!' he shouted at them. 'Immediately.'

'He is not ready,' the ratlings said.

'How do we speak to him?'

'You cannot. The Lord Navigator is searching for escape. You should not question his work.'

Alarms sounded throughout the craft. Grüber shook

with anger. 'We have to make the jump now! The Black Fleet have surrounded us. We have bare minutes! Do you understand?'

The *Pax Imperialis* threw itself between the evacuation fleet and the *Terminus Est* and emptied her flight decks in one vast disgorgement of bombers and fighters. They swarmed out from the magnificent Imperial flagship like a flock of bees in defence of their hive. The crews knew that they were going to their deaths as the battleship turned her armoured prow around and her dorsal batteries began to rake the enemy ship.

There was a brief flash of hope as the vast batteries momentarily overloaded the *Terminus Est's* void shields. That was when the Lunar-class cruiser *Heart of Light* fired her nova cannon.

The immense gun shot a vast, solid metal slug at almost the speed of light. It traced an incandescent streak of white light across the sky, and hit the *Terminus Est* a raking shot along its port side, before exploding amidships. The vast pox-ship lurched through space, trailing a nebula of gas and fluids as fires broke out where there was oxygen enough to support them.

But then the *Terminus Est* returned fire with three great salvos that hit the *Pax Imperialis'* void shields as one, popping its protective bubble within bare seconds, ripping into the superstructure and setting off a salvo of explosions along the great battleship's spine.

Inside the *Lord-Lieutenant Berwicke*, Grüber was shouting at the ratling attendants of the Lord Navigator. 'We're being destroyed. They're being ripped apart. There's only so much time they can give us.'

The ratlings linked arms. 'We cannot interrupt the Lord Navigator.'

'Stand aside!' Grüber ordered them, but they did not move. The ratlings threw themselves before the doorway to the Navigator's chamber as Grüber stepped towards them. The general had become almost still with fury. 'Then we will all die.' He reached for his laspistol. 'And I cannot allow that to happen.'

The warp jump alarms rang out across the evacuation fleet. In every ship, crewmen looked at each other in astonishment and alarm. It seemed almost impossible that the warp should have shown them a way out of the system now, when the jaws of the enemy were closing.

In the *Lord-Lieutenant Berwicke* Grüber looked about him. 'What is happening?'

The ratling attendants didn't know what to say. They stared up, eyes wide, as warning lights strobed through the ship. Low in the craft, the Geller field generators started up with a dull vibration that quickened to a low hum. Lord Navigator Hyppolytus had found a route through the Immaterium. One by one, each of the Imperial ships raised their Geller field and made the desperate leap into the Immaterium.

The troops in the *Lord-Lieutenant Berwicke* were thrown about as the ship entered the warp. The violence of transition did not subside, but went on for hour after hour of terrible vibrations.

In the cargo holds tanks ripped loose from their moorings, but it was on the human crew that the buffeting passage had the most profound effect.

Many were pushed beyond the limits of endurance. No

one had ever seen so many patients with warp sickness. Medicae ran out of mind suppressants as their decks filled with men and women clutching desperately at the shores of sanity. Commissars dispatched those who were driven mad, but soon entire levels of the ship were dedicated to the sick.

Where they were available, Sisters of Battle, priests and military mendicants walked up and down, soothing the incipient madness with prayers. On ships where there was no clergyman or woman available, officers read aloud from books of prayer, or even just the *Uplifting Primer*.

After the tumults began to ease, Grüber had all the military reports he had not yet read brought to him. They filled an entire room with files, memos, regimental reports of cowardice, or failure in the face of the enemy.

But again and again were reports of a winged saint. She had been seen on almost every battlefront. Her miracles had saved unit after unit from impossible odds. Grüber found his hand shaking as he worked through them. He found tears rising.

Grüber had faith in the Emperor.

Three days into the flight there was a knock on the door. Grüber looked up, expecting to see Zabuzkho, but instead a commissar entered: a tall, lean man with a narrow, hawkish look to him, and a long hooked nose.

Grüber stood up to shake the man's hand. 'My name is General Grüber. To whom do I have the pleasure of speaking?'

The commissar held Grüber's hand for a moment too long, as if assessing his character through his handshake. 'Colonel-Commissar Grake,' he said, his voice deep and resonant for a man so thin. He looked down on Grüber, which the general found irritating.

He sat down. 'Greetings. Please sit. How can I help you?'

The commissar sat back, took off his peaked hat and folded one leg over the other. There was stiffness to his movements that suggested an old wound. Grüber waited. He took an instant dislike to the man, though, to be honest, he'd hardly ever met a commissar that he liked – and those he liked, he thought, generally made bad commissars.

'There was a serious breakdown of command in the hours of the evacuation.'

Grüber sat forward and steepled his fingers together. 'Yes. Of course, there was. My troops were evacuating in the face of continuous attack.'

Grake leaned forward. 'There was cowardice on Cadia. Gross failures on the part of your troops to carry out their basic duties.'

Grüber stiffened as he leaned forward. 'There was courage on Cadia. Bravery. Stalwart defiance of the enemy.'

Grake smiled from the corner of his mouth. It was a cold and unpleasant look that showed metal-capped teeth. 'In the last hours of Cadia, I shot fifty-nine men.'

'So I have heard.'

'And?'

'I think that is fifty-nine lives of my brave troops that you wasted. Fifty-nine fewer defenders of the Imperium of Man.'

'In their flight they had discarded their weapons.'

'Yes,' Grüber said. 'I have read the reports. Guardsman Marling and Guardsman Marcus had lost their rifles because they were carrying their wounded fellows.' Grüber fumbled for the relevant paper. 'Yes. Here!' he said defiantly. 'And you also shot the wounded men they had brought to the evacuation point. Guardsman Materel and Sergeant Blenkin. Guardsman Materel had been shot in the arm, which reports say was bound to his chest. Sergeant Blenkin had stepped on a mine and lost her leg from the knee downwards.'

'Sergeants have a responsibility to set a proper example to the others.'

Grüber was trembling with fury. 'Sergeant Blenkin was a veteran of nine years. She had already twice won the Eagle Ordinary, and I have three reports, here, here and here,' he said, waving the papers in the air, 'recommending Sergeant Blenkin for the Ward of Cadia. And you shot her!'

Grüber was standing. He had both fists planted on the desk. 'You shot a woman who had fought with commendation and bravery for nine years, earned some of the highest honours available to a Guardsman, for the crime of dropping her rifle once wounded.'

Grake seemed almost reptilian in his calm. 'Yes,' he said. 'I had to make an example in order to stop panic breaking out. This is not about one or two Guardsmen–'

'Fifty-nine,' Grüber said, sitting back down.

Grake shrugged. '–Or fifty-nine. It is about the ten thousand warriors I got safely off the planet.'

'Other commanders managed to do so without shooting wounded men.'

Grake's blue eyes were cold as steel. He made no response.

Grüber sat forward. 'And what about the thousands you left behind?'

'I was obeying commands.'

Grüber slammed his palm down on the table. 'You are hiding behind other men's orders. I can list ten, twenty places where the orders were disregarded, and we have two hundred thousand more men off the planet because of that.'

'They put the whole operation at risk.'

Grüber bit back his retort and Grake sat forward once more. 'General, the discipline of your warriors is my concern. I want the records, so I can go through them to ascertain who should be executed. I have gone through the files, and found one thousand three hundred and sixteen cases of cowardice that warrant punishment. Give me the list of names and I will deal with them.'

Grüber stared at him. 'No,' he said.

Grake's eyes narrowed slightly. 'Pardon?'

'No.'

Grake smiled again, a chilling glimmer of metal teeth where his own had been knocked out. 'General. I am the representative of the Commissariat.'

'I have pardoned them,' Grüber said. 'And formed a penal division from their number. They will have the honour of leading our next attack.'

Grake was silent for a long time. He spoke slowly, like a gambler laying his cards, one by one, onto the table. 'That is your prerogative.'

'Yes, it is,' Grüber said. 'I have no doubt that they will make up for their sins by fighting with honour and courage. But if you have any doubts about them, then I suggest you lead them.'

Grake smiled. 'You're offering me a penal regiment?'

'Yes.'

Grüber expected the commissar to refuse, but he was

impressed when Grake reached one long, thin hand across the table and shook his hand. 'It will be an honour,' he said.

They had been in the warp for a month when, at last, the announcement came over the ship's loudspeakers.

'Transition imminent.'

Ships were made ready. The initial wave of relief began to stretch thin as the ship was buffeted by head currents that seemed designed to push them back into the maelstrom.

The pressure mounted within the sealed troop hangars. Even experienced passengers swallowed back vomit as the temperature dropped and warp-alarms began to ring out above them. For a millisecond there were faces and hands and gaping maws swirling about the Geller fields. Across the craft stoic men screamed for a moment as the pressure rose in their heads. But at last, it seemed that Lord Navigator Hyppolytus Fremm had found a way back.

Transiting a warp-going spaceship back into real space was like squeezing a splinter of steel from a gangrenous wound. Reality reasserted itself as the warp gave way with a burst of purple-and green-light. The Geller field blinked from existence, and the sudden loss of pressure sucked the warp light back upon itself. The explosion reversed this time, leaving the mile-long *Lord-Lieutenant Berwicke* to slam back into real space at dangerous speed.

The armoured nose section re-entered a full three-point-two seconds before the dorsal enginariums. The bone-crunch of gravity travelled down the length of the craft in a ripple of energies. Lights flickered. Heating systems coughed and gravity generators failed across the troop decks for a stomach-churning moment.

In the bridge, a dozen alarms sounded as the local superstructures failed for an instant. Across the ship, repair teams responded with well-trained speed to popped rivets, leaking bulkheads, boiler overloads. Some decks went entirely dark as reactors strained at the sudden drain of energy. Then the shock of transition passed, the engines began to take the strain, the flicker of amber emergency lighting returned to normal and vast cogitators whirred as they adjusted the gravity generators to the orbital pull of planets and stars.

Grüber was standing on the bridge as the transition happened. He was eager for his first glimpse of Holy Terra. As he stood at the viewport and looked out, Captain Zabuzkho checked the charts.

'Are we there?' Grüber said.

Zabuzkho looked downcast. 'No, sir.'

'Where are we?'

Zabuzkho shook his head. 'I'm not sure.'

SIXTEEN

ELYSION FIELDS

Minka fired as the first warp hound appeared. It was a misshapen thing, with a bunched mane of raging fire, human eyes and a snout thick with curved fangs. The autopistol slug hit it in the chest and did nothing to slow it. She fired again, with the same lack of effect, and now she fired a third time and missed.

A second, third and fourth hound appeared on the heels of the first. Rath cursed, drew his knife and pushed Minka out of the way.

'Cadia stands!' he roared as the baying of hunters filled the air, and the first hound leaped for his throat.

Brother.

His pack brothers had hunted all across Cadia. They had brought their quarry to ground, and torn them apart, and they had gloried in the battle.

He knew the warp-born would come for the humans.

Their souls were daemon-bait, like the light of a deep-sea creature that draws fishes near.

As the warp hound leaped in, Skarp-Hedin sprang forward.

It was fast, but he was faster.

He caught it by the throat. The two of them tumbled to the ground, a rolling ball of fur and fire. He tore its throat out, was on his feet before the second threw itself at him and bowled him backwards, fangs crunching down on his power armour.

He punched his fingers into its eye, digging deep into the matter inside its skull. It was a blow that would have killed anything mortal, but these were beasts of the Immaterium, and the warp hound howled with pain and pleasure as the Space Wolf set one hand on its jaws and yanked, dislocating the jaws and ripping its head from its shoulders.

In an instant it was gone, its spirit howling frustration as it was banished for a moment from the physical realm. In a frenzied blur, he tore them apart. All there was, was the killing. It was supreme. It was glorious.

Brother. It is time. We are leaving.

In a moment, Skarp-Hedin shook his head, and his berserk fury left him. He found himself staring down at the ground, where he had just thrown a warp hound, and it had blinked out of existence as its hold on the corporeal realm failed.

There was a shadow on the floor before him.

He looked up and saw a swirling purple cloud of warp energy.

Something was manifesting in the air above him. He drooled with anticipation as a red figure started to solidify within the cloud: a vast red monster, whip in one hand, great brass axe in the other.

Minka was on her hands and knees, retching as the warp energies swirled about her. She felt the ground shudder. She looked up. A vast shape of red fire stood above her. She closed her eyes as it took a single step forward. Cadia trembled beneath its foot.

Somehow she fired her autopistol but the lead round was lost in the creature's unholy flesh.

Minka scrabbled backwards. The monstrous thing lifted its great axe into the air.

Minka called out to the God-Emperor to witness her defiance. 'In the name of the God-Emperor of Mankind!' she shouted.

There was a flash of white light and the sound of singing. She put her hand up to shield her eyes as a white shape materialised in the air above her.

The winged saint is sublime, transcendent. She has wings of feathers. A silver halo. The angry face of an angel. She hangs in the air above them all. It is impossible to look at her directly.

It is not the only thing about her that defies logic.

In truth, she is not here. She is in ten places at once, fighting the enemies of mankind. She lifts a sword of flaming white, yet it is not the blade that kills, but the power of her truth. Her chin is high. Her face uplifted does not shine with the purple light of the sky, but with the golden light of a radiant sun, a bright Terran day, a throne of incandescent gold. If she speaks words they are like the wind in the mountain forest – a roar of natural power.

Minka tries to stand, but the light is like a mountain gale, pushing her back.

She hears a snarling voice, and knows that it is the warp-born.

Light flashes, or rather darkness flashes in the light, and then she hears a low moan. It is her own voice. It is like the voices of women in childbirth, a groan that is squeezed from inside them. It is a moan of pain, of creation, of exultation.

Minka stands. For a moment she is the saint.

It is her voice speaking.

In the name of the God-Emperor of Mankind.

The white light had gone. Minka fell onto her hands and knees and coughed.

There was blood on her face. She did not know if it was hers or not. Her right hand was scorched red as if she had held a brand in it. She pushed herself to her feet.

'Up!' someone was shouting. Something grabbed her arm.

She could barely see. Her eyes were dazzled still. She felt giddy, felt as she had in her dreams when she saw herself hanging over the city.

She had faith.

Brother, it is time. We are leaving.

Skarp-Hedin turned. There was the lander. He seemed to remember it, and then it all rushed back to him, the assault by Ottar the White, the mounds of the dead, the lander.

The lander.

Its ramps were closed. Its systems were active. He sprinted for the cabin, ran and caught the ladder and hauled himself up. 'I am coming back now,' he voxed as he slammed the cabin release latch. A voice called out to him. It was not his brothers.

He turned, and saw two humans, a male and a female, looking up with faces drawn with terror and exhaustion. 'Help us,' the man said.

Skarp-Hedin was repelled by the word. It was not a word he was used to. It spoke of weakness. Of defeat. He responded with a growl and threw the cabin door open.

'You cannot leave us,' the man said. 'Our fight is not yet done. We have to take revenge.'

Skarp-Hedin paused. Revenge was a word he understood. There were many reasons not to help them. They were weak. They were human. They would slow him down.

Despite that, he turned. 'Can you fly?' he demanded.

Rath nodded.

Skarp-Hedin approved. The Space Wolf reached down and held out a hand. He hauled them up one by one.

The Space Marine turned to them and spoke. Minka stared up. The voice was deep and gravelly. She could not understand the words.

He spoke again, and this time she caught his guttural accent. 'How do you know how to fly?'

Rath nodded. 'Cadian 101st, Airborne,' he said.

The Space Wolf laughed. 'Fly then,' he said. 'I hunt.'

The Space Marine stalked inside and left the two Cadians in the cockpit.

The pilot had been torn apart. The cabin was awash with clots of blood; there was no time to clean the mess. It was a scramble as they got the craft ready to fly.

Rath winced as he slid into the pilot's seat. 'Are you sure you can fly this?' Minka asked.

'Yes,' Rath said, though he didn't sound sure. Minka

watched him work one-handed, pressing the activation studs. His face was pale. His breath seemed laboured. Even the light of his augmetic eye seemed dull. He forced a smile. 'Of course. I was Airborne once.'

The engines came to life on the third try.

Rath pulled on a lever and found it was the wrong one.

He tried each of the levers in front of him and seemed satisfied.

'Right,' he said. 'Here goes.'

The engines roared as he brought them up to full strength, then he put his hands to the controls and took a deep breath. The craft's nose lifted unsteadily. It hung a hundred feet above the ground, its wings shuddering violently.

Rath looked confused. He struggled to keep her level as the craft was buffeted by winds, then found the right lever and pushed the engine nozzles from lift to fly.

It was a tortuous flight. Minka clung on and prayed. Warp creatures flew at them, swatting themselves against the viewport. One of them was sucked into the engine, which rattled for a moment.

'Throne,' Rath hissed, expecting the engine to rupture, but it coughed and spluttered, and then kicked back into flame.

Cadia fell away behind them. Once they were out of immediate danger, the Space Wolf took over, ripping the captain's seat out of its mounting in order to make room for himself.

'Where are we going?' Rath asked.

'My brothers are waiting,' the Space Marine said.

They did not ask any more questions. It was more than

two hours' flight before the Space Wolf strike cruiser appeared before them. It was a grey slab of ceramite, hanging in the void, the bloody light twinkling off the vast turrets of cannons and lance arrays. Minka barely dared breathe as they flew into the shadow of the vast craft.

There were dark openings along its side. It was to one of those that the Space Marine flew them. The yawning gap filled the viewport. Slaved guns tracked them as they flew into the shadowed tunnel.

The Space Wolf brought the lander down with a thud that slammed Minka back against the wall. They were inside a brightly lit landing bay. The Space Wolf stood, kicked the door open and squeezed out, his power armour grating against the doorframe. He leaped the twenty feet down to the floor.

Rath and Minka looked at each other. 'I'll help you,' she said.

Minka helped Rath down. The Space Wolf was waiting for them. 'Come!' he shouted, and waved them to the doorway as servo-attendants moved out from the wall on tracked carriages and began to attend to the lander. Minka slipped down behind Rath.

Skarp-Hedin's footsteps pounded out as he crossed the floor. There were five more Space Marines in grey power armour, standing in two files by the door. Rath needed a medicae, but she didn't dare move. The scale of this ship was built for Adeptus Astartes, not human. Everything was too large.

The Space Wolf called out to her. 'Come!' and she took a step forward.

As she helped Rath along, the waiting Space Marines suddenly lifted their fists and made the sign of the aquila.

Minka froze at the sudden movement, but Skarp-Hedin spoke. 'Do not fear. They're saluting you.'

PART FOUR

CADIA STANDS

ONE

AGRIPINAA SYSTEM

Tithe-servant to Cadia, the forge world of Agripinaa was known as the Orb of a Thousand Scars, its inhabitants sealed within their hive complexes in order to protect them from the toxic atmospheres; eighty million industrial slaves sustained by the agri worlds of Yayor, Dentor and Ulthor.

It was a bastion of a planet, with its own battlefleet and a trio of Ramilies-class starforts in orbit about its surface of mines, factories, refineries and industrial complexes. And it was to Agripinaa that the warp flung the *Lord-Lieutenant Berwicke*, its crew and passengers shaken and dislocated.

Grüber had taken a brief rest. When he woke he found that Lalinc had somehow managed to salvage his dress uniform from Cadia. It was laid out in his antechamber.

Grüber washed his face with a damp cloth and stood over the flat uniform. His fingers touched the rich brocade, and he let it fall back down.

'I think I will stay in military garb,' he said.

'I understand,' Lalinc said.

Grüber nodded. 'Has the Navigator's chamber opened yet?'

'Not yet, sir.'

'Let me know when it does.'

'I have asked to be notified as soon as,' Lalinc said.

Grüber stared at his dress uniform for a long time and picked up his sword. He'd been given it, a century before, when he had been made a full general. It had saved his life more than once. It felt good to hold it again. He pressed the power stud. A thin line of blue energy crackled along its single, curved edge.

He gave it a few swings. It hummed as it cut through the air. There was a knock at his door.

Grüber sheathed his sword, buckled his belt tight. It was now two holes tighter. He had lost weight. They all had. In many ways. Four months earlier, Cadia had had the best troops in the galaxy, but now they were leaner, tougher, harder. And it was his responsibility to lead them.

The knock came again, more urgent this time.

'Come in!' he called.

Lalinc stepped inside. 'Captain Zabuzkho says that Lord Navigator Hyppolytus' chamber will soon open.'

'Thank you,' Grüber said. 'I shall come.'

There was a flurry of activity as Grüber strode through the bridge corridors of the *Lord-Lieutenant Berwicke* and arrived at the doors to the Navigator's chamber. Grüber sniffed. The twinned ratlings were holding each other's hands. Grüber tried to ignore them as the doors to the chamber were unlocked. The seals opened with a hiss, and the doors slid open.

Navigator Hyppolytus did not appear.

Grüber strode forward. The air inside had a musty, dry smell.

'Please,' the ratlings said. 'Do not go in.'

'Where is he?'

'We will look,' they said.

The Lord Navigator appeared slowly, limping down the steps.

The tall man was bowed and bent. The ratlings brought out a chair and held the Lord Navigator's hands as he sat down. He coughed, and Grüber saw blood on the cloth that he held in his hand.

'Lord Navigator?'

Hyppolytus looked up. The silk cloth was knotted about his head. He looked close to death. When he spoke his voice was little more than a rattle.

'General Grüber,' he said. 'We have arrived. Agripinaa Sector.'

'That is correct. You delivered us,' Grüber said. 'Thank you.'

Hyppolytus Fremm closed his eyes and swallowed. 'It was more than I thought I could manage, general. The warp is in such tumult.' He closed his eyes once more and an expression of sickness crossed his face for a moment. 'This was as far as I could manage.'

Grüber had never touched a Navigator before, but he put a hand out to the mutant's and gave it a reassuring squeeze. 'You did well.'

'Did the others make it through?' the Navigator asked.

Grüber did not know how to break the bad news. 'Some,'

he said. 'A handful of tenders. Of the big ships… The *Lady of Gygax* made contact an hour ago. And we have made visual contact with the *Venerable Warrior*.'

Hyppolytus frowned. 'And the others?'

'Nothing,' Grüber said. 'Yet.'

The Navigator closed his eyes.

'Maybe they will come through.'

'Maybe,' the Navigator said. He looked weary.

'You don't have any sign of them?'

The Navigator shook his head. 'Nothing. I tried to show them the way, but the gap was closing even as we made the transition.'

'Have they been lost?'

The Lord Navigator did not answer. 'It is possible that they have been scattered. The warp storm was unlike any I have seen before. But yes, it is possible.'

'Probable?'

The Lord Navigator shook his head.

Grüber took in a deep breath. 'Well. As soon as we make it to Agripinaa, we will make contact with the High Lords of Terra.'

'Yes,' the Navigator said. 'Terra must know.'

As the four surviving ships of the evacuation fleet limped towards the system, Grüber established the fighting strength of the forces that had made it through the warp. It was only ninety thousand men. Ninety thousand from a population of nine hundred million. One in a thousand had survived the fall of Cadia.

Grüber's staff left him alone. They were as stunned as their commander.

An hour passed. Decisions had to be made. It was

Marshal Shai Arrian, a survivor of Kasr Kraf, who had the courage to come and disturb the general's reverie.

He coughed. 'Lord General Grüber...'

Grüber slowly looked up. 'Ninety thousand,' he said. Arrian did not answer. 'How is the Lord Navigator?'

'He is recovering.'

'Is there a way to Terra from here?'

Arrian inclined his head. 'I will ask.'

'Yes, please do.'

There was a long silence. 'I'm not sure he could make another warp transit,' Arrian said.

Grüber nodded. He had dreamt of bringing the news to Terra himself. But it seemed even this small victory was to be denied him.

'Any word from Agripinaa?'

'No, sir,' Arrian said. 'Our astropaths have tried to contact the forge world. But there has been no response.'

In the command chamber aboard the *Lord-Lieutenant Berwicke*, Lalinc went through the reports with General Grüber. They were assessing the armour that they had on board. 'Three Baneblades. I see the *Pugilist* made it, and the *Excalibur*, and the *Macharius Star*.'

'Is that Pask's tank?'

'No, sir. He drove the *Hand of Steel*.'

'Of course. Any news of him?'

'Unfortunately not.'

'Witnesses report that his Titan hunters knocked out two squadrons of Warhounds of Legion Ignatum, before the end.'

Pask was a fine fighter. A little quiet, but heroes often were, he'd found. In his mind, he went over the events on

Cadia. The enemy had not planned the manner of Cadia's demise. It had been an opportunistic attack. A lucky gambit. They had won the battle, he was sure.

Lalinc kept talking, but Grüber had stopped listening. His mind wandered, and he sat forward and said, 'We should decorate Pask. Posthumously. What medals does he have already?'

Lalinc didn't know. 'Well, we should give him something else. Damn it, we should strike a new medal for all the survivors of Cadia.' Grüber mused on the name. 'How's your High Gothic?'

His aide made a face. He was a soldier, not a scholar.

'Arrian!' Grüber called. 'How's your High Gothic?'

'Reasonable,' the marshal said.

'Good,' Grüber said, rubbing his hands together, and started to explain.

It was decided that the medal would be named the 'Invictus Crimson' and that all surviving troops would be awarded it. All Cadians, in fact, who had survived the war. Grüber had been energised by the conversation, but once the medal had been sketched, he sat down and appeared deflated once more.

'What will happen to the Cadian Shock Troopers, now that Cadia is no more?' Lalinc asked suddenly.

Grüber nodded. 'Well. We regroup. We raise more troops. Perhaps the Imperium will give us a new planet to settle.' Grüber rubbed his eyes. 'I can't see the High Lords of Terra rewarding us for defeat.'

'But the years of service,' Lalinc said. 'And besides, we did not fail.'

Grüber nodded. 'We did not. But we shall be blamed.' When something went wrong, great institutions needed scapegoats. 'There are many in the Astra Militarum who are jealous of our status. They are jealous, frankly, that we have always been the foremost,' Grüber said. 'They will see the fall of the Cadian Gate as confirmation that we have failed. They will want to take our place. They will want to demote us. I cannot let that happen.'

'I agree. But what can we do?'

Grüber stood. 'We have to prove that we are a force worth keeping together. If we are in Agripinaa, then we must take the opportunity. I shall send word to Terra. They must hear the story from us first. The Imperium cannot function without us.'

At that moment there was a knock on the door.

'Yes.'

Two men entered. One was a short, broad man; the other was young, with a thick mop of brown hair, a round face and the youthful beginnings of a moustache. Grüber did not know either of them. 'Yes?'

The young man hesitated. 'The captain asked me to come and see you.'

'Why?' Grüber motioned him to come forward. On his chest, his jacket wore a familiar red warning label.

'Sir. I am Sanctioned Psyker Ruut, currently serving with the Cadian Eighty-Fourth.'

'Ah. And this is…?'

The other man stepped forward. 'I am Sergeant Ivann.' He patted his laspistol. 'His minder.'

Psykers were a dangerous weapon. Sometimes they needed to be neutralised.

Grüber turned his attention to Ruut. 'We lost our last astropath in the warp. I want a message sent through to Terra. Can you do it?'

Ruut blanched. 'My astropathic ability is weak, I'm afraid, sir. Even at the best of times it would take an astropathic choir to send a message that far. I am a battle psyker. Telekinesis. Lower delta level. As an astropath, I am kappa at best.'

The man seemed a little slow. Grüber nodded indulgently. 'Can you at least reach Agripinaa? We have had no response from them. There will be a choir there that can relay the message on.'

'Yes, sir. I will do my best.'

'Good. Communicate to them that the Cadian High Command has evacuated the planet, following the collapse of the Cadian Gate. Let the hive lords of Agripinaa know we are in desperate need of provisions and medicae facilities. Reassure them that we are making for Holy Terra, and require a brief stopover. Do not tell them more. The less they know at this point the better.'

Two hours later, Ruut returned. He had a worn look about him.

Grüber looked up, expectantly. 'Yes?'

'I am afraid there is bad news.'

Grüber laughed. He had heard enough bad news for one day. 'Well,' he said, sitting back. 'You had better tell me.'

'I have not managed to contact Agripinaa.' Ruut shook his head. 'I could project my voice out. But I heard nothing.'

'Nothing?'

Ruut shook his head again.

'What does that mean?' Grüber said.

Ruut said nothing. No one wanted to say it out loud. Grüber put his head in his hands. 'Dismissed, Ruut. Lalinc, I am going to lie down. Fetch me as soon as there is news.'

* * *

Next morning Grüber was woken by Lalinc knocking on his door. His adjutant looked like he had dressed hastily. 'Yes?' Grüber said, sitting up from his simple camp bed. He fumbled for the chrono, thinking he had missed his chime, but it was still two hours before ship dawn.

'Sir, we have made first visual contact with Agripinaa.'

'And?'

'Well, I think it is important that you come to see for yourself.'

Grüber took the lift to the captain's bridge, where the night shift was on duty. Arrian was there. The marshal had been working all night, and there were heavy bags under his eyes. Grüber strode across to the viewport. He didn't know what he was supposed to be looking at. 'There,' Arrian said. He pointed to a bright point before them.

'What is it?'

'It is one of the Ramilies starforts.'

'And?'

'It has been destroyed.'

Arrian passed Grüber a pict image. It showed what was left of the Ramilies-class starfort. The cathedral was broken and burned out, its plasma reactor dead.

'And the others?'

There was one more. Both of the vast bastions showed significant signs of damage. 'And the third?'

Arrian made a face. 'It is no longer here.'

'What do you mean, it's no longer here. Has it left?'

'No,' Arrian said. 'From the debris cloud here, I think its reactors went critical.'

'Destroyed.'

Arrian nodded.

'But to destroy a Ramilies... I've never heard of such a thing!'

'Never mind three,' Arrian said.

As they drew closer to Agripinaa, visual contacts began to confirm their greatest fears. Agripinaa had suffered the same fate as Cadia, and she had not had the Cadian Shock Troop defending her.

Her proud defences had been smashed. The wrecks of Battlefleet Agripinaa hung in sedate silence in the void, clouds of ice and gas and frozen flotsam sparkling in the light of the distant sun. The only movement was the front half of a battleship, quickly identified as the *Theseus* from the size of the dorsal lance turrets, which was turning slowly as its floors vented the last of its internal atmosphere.

The majestic battleships and cruisers had been torn apart. Their escorts clung to them like piglets about their sow; but they too were frozen and still and dead.

The *Lord-Lieutenant Berwicke* pushed on through the iron corpses, leading the small flotilla of survivors through the debris field. The sight of Agripinaa killed any hope they might have held on to. The planet – a grey ball of forge-world ash and pollution – was now a vast, black comet, circling slowly in its orbit, a long tail of rock, smoke and debris falling behind.

There was stunned silence on the bridge of the *Lord-Lieutenant Berwicke*.

'Agripinaa, too?' someone said.

No one responded.

'Our enemies seem to have foreseen our every move,' Grüber said.

Again, no one spoke. At last Grüber said, 'Say nothing of this. Nothing at all. Communicate that to the other captains. The men cannot know. They have to have hope.' He looked at each of his commanders in turn. 'Understood?'

They nodded solemnly.

TWO

DEBRIS FIELD, AGRIPINAA SECTOR

There was silence aboard the Sons of Malice cruiser, the *Bronze Minos*.

The figures in the bridge wore archaic power armour of black and white quarters, with trims of brass spikes. They were still as shadows as they stood waiting, and at last a figure moved on the bridge. No one stirred as the new-comer spoke in a low hiss of fangs. 'Agitor.'

'Yes, Junger.'

'We have identified the ships.'

There was a pause before the Agitor nodded. 'Speak.'

'The ships are from Cadia.' The words had a heavy import, and Junger let them fall before saying any more.

The Agitor smiled. 'Abaddon's net was not as tight as he promised us.'

'No, lord. These are Cadians.'

The Agitor paused. He did not turn from the viewscreen

and spoke in a whisper. 'So, Junger. This is all that remains of Cadia's proud armies – a handful of hulks?'

'Yes, Agitor.'

This time the Agitor gave a low chuckle. The sudden noise surprised some of the other figures standing there. 'So. The chance has been given to us to destroy the Sons of Cadia. How could I let this moment pass? When we wipe them out, will they understand the delightful irony of this moment?'

'I doubt it. What do they know? They learn nothing that is true. They will have no idea about us. About the past. About the blood debt they owe us.'

'They won't, will they? It's almost sad. Perhaps we should let them know.'

Junger frowned. 'They would not believe it. We did not remember. Until our eyes were opened.'

The Agitor mused on this.

'We should just kill them,' Junger said.

The Agitor nodded. 'You are right.'

The name of the Sons of Malice Chapter had long since been erased from Imperial records, but they had been loyal once. They were one of the twenty Chapters known as the Astartes Praeses, Chapters devoted to keeping the Cadian Gate secure.

For centuries they had waged a tough and relentless war against the heretics and daemons of the Eye of Terror. The ferocious manner of war-making became a byword for the ruthless and relentless punishment of treachery and heresy, and they prided themselves on the cost they inflicted upon their foes, taking recruits from their home world, Scelus, where tattooed tribes indulged in cannibalism.

It was after millennia of devoted battle that an Imperial Inquisitor, Solomon Pietas, had witnessed the manner of their flesh-eating ceremonies.

Instinct told him that the Chapter had already fallen, and he had brought in a strike attack of Sisters of our Martyred Lady and five regiments of Imperial Guard. The combined force caught the Sons of Malice in one of their eleven-year rites when their guard was down. They attacked the Chapter with melta and fire and fury.

The attack failed utterly. Solomon Pietas was captured and sacrificed in the Chapter's inner chambers, and as word arrived at the High Lords of Terra, the Sons of Malice were offered the chance to repair their sins with a fifty-year crusade.

The Chapter Master had refused. He would accept neither censure nor punishment. But he was a warrior with his own sense of honour. The Imperial envoy was allowed to depart unscathed, the low hiss of the Chapter Master's defiance ringing in his ears.

'We have done nothing wrong,' he had told him. 'We shall not do penance to any.'

It was a misconception that battles were won by strength, or power, or ferocity.

It was certainly something that the Chapter Master of the Sons of Malice believed. Typical of a gene-enhanced member of the Adeptus Astartes. But students of Imperial history knew that martial strength did not decide the victors.

In ancient times a snowstorm or inclement weather might have tilted the balance of battle. The victors were often decided by small, incidental facts. And in the case of the struggle between Inquisitor Solomon Pietas and the Sons of Malice, it was the inquisitor's message that arrived at Holy Terra first.

The Sons of Malice assumed that their long history of service to the Imperium would vindicate them of charges that they considered baseless.

But the inquisitor had sent urgent and skewed accounts to the High Lords of Terra, and with trouble so close to the Cadian Gate, the panicked response of the Imperium was swift and brutal and sudden. An extermination fleet arrived in the Scelus System within months.

They would not listen to any of the Sons of Malice's brief messages. It was war.

The Sons of Malice escaped aboard their battle-barge, the *Labyrinth*, but they left their home world of feral tribesmen undefended, and it was on the feral world that the forces of Cadia descended, scouring the planet of human life in a terrible campaign of fire and murder.

The Chapter had been forced into the Eye of Terror. There, they had fought both the heretics and the Imperium, until at last Abaddon had brought them round to his cause. Despite centuries of heresy, the injustice of their treatment had burned within them. After centuries of fighting and struggle, they had, through stupidity and alarm, been driven into the arms of the enemy whom they had been created to defeat.

The Chapter had chafed for centuries, and it seemed now they had been given a chance to punish the Cadians for the role they had played in their ancient tragedy.

All this was known to the warriors who stood on that bridge.

Agitor Kanath closed his eyes and said a silent prayer of thanks to the power of lawlessness and violence. 'Fate is kind to those who hate,' the Agitor said. 'They destroyed the tribes who were our mother and father. We shall destroy them and eat their souls.'

But it was not just the Sons of Malice who had heard the rumours. All across the Agripinaa Sector, rumour flew. From the vapour world of Yaymar to the subterranean hives of Narsine, heretical warbands of Traitor Astartes gathered like carrion, determined to take their share of whatever glory was on offer.

Word travelled quickly through the warp. Daemons brought their mortal worshippers into the secret, and across the whole sector of what had once been Imperial space – the agri world of Albitern, the island hives of Tabor, the grox-raising plains of Sarlax, from Lelithar, the penal worlds of Bar-el and from proud Malin's Reach – shards of the Black Legion began to gather like vultures who see an old and dying beast fall and struggle to rise.

THREE

AGRIPINAA SECTOR

On the bridge of the *Lord-Lieutenant Berwicke*, the alarm bells started moments before the troop tender *Spear of Aegeas* exploded. Captain Zabuzkho scrolled through the readouts. 'What happened…?'

He knew the captain of that craft well. 'Plasma reactor overload,' one of the flight crew suggested, but then the first lance shots flared out, hitting the next ship, the *Lady of Gygax*, in her exposed belly.

'Raise void shields!' Captain Zabuzkho ordered. 'Now!'

One by one the surviving ships of the evacuation fleet got their void shields up. While the *Spear of Aegeas* burned, the captain of the *Lady of Gygax* ran through emergency protocols in an effort to save his ship. She had suffered critical hull ruptures on all three troop levels. The ship would be lost entirely unless her captain took drastic action. He did not hesitate in opening each of his void gates.

The void sucked out the contents of the chambers. In the space of two minutes, seven thousand veterans of Cadia Tertius were expelled out into the freezing void. Those that forgot to exhale popped like human balloons. They died more quickly.

The others swelled as the water in their skin and muscles evaporated. They lost consciousness. Within two minutes all of them were dead.

The transport *Imperious Georg* was hit by a torpedo in the enginarium, rending the slender lozenge of a craft powerless as the Sons of Malice battle-barge, the *Bronze Minos,* moved alongside.

In a colossal broadside, the Space Marines of the Sons of Malice vented centuries of hatred on the defenceless warriors of seventeen surviving regiments of Cadians aboard the *Imperious Georg.*

The *Venerable Warrior* followed the *Lord-Lieutenant Berwicke* as they accelerated away, but there was no way that the slow transports could outrun a strike cruiser of the Renegade Astartes.

Grüber summoned Lord Navigator Hyppolytus. The abhuman limped into the room with his two ratling attendants. Grüber explained the situation. Was he well enough to take them to Terra?

'The warp will not be any kinder to us than it was last time.'

'You do not think we would survive the jump.'

'I guarantee we would not.'

'And we have no hope of reaching Terra?'

'In these storms, no.'

'Can we fight them off?' Grüber asked Zabuzkho.

The ship's captain shook his head at even the idea of it. 'There is no way.'

'Can we board them?'

The captain laughed. 'We have no boarders. Only landers.'

'Are the landers equipped with boarding devices?'

Zabuzkho shook his head. Grüber's Cadian training told him to make the jump, to attack, to stand and fight and to sacrifice his men. 'We could board them via the landing bays.'

'It would be suicide. Their attack craft would destroy us before we even got close.'

Grüber leaned on the back of the captain's chair. 'Well, it seems we have no choice.'

Grüber closed his eyes. He could see Creed's face in his mind's eye: unshaven, the smell of his morning shot of amasec on his breath, his lip curled into a sneer as he listened to the older generals speak. That was what an old general would do, he told himself. He put his fingers to his forehead and tried to force the ghost of Creed to speak.

Alarms rang as Grüber stood with his eyes closed. The enemy was closing.

At last Grüber spoke. 'Do you know this system, captain?'

Captain Zabuzkho shook his head. 'I have not been in the Agripinaa System before,' he said.

'Anyone else?'

A Naval sub-lieutenant stepped forward. He wore the black velvet greatcoat of Battlefleet Cadia, gold embroidery about his cuffs, and a pair of heirloom laspistols on his left hip. 'Sir. My name is Lieutenant Denyam. I know this system well. I served for ten years at Aurent. I was an officer cadet on a promethium hauler, the *Maya Hope*.'

'Good man. Come here!'

Grüber spelled out what he needed, and the younger man nodded.

'If that is what you want,' he said, 'then the best place would be here.'

He put his finger to a point on the system charts. It was a small moon in an elliptical orbit about Morten's Quay, one of the inner planets of the Agripinaa System. 'Morten's Quay has one moon, Faith's Anchorage. Uninhabited, beyond a few promethium mining facilities. Ice world,' Denyam said.

It was Captain Zabuzkho who spoke. 'If you land on Faith's Anchorage, I will try and draw them off.'

Grüber listened to the captain's plan. Everything about it seemed crazy, but they had no more options before them.

Grüber nodded. 'Right. Then that is it. You will bring us into low orbit and disembark as many troops as possible. As soon as the landers get us off, Zabuzkho, you will proceed at full speed. They will either have to engage us or follow you.'

'If they do not follow me they will destroy you,' Zabuzkho said.

Grüber nodded. 'Yes. They will. But then there is a chance that you can make it to Terra.'

Lalinc stepped forward. 'General Grüber. You should accompany Zabuzkho to Terra.'

'You want me to flee?' Grüber asked. Lalinc tried to explain his point, but Grüber cut him off. 'I would be mortified to leave you behind. Any of you. No. I shall stand and fight with you, and if it is our fate to be killed, then so be it. We shall console ourselves with the hope that word will reach Terra.'

There was silence as his orders sank in. At last Grüber looked up. The faces were all pale with concern. 'Those are my orders. Please broadcast them to the surviving ships.'

Captain Zabuzkho nodded. Orders were relayed down the vox tubes, and the stars in the viewport were starting to pan to the left as the *Lord-Lieutenant Berwicke* changed course.

Grüber drew his shoulders back and forced a smile. The end had come. On the ice moon of Faith's Anchorage, Cadian High Command would make their last stand.

FOUR

FAITH'S ANCHORAGE

Old ship charts were clear: there was only one recorded point of habitation on Faith's Anchorage, a small landing pad and hab-dome on the western icecaps, half a mile from a promethium mining complex.

Grüber examined the maps he had. They could be out of date, but they were all he had to go on. Hab-blocks. Mine head. Landing zone. Store rooms. Kitchen block.

In his mind Grüber drew up rudimentary plans, turning the mining complex into a fortress. Despite repeated calls – on open and encoded wavelengths – the outpost did not answer any requests for information regarding the current strength of the garrison, their supplies of food and equipment, nor any other ancillary details.

'We must assume that there will be nothing,' Grüber said as he put the map down. 'We must take all we need with us.'

* * *

The enemy was closing in, but the Cadians prepared with their customary efficiency, their tech-priests stripping the *Lord-Lieutenant Berwicke* and the *Venerable Warrior* of anything that they would need as the *Lord-Lieutenant Berwicke* slipped into the gravity well of Faith's Anchorage and powered down to disembark. It took less than six hours for all the troops to be ferried to the surface.

They found that the base on Faith's Anchorage had already been wiped out. The generatorium was burned out, the Arvus lighters had been melta-bombed, and the ice was littered with the bodies of the promethium miners.

Grüber was unperturbed. He had a Leman Russ shove the wrecked landers into a rough wall of steel on the east side of the base, then set out his defence ring.

Individual commanders took over their own sectors, setting up enfilading fields of fire, kill zones and a series of fall-back points. Grüber gave the place a cursory look. It seemed ironically fitting: a small, unknown outpost for the pride of Cadia to make their last stand. A trail of landers was ferrying his troops down to the moon. He did not know how many he could get onto the planet.

He could even see the ungainly shapes of the *Lord-Lieutenant Berwicke* and the *Venerable Warrior*. From here each craft looked no bigger than the last joint of his little finger. A third of the way across the sky the strike vessels of their pursuers were approaching. He used his scopes to view them. They looked like six lean snakes slithering towards their prey.

As the Cadians put the last touches to the trenches and firing points, Grüber had the void shield raised about the base. There was a whine as the tech-priests coaxed the generatorium to life, then the void shield flickered and shimmered into being, a buzzing blue dome above them.

If the enemy wanted to engage them then they would have to come down to the surface and slog it out, toe to toe. It would bring the *Lord-Lieutenant Berwicke* and the *Venerable Warrior* valuable time. The two ships had already disengaged, each heading in different directions. The *Venerable Warrior* was making straight for the outer system, its engines flaring blue plasma as they were driven to their utmost.

'Think they'll make it?' Lalinc said.

'I pray so,' Grüber said. His heart began to sink when one of the strike cruisers peeled off from the gathering fleet and made to follow it.

Half an hour later there were distant flashes of lance fire. Grüber took his scopes from Lalinc. He was just in time to see the *Venerable Warrior* explode in a miniature firework.

Grüber cursed under his breath.

'There's always the *Lord-Lieutenant Berwicke*,' Lalinc offered. 'Zabuzkho seems a good captain.'

'I pray so,' Grüber said.

The *Lord-Lieutenant Berwicke* had taken an opposite course, flying close to Agripinaa's sun in an attempt to get lost on the augury scanners. As the chronometer ticked by, it seemed that the *Lord-Lieutenant Berwicke* had escaped. But as night began to fall on Faith's Anchorage, the soldiers that he had set to watch the skies reported that a larger craft had appeared to cut the *Lord-Lieutenant Berwicke* off.

'What craft? Let me see,' Grüber said. They helped him find the spot.

Grüber's augmetic eye focused on the shape of the new ship. It had to be a battle-barge.

'Could it be friendly?' Lalinc asked.

'It might be,' Grüber said, but inside he knew that the *Lord-Lieutenant Berwicke* was doomed. Even here, it seemed, they were caught in a net of steel and fire. And despite their struggles, the enemy was slowly tightening the noose. They used scopes to track the path of the *Lord-Lieutenant Berwicke*.

It ran as close to the sun as it dared.

'They're approaching firing range,' one of his aides reported.

'Go on,' Grüber willed it, punching his thigh, but then his aide reported seeing a sudden flash.

One of the ships was dead.

All of them knew that it had to be the *Lord-Lieutenant Berwicke*. 'I think they tried to engage their Geller fields,' Lalinc said. 'The reactor must have been damaged or the Lord Navigator's strength failed. Either way, the Geller field reactor failed on transition.'

'All hands lost?'

Lalinc nodded.

Grüber accepted the news in stoic silence. Terra would never know what had happened on Cadia. Half an hour later his scouts reported the first sighting of landers making their way down to the planet.

'I should make a speech,' Grüber said. 'Before the end.'

Lalinc looked about and nodded. 'Yes. It would make the men feel better, I'm sure.'

FIVE

THE BATTLE OF FAITH'S ANCHORAGE

Grüber had faced an orbital assault from Renegade Astartes before and knew what it would entail: war on all fronts at once – a blistering attack combined with overwhelming and simultaneous ground and air-based assaults, no doubt with precision strikes on key commanders via drop pod or Thunderhawk.

He prepared, as best as he could, in depth around the domed hab-block. About it there were walls of stacked containers, the kitchen block, a line of wrecked Arvus lighters. Heavy-weapons teams dug foxholes. Any gaps were filled with Aegis lines and ice trenches that offered wide fields of enfilading fire.

Grüber divided the command of the line into four. Each of his best commanders was put in charge of a quarter. They set up their own HQ bastions. Each of the bastions was independent of the others so that if one should fall the others would not be affected. Grüber set up his defence in the domed hab. He kept his tanks back, in a central, mobile reserve, while half his available Baneblades were dug in as massive support bastions, ready to pummel the enemy with their devastating firepower.

A hand-picked bodyguard of Cadian kasrkin accompanied the general as he made his rounds of each of the points of defence. About half his forces had hostile environment suits. The rest made do with greatcoats and a triple issue of Cadian drab, which sufficed.

It was not as if the campaign would last that long, Grüber thought.

Lalinc was scanning the horizon with his scopes. 'They're moving in,' Lalinc said as he faced north.

Grüber gave the skyline a brief glance. He was not worried yet. 'They're just taking their time,' he said. 'We'll know when the attack is coming.'

The first ranging shots came half an hour later: lance strikes from orbit hammering down. The first three hit the ice fields before the bastion. The superheated beams sent a gout of steam and ice up into the air. The fourth hit the void shield and the air crackled with blue light, and then the shot was dissipated and the void shield held.

Grüber looked up and seemed satisfied. He hated the waiting. He just wanted the thing to start. It was easier to react than to kick one's heels.

For twenty minutes the strikers hovered overhead and pummelled the ice fields about them. Lalinc seemed jubilant. 'They're fools!' he shouted over the din as the flat ice fields were churned up. 'They'll have to get through that!'

Grüber put his hand on his sword hilt. 'That won't slow them down.'

Lalinc didn't understand. Grüber pointed. 'They're giving themselves cover.'

Lalinc looked again and saw the flat kill zones were now a confused landscape of ice and crater fields.

At that moment a thin white cloud appeared in the blue of the sky above them. Within seconds there were fifteen, twenty contrails arrowing down towards them. Grüber nodded to Lalinc, and the alarm was sounded, orders repeated, prayers said to the Golden Throne. 'Cadia stands!' Grüber shouted, and the warcry was echoed from trench to trench as the Hydras and Sabre weapon platforms opened up with streams of tracers burning liquid red lines into the sky.

A thrill went through the thousands of Guardsmen. After a hundred days in the burning hell of Cadia, Faith's Anchorage seemed hard but clean. The first drop pods impacted. As the petal doors slammed down, a hail of missiles and bolter fire hosed out in all directions. The effect on the Cadians was minimal, but it forced them to keep their heads down as the second wave of drop pods hit; and this time the giant figures of Renegade Astartes leaped out in their suits of power armour, their once-proud livery of black and white quarters now defaced with heretical symbols and carvings.

Sanctioned Psyker Ruut stood with the command squad of Fifth Bastion, on the north side of the base. Behind them sat the metal bulk of the Baneblade, *Pugilist*. Ruut could feel the fear of the men, the anticipation of battle. It was a heady, almost overpowering sensation as the psychic tension rose to the ultimate pitches, and then the shooting started and he felt the relief and focus of the men about him start to tingle in his toes and fingertips.

'Are you well?' Ivann said.

'Well,' Ruut responded.

Ivaan nodded. It was his job to shoot Ruut should the psyker show signs of corruption. Ivann had shot two of the last three psykers he'd been assigned to. It was good practice to check in regularly. Corruption could come almost instantaneously.

If in doubt, his instructor had always told him, shoot.

'Do you have faith?' Ivann said.

Ruut swayed. 'Faith in the Emperor,' he responded as he felt the wave of psychic power building in him. The natural instinct of an untrained mind was to unleash one's powers the minute a target presented itself. But Imperial-sanctioned psykers were not like wild men and shamans. They were as well honed as a standard issue bayonet, as well disciplined as the troops they served with.

The shooting grew closer. Ruut groaned as he held his power back inside him. A drop pod hit fifty yards to his left, the superheated metal melting a hole in the ice as the assault ramps slammed down.

In an instant, there was a furious firefight as the men and women of Cadia unleashed all they had on the warriors within. A storm of las-bolts and heavy bolter rounds pummelled the drop pod openings, but despite it all, from the steam and smoke and fumes ten power-armoured figures leaped out.

One landed in a trenchwork, his upper torso visible as he slaughtered the unseen Guardsmen within. Another swung his flamer in a low, wide arc, incinerating more Cadians. A third knelt and singled out the bastion's commander from his shoulder epaulettes.

'Sir. Look out!' one of the command squad shouted, pushing the captain sideways, and the round hit the man behind him, spraying red across the back of the trench.

The Baneblade *Macharius Star* covered the southern approaches, where the men of the combined 34th, 98th, 664th and 2003rd Cadians drove the attacking Traitor Marines back into the crater fields. A ferocious firefight strobed the ice. As the Cadians' heavy-weapons teams were engaged, the tanks of the enemy rolled forward.

'Predator,' the chief gunner, Ruslan, reported. He could see its turret, just peeking above an ice shelf, the twinned lascannons traversing as it lined up a shot at them.

'Krak,' he ordered, and the long, pointed, anti-tank shell was slid into the breech of the Baneblade's main battle cannon. There was a slam of metal and the low squeak of the locking mechanism, and then he fired.

The whole tank shook with recoil. It took a moment for him to zero in again. The shell had taken the top off the ice bank, but it looked like the enemy vehicle had escaped. He panned round, looking for another target as the foredeck Demolisher cannon fired, and the fore gunner team whooped.

'Got them!' Yury shouted.

'Well done!' Ruslan called down to him. Yury had started the war as a powder boy, and now he was a better gunner than Ruslan himself. As long as he kept his cool. 'Look for the next one now. Keep focused.'

Ruslan sighted a squadron of bikes racing towards them. There were three, the sidecar gunners engaging the bastion alongside them.

The riders had not seen the Baneblade's turret swing

towards them. It was almost too easy. 'Ready?' Ruslan called. He was so eager for a kill.

'Ready!' his team replied. Ruslan did not wait for a second longer and fired.

The recoil threw them back once more.

The ice erupted in a blizzard of snow. When it cleared there was a crater scattered with dark scraps of burning wreckage. 'Kill,' he confirmed. 'All three of them!'

There was a cheer from the fore and aft gun teams.

'About time you lot helped,' Daniil called out from the port sponson. His lascannon had been jamming on Cadia and he'd spent the entire journey stripping the gun mountings down and fitting it all back together.

Ruslan felt magnanimous now that he'd got his first kill in. 'How's the lascannon moving?' he shouted as he panned for another target.

'Very nicely,' Daniil called back. There was a flash as the lascannon fired. 'You should ask that frekking power-armoured giant…' he said. 'Oh, but you can't, I just shot his head off.' Daniil swung his weapon mountings round, and then there was a sudden flash and bang, and the chamber was filled with fumes.

'What the hell?' Yury shouted, but they all knew what had happened, even before the smoke cleared and Leonid pulled Daniil's body from his seat. Daniil's clothes were burned and smoking. His whole right side was red and raw, the skin burned away.

He flopped sideways, his head chiming a low, dull note on the Baneblade's metal hull. 'Dead,' Leonid said. He dragged Daniil's body to the back, by the magazine.

'Did it overheat?' Ruslan called down, and Yury bent and waved away the smoke. He saw the lascannon trigger at the same time that he saw the neat, round hole that had been blasted through the Baneblade's four-inch ceramite hull.

He was about to speak when a grenade was thrown through the hole.

'Grenade!' His shout gave everyone a moment's warning.

It was not enough. The explosion filled the Baneblade with a storm of metal fragments. The smoke was still clearing when Ruslan saw a leg. He had no idea if it was his. He was still dragging himself up from the floor when heavy footsteps rang out on the top of the tank.

They seemed almost casual as they strode to the back of the great tank and then stopped. Ruslan suddenly understood. The figure was standing above the magazine.

He panicked for a moment, then saw that his gun team had closed the magazine doors.

'Thank the Throne,' he thought, as the silence went on a few seconds longer. The magazine was heavily reinforced with layers of ceramite and ablative shielding. It would take a–

The multi-melta tore through the inches of shielding as if they were wet paper.

Macharius Star was the first Baneblade to die that day.

Sanctioned Psyker Ruut was crouching in the angle of the trench. He kept his head low. The air above him sizzled with ozone. Las-bolts hissed as they hit the snow. The bark of bolters was constant. His pistol remained holstered. His fingers tensed and stretched. He felt the power ready within him.

'Where is your faith?' Ivann hissed. His mentor was just behind him.

'In the Emperor,' Ruut said.

He could feel them coming towards him. Cadians were backing down the trench, their lasrifles at their shoulders, ready.

Suddenly they flew backwards, mass-reactive shells jerking their bodies like marionettes. The ice walls dripped with gobbets of human flesh. There was wet on Ruut's face. He wiped it off, saw blood on his sleeve. He had seen worse.

'Ready?' Ruut said.

Ivann nodded.

'Right,' Ruut said. 'Let's go for it.'

The sanctioned psyker stepped forward. Down the stretch of the trench a black-and-white-armoured Space Marine was striding towards him. The trench reached only as high as his abdomen. In one fist he carried a massive bolter, a dripping chainaxe in the other. The blade buzzed as he came towards Ruut.

The look of the enemy was like that of a lion on its prey, taking in all that it needs to know in an instant. It lifted its boltgun and pressed the trigger down long enough for three mass-reactive bolts to fire. The spent brass shells flew left, across the path of the Space Marine, as the bolter exploded.

It had taken just a finger of Ruut's psychic force to plug the barrel of the boltgun. It was a trick he'd used before. Surprise gave him a moment's advantage.

The Space Marine kept striding forward. If he was at all perturbed he did not show it. He casually dropped his bolter, drew his bolt pistol, gunned his chainaxe to full, and accelerated into a run.

Ruut braced his feet into the trampled ice. He envisaged

a fist of steel in the air about him. He put up a hand, closed his eyes and sent that fist straight towards his foe. His power propelled it forward, as a breath of wind will lift a feather in the air and carry it along. It hit the Renegade full in the chest, went straight through power armour, bone and one of its hearts, came out the other side and buried itself thirty feet into the ice.

Ruut felt its power. He opened his eyes, saw the chain-axe descend.

Ruut's blood sprayed over Ivann's face as the minder fell over himself in horror.

The Space Marine turned and caught him by the foot.

Ivann kicked and squirmed. He fired his laspistol and hit. He must have hit, but the thing seemed immune. Throne! It had a fist-shaped hole through its chest.

Ivann thrashed as the Space Marine dragged him up to its helmet. It lifted him high enough to bring Ivann's face right up to the Space Marine's face plate.

'Are you frightened, little man?' the Renegade hissed in a voice that was chillingly quiet.

Ivann lost control of his bowels. 'How can you still live?' he asked, staring at the gore that dripped from the hole in the thing's chest.

'Because I want *vengeance*,' the Space Marine hissed, and with a sudden jerk of his power-armoured fist he snapped Ivann's neck.

SIX

GRÜBER'S LAST STAND

On the west side of the base, where the kitchen block met the sunken habs, the survivors of fifteen regiments faced off against a horde of howling cultists and mechslaves that had been harvested from Agripinaa's hive forges when the planet had been destroyed. The cultists charged barefoot across the ice and were mown down as they caught on the lines of barbed wire.

But they were just the first assault. Behind them came industrial mechslaves pumped full of stimms, their data-coils replaced with a searing litany of heresy and Chaos bile. It sent their lobotomised minds into a state of frenzy.

A single platoon of Cadian Shock Troopers held the front trench. A Sons of Malice kill squad turned their flank, so they fell back to the Aegis defence line.

The first line knelt as the second fired over their heads, and the third line reloaded. Their lieutenant had lost an arm on Cadia, but he'd taught himself to shoot left-handed. 'First rank!' he shouted, and a salvo of shots stabbed out.

'Second rank!' And again, the shots scythed into the enemy.

'Third rank!'

The mechslaves scrambled over the barbed wire. They leaped the front trench and charged towards the Aegis with all the ferocity of arco-flagellants. The men held their line. 'Fire at will!' The order went out when the mechslaves were twenty feet off, and the lieutenant lowered his bolt pistol and fired, hitting one in the chest and blowing its frail factorum body apart.

The first mechslave attacked the metal Aegis, its buzz-saw throwing yellow sparks into the air. A las-round to the heart stilled the thing, but more of them were gaining the line. The Cadians were mowing the insane creatures down, but it was not enough. Even the wounded bounded and skidded on their own entrails. Only death could stop them. They came forward in a blizzard of razor-scythes, forge-hammers and pain-lashes.

The line of Cadians held firm. Not one man flinched, even as the tide of mechslaves tore into them, and the first, second and third lines disappeared in a spray of red.

On the east side of the compound, the line of wrecked Arvus lighters gave the heavy-weapons teams a broad field of fire over the top of the trench and defence line networks.

There the elite Cadians drove the assault back three times, leaving a field of burning tanks and dying cultists.

As the day wore on the enemy withdrew, but none of the Cadians was fooled.

The heretics had just been testing them.

Now they knew their strengths and weaknesses. The Sons of Malice had bidden their time. They launched their assault under cover of dark, an armoured spearhead plunging straight over the trenches on the west side, right up to the line of stacked containers. The heretic tanks mowed heavy-weapons squads down beneath their tracks, while stragglers were cut down with chainsword and axe before las-bolts drove them back.

The surviving Cadians were pushed back towards the central habs, where Grüber stood, sword in hand.

'We cannot hold!' Lalinc shouted. His left arm was in a crude sling, but he'd drawn his chainsword.

'We *will* hold,' Grüber told him, but he'd known that this moment would come. 'To me!' he shouted, and gathered his kasrkin about him.

In the darkness, las-bolts flashed. Grüber marched out, bellowing the warcry, 'Cadia stands!'

The kasrkin shielded the body of General Grüber with their own.

Their hellguns flashed a bright orange, but many of them were armed with plasma and melta. Their unerring aim punished the enemy; when the cultists charged, they were met with a wall of flame. The kasrkin held their ground as the fiercest made it to their line. There was a furious hand-to-hand struggle, a brutal combat decided by bayonets and knives, rifle-butts and courage. After what seemed an age, the cultists withdrew, dragging their wounded with them.

'Have we won?' someone asked, confused.

Grüber laughed. 'Not until we've killed the Renegade Astartes. Until we meet them there will be no victory.'

As dawn came, the survivors could see the cost of the night's fighting. Their western defences had been over-run, the trenches filled with the bodies of their enemies.

Grüber reorganised his defences. The doorways of the central hab were barricaded, each room and window made defensible. The cultist attacks came again and again, inter-spersed with bombardment from space. The void shield lasted for two days before the generator overheated and there was nothing the tech-priests could do.

Then the base was subjected to a maelstrom of lance and bombardment cannon. At the same time, waves of cultists charged against them.

Mist rose as the bombardment melted the ice. When it seemed that there was nothing worse to come, the onslaught ended, and the handful of stunned and scattered survivors crawled out of the ruins of the hab-block and trenches, looked skywards and saw – in all its terror and magnificence – another orbital assault.

Chaos warbands that had been scouring the Agripinaa Sector flocked to Faith's Anchorage, eager to take their share in the spoils. They all joined in the attack. They came in drop pods and Thunderhawks, and more-ancient craft of brass and black ceramite. There were warbands from the Sons of Slaughter, the Black Legion, Crimson Slaughter and five other Legions. This time there was no counter-fire. The Hydra gun platforms were in ruin, the Baneblades had been destroyed, the survivors of Cadia dead.

The assembled warbands strode forward in their armour of black and brass, blue and gold, dripping red, black and white. They were here to witness, and celebrate, ten thousand years of struggle. It was a warrior from the Sons of Malice who singled General Grüber out. The Space Marine pointed with one hand, while from his other shoulder a black-suckered tentacle flicked about it, like the twitch of an irritated feline.

'Cadian,' he called out. 'It is not too late to turn.' Its tentacle made a gesture of taking in the assembled ring of Chaos Space Marines about them. 'We all started, as you, defending the False Emperor. If you renounce your vows, I will spare you.'

General Grüber stumbled to his feet. His voice was clear and strong, despite the gashes that had been torn through his breastplate. He ignited his power sword as the dreadful monster strode towards him. 'Never!' he shouted as he charged.

SEVEN

PAX IMPERIALIS

General Bendikt stood with Admiral d'Armitage on the bridge of the Emperor-class battleship *Pax Imperialis*, and counted the enemy craft that ringed Faith's Anchorage.

There were five strike cruisers in the assorted colours of Renegade Space Marines, a black battle-barge and a number of modified escorts, their proud heraldry now defaced with the symbols of heresy.

'Can we take them?' Bendikt asked.

The admiral pursed his lips and nodded. 'Yes,' he said. 'I believe we can.'

Bendikt felt a wave of responsibility upon his shoulders. He took in a deep breath and thought of all the other commanders who might be here – but most of all of Creed.

His loss had been the most grievous.

Bendikt was unworthy to lead the forces of Cadia, but there was no one left.

'Good,' he said. 'Then let the attack begin.'

Without a Navigator as able as Hyppolytus Fremm, the evacuation fleet and the surviving ships of Battlefleet Cadia had been scattered across the galaxy by the warp. About half had followed in the wake of the *Lord-Lieutenant Berwicke*, re-entering real space in the far reaches of the Agripinaa System.

The wounded ships had gathered well beyond the elliptical orbit of far-flung Urath and the labour-rich Narsine, and proceeded cautiously into the system. Admiral d'Armitage had imposed strict silence on all ships and crews as his damaged craft went through necessary repairs and refitting. As soon as his Cobra scouts reported a gathering of heretical ships within the orbit of Agripinaa and Morten's Quay, he'd ordered his fleet to move forward at dead slow and to maintain void-silence.

By the time d'Armitage and Bendikt were surveying the Chaos fleet, a lifetime of training had reasserted itself and the forces of Cadia were eager for another fight. A chance to prove themselves. Bendikt would give them that, he promised.

The *Grand Alliance* led Battlefleet Cadia forward, her entire complement of fighters and bombers sitting on the flight decks, ready to go. The heretic ships had been so focused on destroying Grüber that they only suddenly saw, with horror and alarm, that another, much larger Cadian fleet was sailing towards them.

On each bridge, the heretic skeleton crews left behind

were presented with a desperate challenge: to engage or to flee.

Each of the captains on board responded according to their own priorities. For some, it was a chance to seize control of a valuable void-craft; others saw the Imperial fleet and knew that the forces that had met on the ice world of Faith's Anchorage would be lost without them.

But none of the choices were good. It was just a matter of picking the least worst from a range of options. The Hades-class heavy cruiser *Tears of Hate* jabbed forward, attempting to engage the lead Imperial ships with her deadly broadsides and slow them down. Her slave gun crews were hauling the last of her vast shells into the breech when she was struck squarely on the armour-plated nose by a nova cannon shot from the *Golden Farrel*, a Lunar-class cruiser.

The shot detonated with incredible power, ripping the *Tears of Hate* apart. In an instant, nine thousand lives were lost: Black Legion, heretics, cultists and slaves. The void did not care. As the two fleets closed the heretics began to exact a growing toll on the weakened Imperial craft. Assault torpedoes were launched across the void, with Cadians storming Chaos ships and Black Legion kill squads fighting their way through to the enginariums, bridges and void-shield generators, and disabling them with a series of well-laid melta bombs.

The skies above the small moon were thick with flashes of fire and smoke, as debris began to rain down on Faith's Anchorage. In the midst of it all, the *Grand Alliance*'s flight crews tore gaping holes in the enemy craft, but she herself was raked by a pair of broadsides that left her listing to port and unable to steer.

Her course drove her straight into the middle of the Chaos fleet, where she was set upon with merciless fury. There were fights in almost every landing bay as the heretics sought to seize control of the Imperial flagship. It was only the sudden intervention of a lean grey hunter that saved her.

Where the Space Wolves strike cruiser *Stiklestad* came from, no one could tell, but suddenly she appeared between the two ships and took the broadside that was meant to finish off the *Grand Alliance* on her void shields, and then retorted with a broadside of her own, crippling the burning Slaughter-class cruiser, the *Hand of Abaddon*.

The battle was deadly and bloody. Bit by bit the Chaos fleet was broken, destroyed or boarded, the few survivors fleeing sunwards, late arrivals quickly turning back.

After eight hours of relentless Naval fighting, the Chaos forces on Faith's Anchorage faced the same predicament that Grüber's small force had before them. The Imperials held space above them, and Faith's Anchorage was to be their grave.

Admiral d'Armitage led his fleet forward and they unleashed a devastating barrage upon the moon.

'We could destroy it,' he said, as the green light of the holo-pict underlit his face.

'Don't,' Bendikt said. 'Allow my men the opportunity to take revenge.'

'How many do you have?'

Bendikt paused. 'Enough,' he said.

'Think you could take out the forces on the moon?'

Bendikt smiled. 'I am sure of it.'

D'Armitage bowed. 'General Bendikt. My landers are at your disposal. Take revenge for us all.'

EIGHT

NEW CADIA

It took two weeks for the Cadian Shock Troops under Bendikt's command to scour Faith's Anchorage clear of any heretic trace. General Grüber's body was found, and he was buried in a colossal marble mausoleum, all the defenders of Faith's Anchorage laid out in a neat, starlit graveyard about him.

Three Cobras were selected to make the journey to Holy Terra, to bring news of the Cadian Gate's fall, while planet by planet the whole Agripinaa System was cleansed of the enemy, the Naval facilities of Aurent and Morten's Quay were returned to production, and the proud ships of Battlefleet Cadia were brought back to full strength. Bendikt let it be known that Chaeros, the seventh planet in the system, would henceforth be known as New Cadia.

The Space Wolves of the *Stiklestad* did not help in this effort, but they did send a lander across to the *Grand*

Alliance: a sleek grey arrow that filled the main landing bay on the lower port side.

Once the ship was near docking, General Bendikt and Admiral d'Armitage came down to meet it. Neither of them felt entirely comfortable. The Space Wolves had a certain reputation, and a human could not meet a member of the Adeptus Astartes without a tremor of fear running through them, especially after the last months, when they had faced the terror of Space Marines who had lost their way.

The Space Wolves Thunderhawk slowly filled the rectangular mouth of the landing bay and seemed to barely scrape inside. It touched down with a hiss as the incredible weight of the craft settled slowly on the dampeners. The loading ramps lowered and then the carriage clamps disengaged, and the Thunderhawk began to rise into the air, leaving a cargo container behind.

D'Armitage and Bendikt exchanged glances as the Thunderhawk turned and powered out of the landing bay.

'Is it safe?' d'Armitage demanded.

Bendikt ordered his kasrkin squad forward to investigate, but as they approached it two figures appeared from behind the cargo container. They were both dressed in Cadian drab.

'Captain Rath Sturm,' the first declared as he made the sign of the aquila. 'Last surviving member of the Cadian 94th, Kasrkin, the Brothers of Death.'

Bendikt saluted him and turned to the girl.

'Whiteshield Arminka Lesk, Kasr Myrak Defence Force.'

'The Space Wolves carried you from the planet?' Bendikt asked.

It was the girl who spoke. 'Yes, sir.'

'And they brought you here?'

The two soldiers nodded, and the girl said, 'Sir, Lord General, there is something we must show you.' She led him to the back of the vast container. From inside came the scent of earth and rock. Bendikt looked at the thing that lay cushioned there. It was grey and smooth and riddled with holes. It was intimately familiar to anyone who had been on Cadia.

'Impossible,' Bendikt said, but he stepped up onto the ramp, walked inside and put his hand to its side. The stone was dead and cold and still. But it was from Cadia.

'You brought a pylon from Cadia?' Bendikt said.

They nodded. 'Yes, sir.'

'We must make a memorial of it,' he said. 'We must never forget where we came from.'

Minka nodded. Her eyes were hard. 'Never,' she promised him.

Never.

EPILOGUE

PAX IMPERIALIS

Minka sits on her bunk and turns her Whiteshield helmet in her hands.

In a ceremony this morning she was promoted with the other surviving cadets.

She is a Cadian Shock Trooper, even though her planet no longer exists. They are veteran warriors, on course for Holy Terra. This is all she had ever wanted, she thinks, as the troop ship prepares to enter the warp. To leave home. To graduate from the cadets. To fight for the Emperor.

The iron bulkheads rattle as the Geller field generator powers up. A low whine fills the troop hangar.

Rath is lying on the bunk above her. He is smoking a lho-stick. The metal bed creaks as he turns over. He peers down, his augmetic eye glowing red. 'Get some sleep,' he says.

She nods. 'How long will it take?'

His head appears again. 'What?'

'The transition?'

Rath laughs. 'Who knows,' he says, lying back. 'We might never get there.'

Minka knows they will. She lies back and closes her eyes, and for a moment she is a child again, staring into the Eye of Terror.

Her father holds her up, and she shouts at the sky, and the moment is over.

He puts her back down, puts his hands on her shoulders and kisses her head. 'Do you have faith, my child?'

She nods.

'Say it!' he urges.

She speaks the words. 'I have faith in the Emperor.'

Minka opens her eyes. She has seen the Saint. She has faith. They *will* reach Holy Terra.

'We'll get there,' she says.

Rath says nothing for a while. He takes another lho-stick from his breast pocket and lights it, puffs blue smoke into the air, takes a drag. 'Great,' he says at last.

Minka lies back as the alarms begin to ring. There is a lurch as the ship transits into the warp, and she feels bile rise and swallows it back. It is just warp sickness. It will pass. In a month or two, they will arrive at the centre of the Imperium of Man.

A battle has been lost, but the fight will still go on.

She stares up at the bunk above her, where Rath's shape is imprinted through the mattress.

Minka looks to the future. She sees only war.

ABOUT THE AUTHOR

Justin D Hill is the author of the Necromunda
novel *Terminal Overkill*, the Warhammer
40,000 novels *Cadia Stands* and *Cadian
Honour*, the Space Marine Battles novel *Storm
of Damocles* and the short stories 'Last Step
Backwards', 'Lost Hope' and 'The Battle of
Tyrok Fields', following the adventures of
Lord Castellan Ursarkar E. Creed. He has
also written 'Truth Is My Weapon', and the
Warhammer tales 'Golgfag's Revenge' and 'The
Battle of Whitestone'. His novels have won a
number of prizes, as well as being *Washington
Post* and *Sunday Times* Books of the Year. He
lives ten miles uphill from York, where he is
indoctrinating his four children in the 40K lore.

YOUR
NEXT READ

THE WARMASTER
by Dan Abnett

Returning to the crusade's heart after a dangerous mission, Colonel-Commissar Gaunt is
thrust into intrigue while his Ghosts face a threat to their very existence.